Mr. and Mrs. Beresford took possession of the offices of the International Detective Agency....

"Well, I have read every detective novel that has been published in the last ten years," Tuppence said.

"So have I," said Tommy, "but I have a sort of feeling that that wouldn't help us much."

"You always were a pessimist, Tommy. Belief in oneself—that is the great thing."

And then one glorious day, the first client arrived...

"The champion deceiver of our time."
—NEW YORK TIMES

AGATHA CHRISTIE

PARTNERS IN CRIME

BERKLEY BOOKS, NEW YORK

This Berkley book contains the complete text
of the original hardcover edition. It has been
completely reset in a typeface designed for easy
reading, and was printed from new film.

PARTNERS IN CRIME

A Berkley Book/published by arrangement with
Dodd, Mead & Company

PRINTING HISTORY
Dodd, Mead edition published 1929
Dell edition/March 1981
Berkley edition/June 1984

ISBN: 0-425-06798-X

A BERKLEY BOOK TM® 757,375
Berkley Books are published by The Berkley Publishing Group,
200 Madison Avenue, New York, New York 10016.
The name "BERKLEY" and the stylized "B" with design
are trademarks belonging to Berkley Publishing Corporation.

PRINTED IN THE UNITED STATES OF AMERICA

Contents

I

A Fairy In The Flat

Mrs. Thomas Beresford shifted her position on the divan and looked gloomily out of the window of the flat. The prospect was not an extended one, consisting solely of a small block of flats on the other side of the road. Mrs. Beresford sighed and then yawned.

"I wish," she said, "something would happen."

Her husband looked up reprovingly.

"Be careful, Tuppence, this craving for vulgar sensation alarms me."

Tuppence sighed and closed her eyes dreamily.

"So Tommy and Tuppence were married," she chanted, "and lived happily ever afterwards. And six years later they were still living together happily ever afterwards. It is extraordinary," she said, "how different everything always is from what you think it is going to be."

"A very profound statement, Tuppence. But not original. Eminent poets and still more eminent divines have said it before—and, if you will excuse me saying so, have said it better."

"Six years ago," continued Tuppence, "I would have sworn that with sufficient money to buy things with, and with you for a husband, all life would have been one grand sweet song, as one of the poets you seem to know so much about puts it."

"Is it me or the money that palls upon you?" inquired Tommy coldly.

"Palls isn't exactly the word," said Tuppence kindly. "I'm used to my blessings, that's all. Just as one never thinks what a boon it is to be able to breathe through one's nose until one has a cold in the head."

"Shall I neglect you a little?" suggested Tommy. "Take other women about to night clubs. That sort of thing."

"Useless," said Tuppence. "You would only meet me there with other men. And I should know perfectly well that you didn't care for the other women, whereas you would never be quite sure that I didn't care for the other men. Women are so much more thorough."

"It's only in modesty that men score top marks," murmured her husband. "But what is the matter with you, Tuppence? Why this yearning discontent?"

"I don't know. I want things to happen. Exciting things. Wouldn't you like to go chasing German spies again, Tommy? Think of the wild days of peril we went through once. Of course I know you're more or less in the Secret Service now, but it's pure office work."

"You mean you'd like them to send me into darkest Russia disguised as a Bolshevik bootlegger, or something of that sort?"

"That wouldn't be any good," said Tuppence. "They wouldn't let me go with you and I'm the person who wants something to do so badly. Something to do. That is what I keep saying all day long."

"Woman's sphere," suggested Tommy waving his hand.

"Twenty minutes' work after breakfast every morning keeps the flat going to perfection. You have nothing to complain of, have you?"

"Your housekeeping is so perfect, Tuppence, as to be almost monotonous."

"I do like gratitude," said Tuppence.

"You, of course, have got your work," she continued,

"but tell me, Tommy, don't you ever have a secret yearning for excitement, for things to *happen?*"

"No," said Tommy, "at least I don't think so. It is all very well to want things to happen—they might not be pleasant things."

"How prudent men are," sighed Tuppence. "Don't you ever have a wild secret yearning for romance—adventure—life?"

"What *have* you been reading, Tuppence?" asked Tommy.

"Think how exciting it would be," went on Tuppence, "if we heard a wild rapping at the door and went to open it and in staggered a dead man."

"If he was dead he couldn't stagger," said Tommy critically.

"You know what I mean," said Tuppence. "They always stagger in just before they die and fall at your feet just gasping out a few enigmatic words. 'The Spotted Leopard' or something like that."

"I advise a course of Schopenhauer or Emmanuel Kant," said Tommy.

"That sort of thing would be good for you," said Tuppence. "You are getting fat and comfortable."

"I am not," said Tommy indignantly. "Anyway, you do slimming exercises yourself."

"Everybody does," said Tuppence. "When I said you were getting fat I was really speaking metaphorically, you are getting prosperous and sleek and comfortable."

"I don't know what has come over you," said her husband.

"The spirit of adventure," murmured Tuppence. "It is better than a longing for romance anyway. I have that sometimes, too. I think of meeting a man, a really handsome man—"

"You have met me," said Tommy. "Isn't that enough for you?"

"A brown lean man, terrifically strong, the kind of man who can ride anything and lassoes wild horses—"

"Complete with sheepskin trousers and a cowboy hat," interpolated Tommy sarcastically.

"—and has lived in the Wilds," continued Tuppence. "I should like him to fall simply madly in love with me. I should, of course, rebuff him virtuously and be true to my marriage vows but my heart would secretly go out to him."

"Well," said Tommy, "I often wish that I may meet a really beautiful girl. A girl with corn-colored hair who will fall desperately in love with me. Only I don't think I rebuff her—in fact I am quite sure I don't."

"That," said Tuppence, "is naughty temper."

"What," said Tommy, "is really the matter with you, Tuppence? You have never talked like this before."

"No, but I have been boiling up inside for a long time," said Tuppence. "You see it is very dangerous to have everything you want—including enough money to buy things. Of course there are always hats."

"You have got about forty hats already," said Tommy, "and they all look alike."

"Hats are like that," said Tuppence. "They are not really alike. There are *nuances* in them. I saw rather a nice one in Violette's this morning."

"If you haven't anything better to do than going on buying hats you don't need—"

"That's it," said Tuppence. "That's exactly it. If I had something better to do. I suppose I ought to take up good works. Oh, Tommy, I do wish something exciting would happen. I feel—I really do feel it would be good for us. If we could find a fairy—"

"Ah!" said Tommy. "It is curious your saying that."

He got up and crossed the room. Opening a drawer of the writing table he took out a small snapshot print and brought it to Tuppence.

"Oh!" said Tuppence, "So you have got them developed. Which is this, the one you took of this room or the one I took?"

"The one I took. Yours didn't come out. You under exposed it. You always do."

"It is nice for you," said Tuppence, "to think that there is one thing you can do better than me."

"A foolish remark," said Tommy, "but I will let it pass

for the moment. What I wanted to show you was this."

He pointed to a small white speck on the photograph.

"That is a scratch on the film," said Tuppence.

"Not at all," said Tommy. "That, Tuppence, is a fairy."

"Tommy, you idiot."

"Look for yourself."

He handed her a magnifying glass. Tuppence studied the print attentively through it. Seen thus by a slight stretch of fancy the scratch on the film could be imagined to represent a small winged creature perched on the fender.

"It has got wings!" cried Tuppence. "What fun, a real live fairy in our flat. Shall we write to Conan Doyle about it? Oh, Tommy. Do you think she'll give us wishes?"

"You will soon know," said Tommy. "You have been wishing hard enough for something to happen all the afternoon."

At that minute the door opened, and a tall lad of fifteen who seemed undecided as to whether he was a footman or a page boy inquired in a truly magnificent manner:

"Are you at Home, Madam? The front door bell has just rung."

"I wish Albert wouldn't go to the Pictures," sighed Tuppence after she had signified her assent, and Albert had withdrawn. "He's copying a Long Island butler now. Thank goodness I've cured him of asking for people's cards and bringing them to me on a salver."

The door opened again, and Albert announced: "Mr. Carter," much as though it were a Royal title.

"The Chief," muttered Tommy, in great surprise.

Tuppence jumped up with a glad exclamation, and greeted a tall grey-haired man with piercing eyes and a tired smile.

"Mr. Carter, I *am* glad to see you."

"That's good, Mrs. Tommy. Now answer me a question. How's life generally?"

"Satisfactory, but dull," replied Tuppence with a twinkle.

"Better and better," said Mr. Carter. "I'm evidently going to find you in the right mood."

"This," said Tuppence, "sounds exciting."

Albert, still copying the Long Island butler, brought in

tea. When this operation was completed without mishap and the door had closed behind him Tuppence burst out once more.

"You did mean something, didn't you Mr. Carter? Are you going to send us on a mission into darkest Russia?"

"Not exactly that," said Mr. Carter.

"But there is something."

"Yes—there is something. I don't think you are the kind who shrinks from risks, are you, Mrs. Tommy?"

Tuppence's eyes sparkled with excitement.

"There is certain work to be done for the Department— and I fancied—I just fancied—that it might suit you two."

"Go on," said Tuppence.

"I see that you take the Daily Leader," continued Mr. Carter, picking up that journal from the table.

He turned to the advertisement column and indicating a certain advertisement with his finger pushed the paper across to Tommy.

"Read that out," he said.

Tommy complied.

"The International Detective Agency. Theodore Blunt, Manager. Private Inquiries. Large staff of confidential and highly skilled Inquiry Agents. Utmost discretion. Consultations free. 118 Halehan St. W.C."

He looked inquiringly at Mr. Carter. The latter nodded.

"That detective agency has been on its last legs for some time," he murmured. "Friend of mine acquired it for a mere song. We're thinking of setting it going again—say, for a six months' trial. And during that time, of course, it will have to have a Manager."

"What about Mr. Theodore Blunt?" asked Tommy.

"Mr. Blunt has been rather indiscreet, I'm afraid. In fact, Scotland Yard have had to interfere. Mr. Blunt is being detained at His Majesty's expense, and he won't tell us half of what we'd like to know."

"I see, sir," said Tommy. "At least, I think I see."

"I suggest that you have six months' leave from the office. Ill health. And of course if you like to run a detective agency under the name of Theodore Blunt, it's nothing to do with me."

Tommy eyed his Chief steadily.

"Any instructions, sir?"

"Mr. Blunt did some foreign business, I believe. Look out for blue letters with a Russian stamp on them. From a ham merchant anxious to find his wife who came as a Refugee to this country some years ago. Moisten the stamp and you'll find the number 16 written underneath. Make a copy of these letters and send the originals on to me. Also if anyone comes to the office and makes a reference to the number 16, inform me immediately."

"I understand, sir," said Tommy. "And apart from these instructions?"

Mr. Carter picked up his gloves from the table and prepared to depart.

"You can run the Agency as you please. I fancied—" his eyes twinkled a little—"that it might amuse Mrs. Tommy to try her hand at a little detective work."

2

A Pot of Tea

Mr. and Mrs. Beresford took possession of the offices of the International Detective Agency a few days later. They were on the second floor of a somewhat dilapidated building in Bloomsbury. In the small outer office, Albert relinquished the rôle of a Long Island butler, and took up that of office boy, a part which he played to perfection. A paper bag of sweets, inky hands, and a tousled head was his conception of the character.

From the outer office, two doors led into inner offices. On one door was painted the legend "Clerks". On the other "Private". Behind the latter was a small comfortable room furnished with an immense business-like desk, a lot of artistically labeled files, all empty, and some solid leather-seated chairs. Behind the desk sat the pseudo Mr. Blunt trying to look as though he had run a detective agency all his life. A telephone, of course, stood at his elbow. Tuppence and he had rehearsed several good telephone effects, and Albert also had his instructions.

In the adjoining room was Tuppence, a typewriter, the necessary tables and chairs of an inferior type to those in the room of the great Chief, and a gas ring for making tea.

Nothing was wanting, in fact, save clients.

Tuppence, in the first ecstasies of initiation, had a few bright hopes.

"It will be too marvelous," she declared. "We will hunt down murderers, and discover the missing family jewels, and find people who've disappeared and detect embezzlers."

At this point Tommy felt it his duty to strike a more discouraging note.

"Calm yourself, Tuppence, and try and forget the cheap fiction you are in the habit of reading. Our clientele, if we have any clientele at all—will consist solely of husbands who want their wives shadowed, and wives who want their husbands shadowed. Evidence for divorce is the sole prop of private inquiry agents."

"Ugh!" said Tuppence wrinkling a fastidious nose. "We shan't touch divorce cases. We must raise the tone of our new profession."

"Ye-es," said Tommy doubtfully.

And now a week after installation they compare notes rather ruefully.

"Three idiotic women whose husbands go away for weekends," sighed Tommy. "Anyone come whilst I was out at lunch?"

"A fat old man with a flighty wife," sighed Tuppence sadly. "I've read in the papers for years that the divorce evil was growing, but somehow I never seemed to realize it until this last week. I'm sick and tired of saying 'We don't undertake divorce cases.'"

"We've put it in the advertisements now," Tommy reminded her. "So it won't be so bad."

"I'm sure we advertise in the most tempting way too," said Tuppence, in a melancholy voice. "All the same, I'm not going to be beaten. If necessary, I shall commit a crime myself, and you will detect it."

"And what good would that do? Think of my feelings when I bid you a tender farewell at Bow Street—or is it Vine Street?"

"You are thinking of your bachelor days," said Tuppence pointedly.

"The Old Bailey, that is what I mean," said Tommy.

"Well," said Tuppence, "something has got to be done about it. Here we are bursting with talent and no chance of exercising it."

"I always like your cheery optimism, Tuppence. You seem to have no doubt whatever that you have talent to exercise."

"Of course," said Tuppence, opening her eyes very wide.

"And yet you have no expert knowledge whatever."

"Well, I have read every detective novel that has been published in the last ten years."

"So have I," said Tommy, "but I have a sort of feeling that that wouldn't really help us much."

"You always were a pessimist, Tommy. Belief in one-self—that is the great thing."

"Well, you have got it all right," said her husband.

"Of course it is all right in detective stories," said Tuppence thoughtfully, "because one works backwards. I mean if one knows the solution one can arrange the clues. I wonder now—"

She paused, wrinkling her brows.

"Yes?" said Tommy, inquiringly.

"I have got a sort of an idea," said Tuppence. "It hasn't quite come yet but it's coming." She rose resolutely. "I think I shall go and buy that hat I told you about."

"Oh God!" said Tommy. "Another hat!"

"It's a very nice one," said Tuppence with dignity.

She went out with a resolute look on her face.

Once or twice in the following days Tommy inquired curiously about the idea. Tuppence merely shook her head and told him to give her time.

And then, one glorious morning, the first client arrived, and all else was forgotten.

There was a knock on the outer door of the office and Albert, who had just placed an acid drop between his lips, roared out an indistinct 'come in'. He then swallowed the acid drop whole in his surprise and delight. For this looked like the Real Thing.

A tall young man, exquisitely and beautifully dressed,

stood hesitating in the doorway.

"A toff, if ever there was one," said Albert to himself. His judgment in such matters was good.

The young man was about twenty-four years of age, had beautifully slicked-back hair, a tendency to pink rims round the eyes, and practically no chin to speak of.

In an ecstasy, Albert pressed a button under his desk, and almost immmediately a perfect fusilade of typing broke out from the direction of "Clerks". Tuppence had rushed to the post of duty. The effect of this hum of industry was to overawe the young man still further.

"I say," he remarked. "Is this the whatnot—detective agency—Blunt's Brilliant Detectives? All that sort of stuff, you know? Eh?"

"Did you want, sir, to speak to Mr. Blunt himself?" inquired Albert, with an air of doubt as to whether such a thing could be managed.

"Well—yes, laddie, that was the jolly old idea. Can it be done?"

"You haven't an appointment, I suppose?"

The visitor became more and more apologetic.

"Afraid I haven't."

"It's always wise, sir, to ring up on the phone first. Mr. Blunt is so terribly busy. He's engaged on the telephone at the moment. Called into consultation by Scotland Yard."

The young man seemed suitably impressed.

Albert lowered his voice, and imparted information in a friendly fashion.

"Important theft of documents from a Government Office. They want Mr. Blunt to take up the case."

"Oh! really. I say. He must be no end of a fellow."

"The Boss, sir," said Albert, "is It."

The young man sat down on a hard chair, completely unconscious of the fact that he was being subjected to keen scrutiny by two pairs of eyes looking through cunningly contrived peep holes—those of Tuppence, in the intervals of frenzied typing, and those of Tommy awaiting the suitable moment.

Presently a bell rang with violence on Albert's desk.

"The Boss is free now. I will find out whether he can see you," said Albert, and disappeared through the door marked "Private."

He reappeared immediately.

"Will you come this way, sir?"

The visitor was ushered into the private office, and a pleasant faced young man with red hair and an air of brisk capability rose to greet him.

"Sit down. You wished to consult me? I am Mr. Blunt."

"Oh! Really. I say, you're awfully young, aren't you?"

"The day of the Old Men is over," said Tommy waving his hand. "Who caused the War? The Old Men. Who is responsible for the present state of unemployment? The Old Men. Who is responsible for every single rotten thing that has happened? Again I say, the Old Men!"

"I expect you are right," said the client. "I know a fellow who is a poet—at least he says he is a poet—and he always talks like that."

"Let me tell you this, sir, not a person on my highly trained staff is a day over twenty-five. That is the truth."

Since the highly trained staff consisted of Tuppence and Albert, the statement was truth itself.

"And now—the facts," said Mr. Blunt.

"I want you to find someone that's missing," blurted out the young man.

"Quite so. Will you give me the details?"

"Well, you see, it's rather difficult. I mean, it's a frightfully delicate business and all that. She might be frightfully waxy about it. I mean—well, it's so dashed difficult to explain."

He looked helplessly at Tommy. Tommy felt annoyed. He had been on the point of going out to lunch, but he foresaw that getting the facts out of this client would be a long and tedious business.

"Did she disappear of her own free will, or do you suspect abduction?" he demanded crisply.

"I don't know," said the young man. "I don't know anything."

Tommy reached for a pad and pencil.

"First of all," he said, "will you give me your name? My office boy is trained never to ask names. In that way consultations can remain completely confidential."

"Oh! rather," said the young man. "Jolly good idea. My name—er—my name's Smith."

"Oh! no," said Tommy. "The real one, please."

His visitor looked at him in awe.

"Er—St. Vincent," he said. "Lawrence St. Vincent."

"It's a curious thing," said Tommy, "how very few people there are whose real name is Smith. Personally, I don't know anyone called Smith. But nine men out of ten who wish to conceal their real name give that of Smith. I am writing a monograph upon the subject."

At that moment a buzzer purred discreetly on his desk. That meant that Tuppence was requesting to take hold. Tommy, who wanted his lunch, and who felt profoundly unsympathetic towards Mr. St. Vincent, was only too pleased to relinquish the helm.

"Excuse me," he said, and picked up the telephone.

Across his face there shot rapid changes—surprise, consternation, slight elation.

"You don't say so," he said into the phone. "The Prime Minister himself? Of course, in that case, I will come round at once."

He replaced the receiver on the hook, and turned to his client.

"My dear sir, I must ask you to excuse me. A most urgent summons. If you will give the facts of the case to my confidential secretary, she will deal with them."

He strode to the adjoining door.

"Miss Robinson."

Tuppence, very neat and demure with smooth black head and dainty collar and cuffs, tripped in. Tommy made the necessary introductions and departed.

"A lady you take an interest in has disappeared, I understand, Mr. St. Vincent," said Tuppence, in her soft voice, as she sat down and took up Mr. Blunt's pad and pencil. "A young lady?"

"Oh! rather," said Mr. St. Vincent. "Young—and—

and—awfully good-looking and all that sort of thing."

Tuppence's face grew grave.

"Dear me," she murmured. "I hope that—"

"You don't think anything's really happened to her?" demanded Mr. St. Vincent, in lively concern.

"Oh! we must hope for the best," said Tuppence, with a kind of false cheerfulness which depressed Mr. St. Vincent horribly.

"Oh! look here, Miss Robinson. I say, you must do something. Spare no expense. I wouldn't have anything happen to her for the world. You seem awfully sympathetic, and I don't mind telling you in confidence that I simply worship the ground that girl walks on. She's a topper, an absolute topper."

"Please tell me her name and all about her."

"Her name's Janet—I don't know her second name. She works in a hat shop—Madame Violette's in Brook Street—but she's as straight as they make them. Has ticked me off no end of times—I went round there yesterday—waiting for her to come out—all the others came, but not her. Then I found that she'd never turned up that morning to work at all—sent no message either—old Madame was furious about it. I got the address of her lodgings, and I went round there. She hadn't come home the night before, and they didn't know where she was. I was simply frantic. I thought of going to the police. But I knew that Janet would be absolutely furious with me for doing that if she were really all right and had gone off on her own. Then I remembered that she herself had pointed out your advertisement to me one day in the paper and told me that one of the women who'd been in buying hats had simply raved about your ability and discretion and all that sort of thing. So I toddled along here right away."

"I see," said Tuppence. "What is the address of her lodgings?"

The young man gave it to her.

"That's all, I think," said Tuppence reflectively. "That is to say—am I to understand that you are engaged to this young lady?"

Mr. St. Vincent turned a brick red.

"Well, no—not exactly. I never said anything. But I can tell you this, I mean to ask her to marry me as soon as ever I see her—if I ever do see her again."

Tuppence laid aside her pad.

"Do you wish for our special twenty-four hour service?" she asked, in business-like tones.

"What's that?"

"The fees are doubled, but we put all our available staff on to the case. Mr. St. Vincent, if the lady is alive, I shall be able to tell you where she is by this time to-morrow."

"What? I say, that's wonderful."

"We only employ experts—and we guarantee results," said Tuppence crisply.

"But I say, you know. You must have the most topping staff."

"Oh! we have," said Tuppence. "By the way, you haven't given me a description of the young lady."

"She's got the most marvelous hair—sort of golden, but very deep, like a jolly old sunset—that's it, a jolly old sunset. You know, I never noticed things like sunsets until lately. Poetry too, there's a lot more in poetry than I ever thought."

"Red hair," said Tuppence unemotionally, writing it down. "What height should you say the lady was?"

"Oh! tallish, and she's got ripping eyes, dark blue, I think. And a sort of decided manner with her—takes a fellow up short sometimes."

Tuppence wrote down a few words more, then closed her note book and rose.

"If you will call here to-morrow at two o'clock, I think we shall have news of some kind for you," she said. "Good morning, Mr. St. Vincent."

When Tommy returned Tuppence was just consulting a page of Debrett.

"I've got all the details," she said succinctly. "Lawrence St. Vincent is the nephew and heir of the Earl of Cheriton. If we pull this through we shall get publicity in the highest places."

Tommy read through the notes on the pad.

"What do you really think has happened to the girl?" he asked.

"I think," said Tuppence, "that she has fled at the dictates of her heart, feeling that she loves this young man too well for her peace of mind."

Tommy looked at her doubtfully.

"I know they do it in books," he said, "but I've never known any girl who did it in real life."

"No?" said Tuppence. "Well, perhaps you're right. But I daresay Lawrence St. Vincent will swallow that sort of slush. He's full of romantic notions just now. By the way, I guaranteed results in twenty-four hours—our special service."

"Tuppence—you congenital idiot, what made you do that?"

"The idea just came into my head. I thought it sounded rather well. Don't you worry. Leave it to Mother. Mother knows best."

She went out, leaving Tommy profoundly dissatisfied.

Presently he rose, sighed, and went out to do what could be done, cursing Tuppence's over-fervent imagination.

When he returned weary and jaded at half past four, he found Tuppence extracting a bag of biscuits from their place of concealment in one of the files.

"You look hot and bothered," she remarked. "What have you been doing?"

Tommy groaned.

"Making a round of the Hospitals with that girl's description."

"Didn't I tell you to leave it to me?" demanded Tuppence.

"You can't find that girl single-handed before two o'clock tomorrow."

"I can—and what's more, I have!"

"You have? What do you mean?"

"A simple problem, Watson, very simple indeed."

"Where is she now?"

Tuppence pointed a hand over her shoulder.

"She's in my office next door."

"What is she doing there?"

Tuppence began to laugh.

"Well," she said, "early training will tell, and with a kettle, a gas ring, and half a pound of tea staring her in the face, the result is a foregone conclusion.

"You see," continued Tuppence gently. "Madame Violette's is where I go for my hats, and the other day I ran across an old pal of Hospital days amongst the girls there. She gave up nursing after the War and started a hat shop, failed, and took this job at Madame Violette's. We fixed up the whole thing between us. She was to rub the advertisement well into young St. Vincent, and then disappear. Wonderful efficiency of Blunt's Brilliant Detectives. Publicity for us, and the necessary fillip to young St. Vincent to bring him to the point of proposing. Janet was in despair about it."

"Tuppence," said Tommy, "you take my breath away! The whole thing is the most immoral business I ever heard of. You aid and abet this young man to marry out of his class—"

"Stuff," said Tuppence. "Janet is a splendid girl—and the queer thing is that she really adores that weak-kneed young man. You can see with half a glance what *his* family needs. Some good red blood in it. Janet will be the making of him. She'll look after him like a mother, ease down the cocktails and the night clubs and make him lead a good healthy country gentleman's life. Come and meet her."

Tuppence opened the door of the adjoining office and Tommy followed her.

A tall girl with lovely auburn hair, and a pleasant face, put down the steaming kettle in her hand, and turned with a smile that disclosed an even row of white teeth.

"I hope you'll forgive me, Nurse Cowley—Mrs. Beresford, I mean. I thought that very likely you'd be quite ready for a cup of tea yourself. Many's the pot of tea you've made for me in the Hospital at three o'clock in the morning."

"Tommy," said Tuppence. "Let me introduce you to my old friend, Nurse Smith."

"Smith, did you say? How curious!" said Tommy, shaking hands. "Eh? Oh! nothing—a little monograph that I was thinking of writing."

"Pull yourself together, Tommy," said Tuppence.

She poured him out a cup of tea.

"Now, then, let's all drink together. Here's to the success of the International Detective Agency. Blunt's Brilliant Detectives! May they never know failure!"

3

The Affair of
The Pink Pearl

"What on earth are you doing?" demanded Tuppence, as she entered the inner sanctum of the International Detective Agency—(Slogan—Blunt's Brilliant Detectives) and discovered her lord and master prone on the floor in a sea of books.

Tommy struggled to his feet.

"I was trying to arrange these books on the top shelf of that cupboard," he complained. "And the damned chair gave way."

"What are they, anyway?" asked Tuppence, picking up a volume. 'The Hound of the Baskervilles.' I wouldn't mind reading that again some time."

"You see the idea?" said Tommy, dusting himself with care. "Half hours with the Great Masters—that sort of thing. You see, Tuppence, I can't help feeling that we are more or less amateurs at this business—of course amateurs in one sense we cannot help being, but it would do no harm to acquire the technique, so to speak. These books are detective stories by the leading masters of the art. I intend to try different styles, and compare results."

"H'm," said Tuppence. "I often wonder how those detectives would have got on in real life." She picked up another volume. "You'll find a difficulty in being a Thorndyke. You've no medical experience, and less legal, and I never heard that science was your strong point."

"Perhaps not," said Tommy. "But at any rate I've bought a very good camera, and I shall photograph footprints and enlarge the negatives and all that sort of thing. Now, mon ami, use your little grey cells—what does this convey to you?"

He pointed to the bottom shelf of the cupboard. On it lay a somewhat futuristic dressing gown, a turkish slipper, and a violin.

"Obvious, my dear Watson," said Tuppence.

"Exactly," said Tommy. "The Sherlock Holmes touch."

He took up the violin and drew the bow idly across the strings, causing Tuppence to give a wail of agony.

At that moment the buzzer rang on the desk, a sign that a client had arrived in the outer office and was being held in parley by Albert, the office boy.

Tommy hastily replaced the violin in the cupboard and kicked the books behind the desk.

"Not that there's any great hurry," he remarked. "Albert will be handing them out the stuff about my being engaged with Scotland Yard on the phone. Get into your office and start typing, Tuppence. It makes the office sound busy and active. No, on second thoughts, you shall be taking notes in shorthand from my dictation. Let's have a look before we get Albert to send the victim in."

They approached the peephole which had been artistically contrived so as to command a view of the outer office.

The client was a girl of about Tuppence's age, tall and dark with a rather haggard face and scornful eyes.

"Clothes cheap and striking," remarked Tuppence. "Have her in, Tommy."

In another minute the girl was shaking hands with the celebrated Mr. Blunt, whilst Tuppence sat by with eyes demurely downcast, and pad and pencil in hand.

"My confidential secretary, Miss Robinson," said Mr. Blunt with a wave of the hand. "You may speak freely before her." Then he lay back for a minute, half closed his eyes and remarked in a tired tone: "You must find traveling in a bus very crowded at this time of day."

"I came in a taxi," said the girl.

"Oh!" said Tommy aggrieved. His eyes rested reproachfully on a blue bus ticket protruding from her glove. The girl's eyes followed his glance, and she smiled and drew it out.

"You mean this? I picked it up on the pavement. A little neighbor of ours collects them."

Tuppence coughed, and Tommy threw a baleful glare at her.

"We must get to business," he said briskly. "You are in need of our services, Miss—?"

"Kingston Bruce is my name," said the girl. "We live at Wimbledon. Last night a lady who is staying with us lost a valuable pink pearl. Mr. St. Vincent was also dining with us, and during dinner he happened to mention your firm. My mother sent me off to you this morning to ask you if you would look into the matter for us."

The girl spoke sullenly, almost disagreeably. It was clear as daylight that she and her mother had not agreed over the matter. She was here under protest.

"I see," said Tommy, a little puzzled. "You have not called in the police?"

"No," said Miss Kingston Bruce, "we haven't. It would be idiotic to call in the police and then find that the silly thing had rolled under the fireplace, or something like that."

"Oh!" said Tommy. "Then the jewel may only be lost after all?"

Miss Kingston Bruce shrugged her shoulders.

"People make such a fuss about things," she murmured.

Tommy cleared his throat.

"Of course," he said doubtfully. "I am extremely busy just now—"

"I quite understand," said the girl rising to her feet. There was a quick gleam of satisfaction in her eyes which Tuppence, for one, did not miss.

"Nevertheless," continued Tommy, "I think I can manage

to run down to Wimbledon. Will you give me the address, please?"

"The Laurels, Edgeworth Road."

"Make a note of it, please, Miss Robinson."

Miss Kingston Bruce hesitated, then said rather ungraciously:

"We'll expect you then. Good morning."

"Funny girl," said Tommy. "I couldn't quite make her out."

"I wonder if she stole the thing herself," remarked Tuppence meditatively. "Come on, Tommy, let's put away these books and take the car and go down there. By the way, who are you going to be, Sherlock Holmes still?"

"I think I need practice for that," said Tommy. "I came rather a cropper over that bus ticket, didn't I?"

"You did," said Tuppence. "If I were you I shouldn't try too much on that girl—she's as sharp as a needle. She's unhappy too, poor devil."

"I suppose you know all about her already," said Tommy with sarcasm, "simply from looking at the shape of her nose!"

"I'll tell you my idea of what we shall find at The Laurels," said Tuppence, quite unmoved. "A household of snobs, very keen to move in the best society; the father, if there is a father, is sure to have a military title. The girl falls in with their way of life and despises herself for doing so."

Tommy took a last look at the books now neatly ranged upon a shelf.

"I think," he said thoughtfully, "that I shall be Thorndyke to-day."

"I shouldn't have thought there was anything medico-legal about this case," remarked Tuppence.

"Perhaps not," said Tommy. "But I'm simply dying to use that new camera of mine! It's supposed to have the most marvelous lens that ever was or ever could be."

"I know those kind of lenses," said Tuppence. "By the time you've adjusted the shutter and stopped down and calculated the exposure and kept your eye on the spirit level, your brain gives out, and you yearn for the simple Brownie."

"Only an unambitious soul is content with the simple Brownie."

"Well, I bet I shall get better results with it than you will."

Tommy ignored this challenge.

"I ought to have a 'Smoker's Companion'," he said regretfully. "I wonder where one buys them?"

"There's always the patent corkscrew Aunt Araminta gave you last Xmas," said Tuppence helpfully.

"That's true," said Tommy. "A curious looking engine of destruction I thought it at the time, and rather a humorous present to get from a strictly teetotal aunt."

"I," said Tuppence, "shall be Polton."

Tommy looked at her scornfully.

"Polton indeed. You couldn't begin to do one of the things that he does."

"Yes, I can," said Tuppence. "I can rub my hands together when I'm pleased. That's quite enough to get on with. I hope you're going to take plaster casts of footprints?"

Tommy was reduced to silence. Having collected the corkscrew they went round to the garage, got out the car and started for Wimbledon.

The Laurels was a big house. It ran somewhat to gables and turrets, had an air of being very newly painted, and was surrounded with neat flower beds filled with scarlet geraniums.

A tall man with a close-cropped white moustache, and an exaggeratedly martial bearing opened the door before Tommy had time to ring.

"I've been looking out for you," he explained fussily. "Mr. Blunt, is it not? I am Colonel Kingston Bruce. Will you come into my study?"

He led them into a small room at the back of the house.

"Young St. Vincent was telling me wonderful things about your firm. I've noticed your advertisements myself. This guaranteed twenty-four hours service of yours—a marvelous notion. That's exactly what I need."

Inwardly anathematizing Tuppence for her irresponsi-

bility in inventing this brilliant detail, Tommy replied: "Just
so, Colonel."

"The whole thing is most distressing, sir, most distressing."

"Perhaps you would kindly give me the facts," said
Tommy, with a hint of impatience.

"Certainly I will—at once. We have at the present moment staying with us a very old and dear friend of ours,
Lady Laura Barton. Daughter of the late Earl of Carroway.
The present Earl, her brother, made a striking speech in the
House of Lords the other day. As I say, she is an old and
dear friend of ours. Some American friends of mine who
have just come over, the Hamilton Betts, were most anxious
to meet her. 'Nothing easier,' I said. 'She is staying with
me now. Come down for the week-end.' You know what
Americans are about titles, Mr. Blunt."

"And others besides Americans sometimes, Colonel
Kingston Bruce."

"Alas! only too true, my dear sir. Nothing I hate more
than a snob. Well, as I was saying, the Betts came down
for the week-end. Last night—we were playing Bridge at
the time—the clasp of a pendant Mrs. Hamilton Betts was
wearing broke, so she took it off and laid it down on a small
table, meaning to take it upstairs with her when she went.
This, however, she forgot to do. I must explain, Mr. Blunt,
that the pendant consisted of two small diamond wings, and
a big pink pearl depending from them. The pendant was
found this morning lying where Mrs. Betts had left it, but
the pearl, a pearl of enormous value, had been wrenched
off."

"Who found the pendant?"

"The parlormaid—Gladys Hill."

"Any reason to suspect her?"

"She has been with us some years, and we have always
found her perfectly honest. But, of course, one never
knows—"

"Exactly. Will you describe your staff, and also tell me
who was present at dinner last night?"

"There is the cook—she has been with us only two

months, but then she would have no occasion to go near the drawing-room—the same applies to the kitchen maid. Then there is the housemaid, Alice Cummings. She also has been with us for some years. And Lady Laura's maid, of course. She is French."

Colonel Kingston Bruce looked very impressive as he said this. Tommy, unaffected by the revelation of the maid's nationality, said: "Exactly. And the party at dinner?"

"Mr. and Mrs. Betts, ourselves—(my wife and daughter)—and Lady Laura. Young St. Vincent was dining with us, and Mr. Rennie looked in after dinner for a while."

"Who is Mr. Rennie?"

"A most pestilential fellow—an arrant socialist. Good looking, of course, and with a certain specious power of argument. But a man, I don't mind telling you, whom I wouldn't trust a yard. A dangerous sort of fellow."

"In fact," said Tommy drily, "it is Mr. Rennie whom you suspect?"

"I do, Mr. Blunt. I'm sure, holding the views he does, that he can have no principles whatsoever. What could have been easier for him than to have quietly wrenched off the pearl at a moment when we were all absorbed in our game? There were several absorbing moments—a redoubled No Trump hand, I remember, and also a painful argument when my wife had the misfortune to revoke."

"Quite so," said Tommy. "I should just like to know one thing—what is Mrs. Betts's attitude in all this?"

"She wanted me to call in the police," said Colonel Kingston Bruce reluctantly. "That is, when we had searched everywhere in case the pearl had only dropped off."

"But you dissuaded her?"

"I was very averse to the idea of publicity and my wife and daughter backed me up. Then my wife remembered young St. Vincent speaking about your firm at dinner last night—and the twenty-four hours special service."

"Yes," said Tommy, with a heavy heart.

"You see, in any case no harm will be done. If we call in the police to-morrow, it can be supposed that we thought the jewel merely lost and were hunting for it. By the way, nobody has been allowed to leave the house this morning."

"Except your daughter, of course," said Tuppence, speaking for the first time.

"Except my daughter," agreed the Colonel. "She volunteered at once to go and put the case before you."

Tommy rose.

"We will do our best to give you satisfaction, Colonel," he said. "I should like to see the drawing-room, and the table on which the pendant was laid down. I should also like to ask Mrs. Betts a few questions. After that, I will interview the servants—or rather my assistant, Miss Robinson, will do so."

He felt his nerve quailing before the terrors of questioning the servants.

Colonel Kingston Bruce threw open the door, and led them across the hall. As he did so, a remark came to them clearly through the open door of the room they were approaching, and the voice that uttered it was that of the girl who had come to see them that morning.

"You know perfectly well, mother," she was saying, "that she *did* bring home a teaspoon in her muff."

In another minute they were being introduced to Mrs. Kingston Bruce, a plaintive lady with a languid manner. Miss Kingston Bruce acknowledged their presence with a short inclination of the head. Her face was more sullen than ever.

Mrs. Kingston Bruce was voluble.

"—but I know who *I* think took it," she ended. "That dreadful socialist young man. He loves the Russians and the Germans and hates the English—what else can you expect?"

"He never touched it," said Miss Kingston Bruce fiercely. "I was watching him—all the time. I couldn't have failed to see if he had."

She looked at them defiantly with her chin up.

Tommy created a diversion by asking for an interview with Mrs. Betts. When Mrs. Kingston Bruce had departed accompanied by her husband and daughter to find Mrs. Betts, he whistled thoughtfully.

"I wonder," he said gently, "who it was who had a teaspoon in her muff?"

"Just what I was thinking," replied Tuppence.

Mrs. Betts, followed by her husband, burst into the room. She was a big woman, with a determined voice. Mr. Hamilton Betts looked dyspeptic and subdued.

"I understand, Mr. Blunt, that you are a private inquiry agent, and one who hustles things through at a great rate?"

"Hustle," said Tommy, "is my middle name, Mrs. Betts. Let me ask you a few questions."

Thereafter things proceeded rapidly. Tommy was shown the damaged pendant, the table on which it had lain, and Mr. Betts emerged from his taciturnity to mention the value, in dollars, of the stolen pearl.

And withal, Tommy felt an irritating certainty that he was not getting on.

"I think that will do," he said at length. "Miss Robinson, will you kindly fetch the special photographic apparatus from the hall?"

Miss Robinson complied.

"A little invention of my own," said Tommy. "In appearance, you see, it is just like an ordinary camera."

He had some slight satisfaction in seeing that the Betts were impressed.

He photographed the pendant, the table on which it had lain, and took several general views of the apartment. Then "Miss Robinson" was delegated to interview the servants, and in view of the eager expectancy on the faces of Colonel Kingston Bruce and Mrs. Betts, Tommy felt called upon to say a few authoritative words.

"The position amounts to this," he said. "Either the pearl is still in the house, or it is not still in the house."

"Quite so," said the Colonel with more respect than was, perhaps, quite justified by the nature of the remark.

"If it is not in the house, it may be anywhere—but if it is in the house, it must necessarily be concealed somewhere—"

"And a search must be made," broke in Colonel Kingston Bruce. "Quite so. I give you carte blanche, Mr. Blunt.

Search the house from attic to cellar."

"Oh! Charles," murmured Mrs. Kingston Bruce tearfully. "Do you think that is wise? The servants won't *like* it. I'm sure they'll leave."

"We will search their quarters last," said Tommy soothingly. "The thief is sure to have hidden the gem in the most unlikely place."

"I seem to have read something of the kind," agreed the Colonel.

"Quite so," said Tommy. "You probably remember the case of Rex *v.* Bailey which created precedent."

"Oh—er—yes," said the Colonel looking puzzled.

"Now, the most unlikely place is in the apartments of Mrs. Betts," continued Tommy.

"My! Wouldn't that be too cute?" said Mrs. Betts admiringly.

Without more ado, she took him up to her room where Tommy once more made use of the special photographic apparatus.

Presently Tuppence joined him there.

"You have no objection, I hope, Mrs. Betts, to my assistant's looking through your wardrobe?"

"Why, not at all. Do you need me here any longer?"

Tommy assured her that there was no need to detain her, and Mrs. Betts departed.

"We might as well go on bluffing it out," said Tommy. "But personally I don't believe we've got a dog's chance of finding the thing. Curse you and your twenty-four hours stunt, Tuppence."

"Listen," said Tuppence. "The servants are all right, I'm sure, but I managed to get something out of the French maid. It seems that when Lady Laura was staying here a year ago, she went out to tea with some friends of the Kingston Bruces', and when she got home a teaspoon fell out of her muff. Everyone thought it must have fallen in by accident. But, talking about similar robberies, I got hold of a lot more. Lady Laura is always staying about with people. She hasn't got a bean, I gather, and she's out for comfortable quarters with people to whom a title still means something. It may be a coincidence—or it may be something more, but five distinct thefts have taken place whilst she has been staying in various houses, sometimes trivial things, sometimes valuable jewels."

"Whew!" said Tommy, and gave vent to a prolonged whistle. "Where's the old bird's room, do you know?"

"Just across the passage."

"Then I think, I rather think, that we'll just slip across and investigate."

The room opposite stood with its door ajar. It was a spacious apartment, with white enameled fitments and rose pink curtains. An inner door led to a bathroom. At the door of this appeared a slim dark girl, very neatly dressed.

Tuppence checked the exclamation of astonishment on the girl's lips.

"This is Elise, Mr. Blunt," she said primly. "Lady Laura's maid."

Tommy stepped across the threshold of the bathroom, and approved inwardly its sumptuous and up to date fittings. He set to work to dispel the wide stare of suspicion on the French girl's face.

"You are busy with your duties, eh, Mademoiselle Elise?"

"Yes, Monsieur, I clean Milady's bath."

"Well, perhaps you'll help me with some photography instead. I have a special kind of camera here, and I am photographing the interiors of all the rooms in this house."

He was interrupted by the communicating door to the bedroom banging suddenly behind him. Elise jumped at the sound.

"What did that?"

"It must have been the wind," said Tuppence.

"We will come into the other room," said Tommy.

Elise went to open the door for them, but the door knob rattled aimlessly.

"What's the matter?" said Tommy sharply.

"Ah, Monsieur, but somebody must have locked it on the other side." She caught up a towel and tried again. But this time the door handle turned easily enough, and the door swung open.

"*Voila ce qui est curieux*. It must have stuck," said Elise. There was no one in the bedroom.

Tommy fetched his apparatus. Tuppence and Elise worked under his orders. But again and again his glance went back to the communicating door.

"I wonder," he said between his teeth. "I wonder why that door stuck?"

He examined it minutely, shutting and opening it. It fitted perfectly.

"One picture more," he said with a sigh. "Will you loop back that rose curtain, Mademoiselle Elise? Thank you. Just hold it so."

The familiar click occurred. He handed a glass slide to Elise to hold, relinquished the tripod to Tuppence, and carefully readjusted and closed the camera.

He made some easy excuse to get rid of Elise, and as soon as she was out of the room, he caught hold of Tuppence and spoke rapidly.

"Look here, I've got an idea. Can you hang on here? Search all the rooms—that will take some time. Try and get an interview with the old bird—Lady Laura—but don't alarm her. Tell her you suspect the parlormaid. But whatever you do, don't let her leave the house. I'm going off in the car. I'll be back as soon as I can."

"All right," said Tuppence. "But don't be too cocksure. You've forgotten one thing."

"What's that?"

"The girl. There's something funny about that girl. Listen, I've found out the time she started from the house this morning. It took her two hours to get to our office. That's nonsense. Where did she go before she came to us?"

"There's something in that," admitted her husband. "Well, follow up any old clue you like, but don't let Lady Laura leave the house. What's that?"

His quick ear had caught a faint rustle outside on the landing. He strode across to the door, but there was no one to be seen.

"Well, so long," he said. "I'll be back as soon as I can."

4
The Affair of
The Pink Pearl (continued)

Tuppence watched him drive off in the car with a faint misgiving. Tommy was very sure—she herself was not so sure. There were one or two things she did not quite understand.

She was still standing by the window, watching the road, when she saw a man leave the shelter of a gateway opposite, cross the road and ring the bell.

In a flash Tuppence was out of the room and down the stairs. Gladys Hill the parlormaid, was emerging from the back part of the house, but Tuppence motioned her back authoritatively. Then she went to the front door and opened it.

A lanky young man with ill-fitting clothes, and eager dark eyes was standing on the step.

He hesitated a moment, and then said:

"Is Miss Kingston Bruce in?"

"Will you come inside?" said Tuppence.

She stood aside to let him enter, closing the door.

"Mr. Rennie, I think?" she said sweetly.

He shot a quick glance at her.

"Er—yes."

"Will you come in here, please?"

She opened the study door. The room was empty, and Tuppence entered it after him, closing the door behind her. He turned on her with a frown.

"I want to see Miss Kingston Bruce."

"I am not quite sure that you can," said Tuppence composedly.

"Look here, who the devil are you?" said Mr. Rennie rudely.

"International Detective Agency," said Tuppence succinctly—and noticed Mr. Rennie's uncontrollable start.

"Please sit down, Mr. Rennie," she went on. "To begin with, we know all about Miss Kingston Bruce's visit to you this morning."

It was a bold guess, but it succeeded. Perceiving his consternation, Tuppence went on quickly.

"The recovery of the pearl is the great thing, Mr. Rennie. No one in this house is anxious for—publicity. Can't we come to some arrangement?"

The young man looked at her keenly.

"I wonder how much you know," he said thoughtfully. "Let me think for a moment."

He buried his head in his hands—then asked a most unexpected question.

"I say, is it really true that young St. Vincent is engaged to be married?"

"Quite true," said Tuppence. "I know the girl."

Mr. Rennie suddenly became confidential.

"It's been hell," he confided. "They've been asking him here morning, noon and night—chucking Beatrice at his head. All because he'll come into a title some day. If I had my way—"

"Don't let's talk politics," said Tuppence hastily. "Do you mind telling me, Mr. Rennie, why you think Miss Kingston Bruce took the pearl?"

"I—I don't."

"You do," said Tuppence calmly. "You wait to see the detective, as you think, drive off and the coast clear, and then you come and ask for her. It's obvious. If you'd taken the pearl yourself, you wouldn't be half so upset."

"Her manner was so odd," said the young man. "She came this morning and told me about the robbery, explaining that she was on her way to a firm of private detectives. She seemed anxious to say something, and yet not able to get it out."

"Well," said Tuppence. "All I want is the pearl. You'd better go and talk to her."

But at that moment Colonel Kingston Bruce opened the door.

"Lunch is ready, Miss Robinson. You will lunch with us, I hope. The—"

Then he stopped and glared at the guest.

"Cleary," said Mr. Rennie, "you don't want to ask me to lunch. All right, I'll go."

"Come back later," whispered Tuppence, as he passed her.

Tuppence followed Colonel Kingston Bruce, still growling into his moustache about the pestilential impudence of some people, into a massive dining-room where the family was already assembled. Only one person present was unknown to Tuppence.

"This, Lady Laura, is Miss Robinson who is kindly assisting us."

Lady Laura bent her head, and then proceeded to stare at Tuppence through her pince nez. She was a tall thin woman, with a sad smile, a gentle voice, and very hard shrewd eyes. Tuppence returned her stare, and Lady Laura's eyes dropped.

After lunch Lady Laura entered into conversation with an air of gentle curiosity. How was the inquiry proceeding? Tuppence laid suitable stress on the suspicion attaching to the parlormaid, but her mind was not really on Lady Laura. Lady Laura might conceal teaspoons and other articles in her clothing, but Tuppence felt fairly sure that she had not taken the pink pearl.

Presently Tuppence proceeded with her search of the house. Time was going on. There was no sign of Tommy, and, what mattered far more to Tuppence, there was no sign of Mr. Rennie. Suddenly Tuppence came out of a bedroom and collided with Beatrice Kingston Bruce who was going down stairs. She was fully dressed for the street.

"I'm afraid," said Tuppence, "that you mustn't go out just now."

The other girl looked at her haughtily.

"Whether I go out or not is no business of yours," she said coldly.

"It is my business whether I communicate with the police or not, though," said Tuppence.

In a minute the girl had turned ashy pale.

"You mustn't—you mustn't—I won't go out—but don't do that." She clung to Tuppence beseechingly.

"My dear Miss Kingston Bruce," said Tuppence smiling. "The case has been perfectly clear to me from the start—I—"

But she was interrupted. In the stress of her encounter with the girl, Tuppence had not heard the front door bell. Now, to her astonishment, Tommy came bounding up the stairs, and in the hall below she caught sight of a big burly man in the act of removing a bowler hat.

"Detective Inspector Marriot of Scotland Yard," he said with a grin.

With a cry, Beatrice Kingston Bruce tore herself from Tuppence's grasp and dashed down the stairs, just as the front door was opened once more to admit Mr. Rennie.

"Now you *have* torn it," said Tuppence bitterly.

"Eh?" said Tommy, hurrying into Lady Laura's room. He passed on into the bathroom, and picked up a large cake of soap which he brought out in his hands. The Inspector was just mounting the stairs.

"She went quite quietly," he announced. "She's an old hand, and knows when the game is up. What about the pearl?"

"I rather fancy," said Tommy, handing him the soap, "that you'll find it in here."

The Inspector's eyes lit up appreciatively.

"An old trick, and a good one. Cut a cake of soap in half, scoop out a place for the jewel, clap it together again, and smooth the join well over with hot water. A very smart piece of work on your part, sir."

Tommy accepted the compliment gracefully. He and Tuppence descended the stairs. Colonel Kingston Bruce rushed at him and shook him warmly by the hand.

"My dear sir, I can't thank you enough. Lady Laura wants to thank you also—"

"I am glad we have given you satisfaction," said Tommy. "But I'm afraid I can't stop. I have a most urgent appointment. Member of the Cabinet."

He hurried out to the car and jumped in. Tuppence jumped in beside him.

"But Tommy," she cried. "Haven't they arrested Lady Laura, after all?"

"Oh!" said Tommy. "Didn't I tell you? They've not arrested Lady Laura. They've arrested Elise."

"You see," he went on, as Tuppence sat dumbfounded, "I've often tried to open a door with soap on my hands myself. It can't be done—your hands slip. So I wondered what Elise could have been doing with the soap to get her hands as soapy as all that. She caught up a towel, you remember, so there were no traces of soap on the handle afterwards. But it occurred to me that if you were a professional thief, it wouldn't be a bad plan to be maid to a lady suspected of kleptomania who stayed about a good deal in different houses. So I managed to get a photo of her as well as of the room, induced her to handle a glass slide and toddled off to dear old Scotland Yard. Lightning development of negative, successful identification of finger-prints—and photo. Elise was a long lost friend. Useful place, Scotland Yard."

"And to think," said Tuppence, finding her voice, "that those two young idiots were only suspecting each other in that weak way they do it in books. But why didn't you tell me what you were up to when you went off?"

"In the first place, I suspected that Elise was listening on the landing, and in the second place—"

"Yes?"

"My learned friend forgets," said Tommy. "Thorndyke

never tells until the last moment. Besides, Tuppence, you and your pal Janet Smith put one over on me last time. This makes us all square."

5

The Adventure of
The Sinister Stranger

"It's been a darned dull day," said Tommy, and yawned widely.

"Nearly tea time," said Tuppence and also yawned.

Business was not brisk in the International Detective Agency. The eagerly expected letter from the ham merchant had not arrived and bona fide cases were not forthcoming.

Albert, the office boy, entered with a sealed package which he laid on the table.

"The Mystery of the Sealed Packet," murmured Tommy. "Did it contain the fabulous pearls of the Russian Grand Duchess? Or was it an infernal machine destined to blow Blunt's Brilliant Detectives to pieces?"

"As a matter of fact," said Tuppence, tearing open the package, "it's my wedding present to Francis Haviland. Rather nice, isn't it?"

Tommy took a slender silver cigarette case from her outstretched hand, noted the inscription engraved in her own handwriting: *Francis from Tuppence*, opened and shut the case, and nodded approvingly.

"You do throw your money about, Tuppence," he remarked. "I'll have one like it, only in gold, for my birthday

next month. Fancy wasting a thing like that on Francis
Haviland, who always was and always will be one of the
most perfect asses God ever made!"

"You forget I used to drive him about during the War,
when he was a General. Ah! those were the good old days."

"They were," agreed Tommy. "Beautiful women used
to come and squeeze my hand in Hospital, I remember. But
I don't send them all wedding presents. I don't believe the
bride will care much for this gift of yours, Tuppence."

"It's nice and slim for the pocket, isn't it?" said Tuppence
disregarding his remarks.

Tommy slipped it into his own pocket.

"Just right," he said approvingly. "Hullo, here is Albert
with the afternoon post. Very possibly the Duchess of Perthe-
shire is commissioning us to find her prize Peke."

They sorted through the letters together. Suddenly Tommy
gave vent to a prolonged whistle, and held up one of them
in his hand.

"A blue letter with a Russian stamp on it. Do you remember what the Chief said? We were to look out for letters
like that."

"How exciting," said Tuppence. "Something has happened at last. Open it and see if the contents are up to
schedule. A ham merchant, wasn't it? Half a minute. We
shall want some milk for tea. They forgot to leave it this
morning. I'll send Albert out for it."

She returned from the outer office, after despatching
Albert on his errand, to find Tommy holding the blue sheet
of paper in his hand.

"As we thought, Tuppence," he remarked. "Almost word
for word what the Chief said."

Tuppence took the letter from him and read it.

It was couched in careful stilted English, and purported
to be from one Gregor Feodorsky who was anxious for news
of his wife. The International Detective Agency was urged
to spare no expense in doing their utmost to trace her.
Feodorsky himself was unable to leave Russia at the moment
owing to a crisis in the Pork trade.

"I wonder what it really means," said Tuppence thoughtfully, smoothing out the sheet on the table in front of her.

"Code of some kind, I suppose," said Tommy. "That's not our business. Our business is to hand it over to the Chief as soon as possible. Better just verify it by soaking off the stamp and seeing if the number 16 is underneath."

"All right," said Tuppence. "But I should think—"

She stopped dead, and Tommy, surprised by her sudden pause, looked up to see a man's burly figure blocking the doorway.

The intruder was a man of commanding presence, squarely built, with a very round head and a powerful jaw. He might have been about forty-five years of age.

"I must beg your pardon," said the stranger, advancing into the room, hat in hand. "I found your outer office empty, and this door open, so I ventured to intrude. This is Blunt's International Detective Agency, is it not?"

"Certainly it is."

"And you are, perhaps, Mr. Blunt? Mr. Theodore Blunt?"

"I am Mr. Blunt. You wished to consult me? This is my secretary, Miss Robinson."

Tuppence inclined her head gracefully, but continued to scruitinise the stranger narrowly through her downcast eyelashes. She was wondering how long he had been standing in the doorway, and how much he had seen and heard. It did not escape her observation that even while he was talking to Tommy, his eyes kept coming back to the blue paper in her hand.

Tommy's voice, sharp with a warning note, recalled her to the needs of the moment.

"Miss Robinson, please, take notes. Now, sir, will you kindly state the matter on which you wish to have my advice?"

Tuppence reached for her pad and pencil.

The big man began in rather a harsh voice.

"My name is Bower. Dr. Charles Bower. I live in Hampstead where I have a practice. I have come to you, Mr. Blunt, because several rather strange occurrences have happened lately."

"Yes, Dr. Bower?"

"Twice in the course of the last week, I have been summoned by telephone to an urgent case—in each case to find that the summons has been a fake. The first time I thought a practical joke had been played upon me, but on my return the second time, I found that some of my private papers had been displaced and disarranged, and I now believe that the same thing had happened the first time. I made an exhaustive search and came to the conclusion that my whole desk had been thoroughly ransacked, and the various papers replaced hurriedly."

Dr. Bower paused, and gazed at Tommy.

"Well, Mr. Blunt?"

"Well, Dr. Bower," replied the young man smiling.

"What do you think of it, eh?"

"Well, first I should like the facts. What do you keep in your desk?"

"My private papers."

"Exactly. Now, what do those private papers consist of? What value are they to the common thief—or any particular person?"

"To the common thief I cannot see that they would have any value at all, but my notes on certain obscure alkaloids would be of interest to anyone possessed of technical knowledge on the subject. I have been making a study of such matters for the last few years. These alkaloids are deadly and virulent poisons, and are, in addition, almost untraceable. They yield no known reactions."

"The secret of them would be worth money, then?"

"To unscrupulous persons, yes."

"And you suspect—whom?"

The doctor shrugged his massive shoulders.

"As far as I can tell, the house was not entered forcibly from the outside. That seems to point to some member of my household, and yet I cannot believe—" He broke off abruptly, then began again, his face very grave.

"Mr. Blunt, I must place myself in your hands unreservedly. I dare not go to the police in the matter. Of my three servants I am almost entirely sure. They have served me long and faithfully. Still, one never knows. Then I have living with me my two nephews, Bertram and Henry. Henry is a good boy—a very good boy—he has never caused me any anxiety, an excellent hard-working young fellow. Bertram, I regret to say, is of quite a different character—wild, extravagant, and persistently idle."

"I see," said Tommy thoughtfully. "You suspect your nephew Bertram of being mixed up in this business. Now I don't agree with you. I suspect the good boy—Henry."

"But why?"

"Tradition. Precedent." Tommy waved his hand airily. "In my experience, the suspicious characters are always innocent—and vice versa, my dear sir. Yes, decidedly, I suspect Henry."

"Excuse me, Mr. Blunt," said Tuppence, interrupting in a deferential voice. "Did I understand Dr. Bower to say that these notes on—er—obscure alkaloids—are kept in the desk with the other papers?"

"They are kept in the desk, my dear young lady, but in a secret drawer, the position of which is known only to myself. Hence they have so far defied the search."

"And what exactly do you want me to do, Dr. Bower?" asked Tommy. "Do you anticipate that a further search will be made?"

"I do, Mr. Blunt. I have every reason to believe so. This afternoon, I received a telegram from a patient of mine whom I ordered to Bournemouth a few weeks ago. The telegram states that my patient is in a critical condition, and begs me to come down at once. Rendered suspicious by the events I have told you of, I myself despatched a telegram, prepaid, to the patient in question, and elicited the fact that he was in good health and had sent no summons to me of any kind. It occurred to me that if I pretended to have been taken in, and duly departed to Bournemouth, we should have a very good chance of finding the miscreants at work. They—or he—will doubtless wait until the household has retired to bed before commencing operations. I suggest that you should meet me outside my house at eleven o'clock this evening, and we will investigate the matter together."

"Hoping, in fact, to catch them in the act." Tommy drummed thoughtfully on the table with a paper knife. "Your plan seems to me an excellent one, Dr. Bower. I cannot see any hitch in it. Let me see, your address is—?"

"The Larches, Hangman's Lane—rather a lonely part, I am afraid. But we command magnificent views over the Heath."

"Quite so." said Tommy.

The visitor rose.

"Then I shall expect you to-night, Mr. Blunt. Outside The Larches at—shall we say, five minutes to eleven—to be on the safe side?"

"Certainly. Five minutes to eleven. Good afternoon, Dr. Bower."

Tommy rose, pressed the buzzer on his desk, and Albert appeared to show the client out. The doctor walked with a decided limp, but his powerful physique was evident in spite of it.

"An ugly customer to tackle," murmured Tommy to himself. "Well, Tuppence, old girl, what do you think of it?"

"I'll tell you in one word," said Tuppence. *Clubfoot!*"

"What?"

"I said Clubfoot! My study of the Classics has not been in vain. Tommy, this thing's a plant. Obscure alkaloids indeed—I never heard a weaker story."

"Even I did not find it very convincing," admitted her husband.

"Did you see his eyes on the letter? Tommy, he's one of the gang. They've got wise to the fact that you're not the real Mr. Blunt, and they're out for our blood."

"In that case," said Tommy, opening the side cupboard, and surveying his rows of books with an affectionate eye. "Our rôle is easy to select. We are the brothers Okewood! And I am Desmond," he added firmly.

Tuppence shrugged her shoulders.

"All right. Have it your own way. I'd just as soon be Francis. Francis was much the more intelligent of the two. Desmond always gets into a mess, and Francis turns up as the gardener or something in the nick of time, and saves the situation."

"Ah!" said Tommy, "but I shall be a super Desmond! When I arrive at The Larches—"

Tuppence interrupted him unceremoniously.

"You're not going to Hampstead to-night?"

"Why not?"

"Walk into a trap with your eyes shut!"

"No, my dear girl, walk into a trap with my eyes open. There's a lot of difference. I think our friend Dr. Bower will get a little surprise."

"I don't like it," said Tuppence. "You know what happens when Desmond disobeys the Chief's orders, and acts on his own. Our orders were quite clear. To send on the letters at once and to report immediately on anything that happened."

"You've not got it quite right," said Tommy. "We were to report immediately if anyone came in and mentioned the number 16. Nobody has."

"That's a quibble," said Tuppence.

"It's no good. I've got a fancy for playing a lone hand. My dear old Tuppence, I shall be all right. I shall go armed to the teeth. The essence of the whole thing is that I shall be on my guard and they won't know it. The Chief will be patting me on the back for a good night's work."

"Well," said Tuppence. "I don't like it. That man's as strong as a gorilla."

"Ah!" said Tommy, "but think of my blue-nosed automatic."

The door of the outer office opened and Albert appeared. Closing the door behind him, he approached them with an envelope in his hand.

"A gentleman to see you," said Albert. "When I began the usual stunt of saying you were engaged with Scotland Yard, he told me he knew all about that. Said he came from Soctland Yard himself! And he wrote something on a card and stuck it up in this envelope."

Tommy took the envelope and opened it. As he read the card, a grin passed across his face.

"The gentleman was amusing himself at your expense by speaking the truth, Albert," he remarked. "Show him in."

He tossed the card to Tuppence. It bore the name Detective Inspector Dymchurch, and across it was scrawled in pencil—"A friend of Marriot's."

In another minute the Scotland Yard detective was entering the inner office. In appearance, Inspector Dymchurch was of the same type as Inspector Marriot, short and thick set, with shrewd eyes.

"Good afternoon," said the detective breezily. "Marriot's away in South Wales, but before he went, he asked me to keep an eye on you two, and on this place in general. Oh! bless you, sir," he went on, as Tommy seemed about to interrupt him, *"we* know all about it. It's not our department, and we don't interfere. But somebody's got wise lately to the fact that all is not what it seems. You've had a gentleman here this afternoon. I don't know what he called himself, and I don't know what his real name is, but I know just a little about him. Enough to want to know more. Am I right in assuming that he made a date with you for some particular spot this evening?"

"Quite right."

"I thought as much. 16 Westerham Road, Finsbury Park? Was that it?"

"You're wrong there," said Tommy with a smile. "Dead wrong. The Larches, Hampstead."

Dymchurch seemed honestly taken aback. Clearly he had not expected this.

"I don't understand it," he muttered. "It must be a new layout. The Larches, Hampstead, you said?"

"Yes. I'm to meet him there at eleven o'clock tonight."

"Don't you do it, sir."

"There!" burst from Tuppence.

Tommy flushed.

"If you think, Inspector—" he began heatedly.

But the Inspector raised a soothing hand.

"I'll tell you what I think, Mr. Blunt. The place you want to be at eleven o'clock to-night is here in this office."

"What?" cried Tuppence, astonished.

"Here in this office. Never mind how I know—departments overlap sometimes—but you got one of those famous "Blue" letters to-day. Old what's his name is after that. He lures you up to Hampstead, makes quite sure of your being out of the way, and steps in here at night when all the building is empty and quiet to have a good search round at his leisure."

"But why should he think the letter would be here? He'd know I should have it on me or else have passed it on."

"Begging your pardon, sir, that's just what he wouldn't know. He may have tumbled to the fact that you're not the original Mr. Blunt, but he probably thinks that you're a bona fide gentleman who's bought the business. In that case, the letter would be all in the way of regular business and would be filed as such."

"I see," said Tuppence.

"And that's just what we've got to let him think. We'll catch him red handed here to-night."

"So that's the plan, is it?"

"Yes. It's the chance of a lifetime. Now, let me see, what's the time? Six o'clock. What time do you usually leave here, sir?"

"About six."

"You must seem to leave the place as usual. Actually we'll sneak back to it as soon as possible. I don't believe they'll come here till about eleven, but of course they might. If you'll excuse me, I'll just go and take a look round outside and see if I can make out anyone watching the place."

Dymchurch departed, and Tommy began an argument with Tuppence.

It lasted some time and was heated and acrimonious. In the end Tuppence suddenly capitulated.

"All right," she said. "I give in. I'll go home, and sit there like a good little girl whilst you tackle crooks and hob nob with detectives—but you wait, young man. I'll be even with you yet for keeping me out of the fun."

Dymchurch returned at that moment.

"Coast seems clear enough," he said. "But you can't tell.

Better seem to leave in the usual manner. They won't go on watching the place once you've gone."

Tommy called Albert, and gave him instructions to lock up.

Then the four of them made their way to the garage near by where the car was usually left. Tuppence drove and Albert sat beside her. Tommy and the detective sat behind.

Presently they were held up by a block in the traffic. Tuppence looked over her shoulder and nodded. Tommy and the detective opened the right hand door, and stepped out into the middle of Oxford Street. In a minute or two Tuppence drove on.

6

The Adventure of
The Sinister Stranger (continued)

"Better not go in just yet," said Dymchurch as he and Tommy hurried into Haleham Street. "You've got the key all right?"

Tommy nodded.

"Then what about a bite of dinner? It's early, but there's a little place here right opposite. We'll get a table by the window, so that we can watch the place all the time."

They had a very welcome little meal, in the manner the detective had suggested. Tommy found Inspector Dymchurch quite an entertaining companion. Most of his official work had lain amongst international spies, and he had tales to tell which astonished his simple listener.

They remained in the little Restaurant until eight o'clock when Dymchurch suggested a move.

"It's quite dark now, sir," he explained. "We shall be able to slip in without anyone being the wiser."

It was, as he said, quite dark. They crossed the road, looked quickly up and down the deserted street, and slipped inside the entrance. Then they mounted the stairs, and Tommy inserted his key in the lock of the outer office.

Just as he did so, he heard, as he thought, Dymchurch whistle beside him.

"What are you whistling for?" he asked sharply.

"*I* didn't whistle," said Dymchurch, very much astonished, "I thought *you* did."

"Well, someone—" began Tommy.

He got no further. Strong arms seized him from behind, and before he could cry out, a pad of something sweet and sickly was pressed over his mouth and nose.

He struggled valiantly, but in vain. The chloroform did its work. His head began to whirl and the floor heaved up and down in front of him. Choking, he lost consciousness. . . .

He came to himself painfully but in full possession of his faculties. The chloroform had been only a whiff. They had kept him under long enough to force a gag into his mouth and ensure that he did not cry out.

When he came to himself, he was half lying, half sitting, propped against the wall in a corner of his own inner office. Two men were busily turning out the contents of the desk, and ransacking the cupboards, and as they worked they cursed freely.

"Swelp me, guvnor," said the taller of the two hoarsely, "We've turned the whole b——y place upside down and inside out. It's not there."

"It must be here," snarled the other. "It isn't on him. And there's no other place it can be."

As he spoke he turned, and to Tommy's utter amazement he saw that the last speaker was none other than Inspector Dymchurch. The latter grinned when he saw Tommy's astonished face.

"So our young friend is awake again," he said. "And a little surprised—yes, a little surprised. But it was so simple. We suspect that all is not as it should be with the International Detective Agency. I volunteer to find out if that is so, or not. If the new Mr. Blunt is indeed a spy, he will be suspicious, so I send first my dear old friend Carl Bauer. Carl is told to act suspiciously and pitch an improbable tale. He does so and then I appear on the scene. I use the name of Inspector Marriot to gain confidence. The rest is easy."

He laughed.

Tommy was dying to say several things, but the gag in his mouth prevented him. Also, he was dying to *do* several things—mostly with his hands and feet—but alas, that too had been attended to. He was securely bound.

The thing that amazed him most was the astounding change in the man standing over him. As Inspector Dymchurch, the fellow had been a typical Englishman. Now, no one could have mistaken him for a moment for anything but a well educated foreigner who talked English perfectly without trace of accent.

"Coggins, my good friend," said the erstwhile Inspector, addressing his ruffianly looking associate. "Take your life preserver and stand by the prisoner. I am going to remove the gag. You understand, my dear Mr. Blunt, do you not, that it would be criminally foolish on your part to cry out? But I am sure you do. For your age, you are quite an intelligent lad."

Very deftly he removed the gag, and stepped back.

Tommy eased his stiff jaws, rolled his tongue round his mouth, swallowed twice—and said nothing at all.

"I congratulate you on your restraint," said the other. "You appreciate the position, I see. Have you nothing at all to say?"

"What I have to say will keep," said Tommy. "And it won't spoil by waiting."

"Ah! What I have to say will not keep. In plain English, Mr. Blunt, where is that letter?"

"My dear fellow, I don't know," said Tommy cheerfully. "I haven't got it. But you know that as well as I do. I should go on looking about if I were you. I like to see you and friend Coggins playing Hide and Seek together."

The other's face darkened.

"You are pleased to be flippant, Mr. Blunt. You see that square box over there. That is Coggins' little outfit. In it there is vitriol . . . yes, vitriol . . . and irons that can be heated in the fire, so that they are red hot and burn . . ."

Tommy shook his head sadly.

"An error in diagnosis," he murmured. "Tuppence and I labelled this adventure wrong. It's not a Clubfoot story.

It's a Bull Dog Drummond, and you are the inimitable Carl Peterson."

"What is this nonsense you are talking?" snarled the other.

"Ah!" said Tommy. "I see you are unacquainted with the Classics. A pity."

"Ignorant fool! Will you do what we want or will you not? Shall I tell Coggins to get out his tools and begin?"

"Don't be so impatient," said Tommy. "Of course I'll do what you want, as soon as you tell me what it is. You don't suppose I want to be carved up like a filleted sole and fried on a gridiron? I loathe being hurt."

Dymchurch looked at him in contempt.

"Gott! What cowards are these English."

"Common sense, my dear fellow, merely common sense. Leave the vitriol alone, and let us come down to brass tacks."

"I want the letter."

"I've already told you I haven't got it."

"We know that—we also know who must have it. The girl."

"Very possibly you're right," said Tommy. "She may have slipped it into her handbag when your pal Carl startled us."

"Oh, you do not deny. That is wise. Very good, you will write to this Tuppence, as you call her, bidding her bring the letter here immediately."

"I can't do that," began Tommy.

The other cut in before he had finished the sentence.

"Ah! You can't? Well, we shall soon see. Coggins!"

"Don't be in such a hurry," said Tommy. "And do wait for the end of the sentence. I was going to say that I can't do that unless you untie my arms. Hang it all, I'm not one of those freaks who can write with their noses or their elbows."

"You are willing to write, then?"

"Of course. Haven't I been telling you so all along? I'm all out to be pleasant and obliging. You won't do anything unkind to Tuppence, of course. I'm sure you won't. She's such a nice girl."

"We only want the letter," said Dymchurch, but there was a singularly unpleasant smile on his face.

At a nod from him, the brutal Coggins knelt down and unfastened Tommy's arms. The latter swung them to and fro.

"That's better," he said cheerfully. "Will kind Coggins hand me my fountain pen? It's on the table, I think, with my other miscellaneous property."

Scowling, the man brought it to him, and provided a sheet of paper.

"Be careful what you say," Dymchurch said menacingly. "We leave it to you, but failure means—death—and slow death at that."

"In that case," said Tommy, "I will certainly do my best."

He reflected a minute or two, then began to scribble rapidly.

"How will this do?" he asked, handing over the completed epistle.

Dear Tuppence,
   Can you come along at once and bring that blue letter with you? We want to decode it here and now.
                              In haste
                              Francis

"Francis?" queried the bogus Inspector, with lifted eyebrows. "Was that the name she called you?"

"As you weren't at my christening," said Tommy, "I don't suppose you can know whether it's my name or not. But I think the cigarette case you took from my pocket is a pretty good proof that I'm speaking the truth."

The other stepped over to the table and took up the case, read "Francis from Tuppence," with a faint grin and laid it down again.

"I am glad to find you are behaving so sensibly," he said. "Coggins, give that note to Vassily. He is on guard outside. Tell him to take it at once."

The next twenty minutes passed slowly, the ten minutes after that more slowly still. Dymchurch was striding up and down with a face that grew darker and darker. Once he turned menacingly on Tommy.

"If you have dared to double cross us..." he growled.

"If we'd had a pack of cards here, we might have had a game of picquet to pass the time," drawled Tommy. "Women always keep one waiting. I hope you're not going to be unkind to little Tuppence when she comes?"

"Oh! no," said Dymchurch. "We shall arrange for you to go to the same place—together."

"Will you, you swine," said Tommy under his breath.

Suddenly there was a stir in the outer office. A man whom Tommy had not yet seen poked his head in and growled something in Russian.

"Good," said Dymchurch. "She is coming—and coming alone."

For a moment a faint anxiety caught at Tommy's heart.

The next minute he heard Tuppence's voice.

"Oh! there you are, Inspector Dymchurch. I've brought the letter. Where is Francis?"

With the last words she came through the door, and Vassily sprang on her from behind, clapping his hand over her mouth. Dymchurch tore the handbag from her grasp, and turned over its contents in a frenzied search.

Suddenly he uttered an ejaculation of delight and held up a blue envelope with a Russian stamp on it. Coggins gave a hoarse shout.

And just in that minute of triumph, the other door, the door into Tuppence's own office, opened noiselessly and Inspector Marriot and two men armed with revolvers stepped into the room, with the sharp command: "Hands Up!"

There was no fight. The others were taken at a hopeless disadvantage. Dymchurch's automatic lay on the table, and the two others were not armed.

"A very nice little haul," said Inspector Marriot with approval, as he snapped on the last pair of handcuffs. "And we'll have more as time goes on, I hope."

White with rage, Dymchurch glared at Tuppence.

"You little devil," he snarled, "It was you put them on to us."

"It wasn't all my doing. I ought to have guessed, I admit, when you brought in the number sixteen this afternoon. But it was Tommy's note clinched matters. I rang up Inspector Marriot, got Albert to meet him with the duplicate key of the office, and came along myself with the empty blue envelope in my bag. The letter I forwarded according to my instructions as soon as I had parted from you two this afternoon."

But one word had caught the other's attention.

"Tommy?" he queried.

Tommy who had just been released from his bonds came towards them.

"Well done, brother Francis," he said to Tuppence, taking both her hands in his. And to Dymchurch: "As I told you, my dear fellow, you really ought to read the Classics."

7

Finessing The King

It was a wet Wednesday in the offices of the International Detective Agency. Tuppence let the Daily Leader fall idly from her hand.

"Do you know what I've been thinking, Tommy?"

"It's impossible to say," replied her husband. "You think of so many things, and you think of them all at once."

"I think it's time we went dancing again."

Tommy picked up the Daily Leader hastily.

"Our advertisement looks well," he remarked, his head on one side. "Blunt's Brilliant Detectives. Do you realise, Tuppence, that you and you alone are Blunt's Brilliant Detectives? There's glory for you, as Humpty Dumpty would say."

"I was talking about dancing."

"There's a curious point that I have observed about newspapers. I wonder if you have ever noticed it. Take these three copies of the Daily Leader. Can you tell me how they differ one from the other?"

Tuppence took them with some curiosity.

"It seems fairly easy," she remarked witheringly. "One is to-day's, one is yesterday's, and one is the day before's."

"Positively scintillating, my dear Watson. But that was not my meaning. Observe the headline, 'The Daily Leader.' Compare the three—do you see any difference between them?"

"No, I don't," said Tuppence, "and what's more, I don't believe there is any."

Tommy sighed, and brought the tips of his fingers together in the most approved Sherlock Holmes fashion.

"Exactly. Yet you read the papers as much—in fact, more than I do. But I have observed and you have not. If you will look at today's Daily Leader, you will see that in the middle of the downstroke of the D is a small white dot, and there is another in the L of the same word. But in yesterday's paper the white dot is not in DAILY at all. There are two white dots in the L of LEADER. That of the day before again has two dots in the D of DAILY. In fact, the dot, or dots, are in a different position every day."

"Why?" asked Tuppence.

"That's a journalistic secret."

"Meaning you don't know, and can't guess."

"I will merely say this—the practice is common to all newspapers."

"Aren't you clever?" said Tuppence. "Especially at drawing red herrings across the track. Let's go back to what we were talking about before."

"What were we talking about?"

"The Three Arts Ball."

Tommy groaned.

"No, no, Tuppence. Not the Three Arts Ball. I'm not young enough. I assure you I'm not young enough."

"When I was a nice young girl," said Tuppence, "I was brought up to believe that men—especially husbands—were dissipated beings, fond of drinking and dancing and staying up late at night. It took an exceptionally beautiful and clever wife to keep them at home. Another illusion gone! All the wives I know are hankering to go out and dance, and weeping because their husbands will wear bedroom slippers and go to bed at half past nine. And you do dance so nicely, Tommy dear."

"Gently with the butter, Tuppence."

"As a matter of fact," said Tuppence, "It's not purely for pleasure that I want to go. I'm intrigued by this advertisement."

She picked up the Daily Leader again, and read it out.

"I should go three hearts. 12 tricks. Ace of Spades. Necessary to finesse the King."

"Rather an expensive way of learning Bridge," was Tommy's comment.

"Don't be an ass. That's nothing to do with Bridge. You see, I was lunching with a girl yesterday at the Ace of Spades. It's a queer little underground den in Chelsea, and she told me that it's quite the fashion at these big shows to trundle round there in the course of the evening for bacon and eggs and Welsh Rabbits—Bohemian sort of stuff. It's got screened off booths all round it. Pretty hot place, I should say."

"And your idea is—?"

"Three hearts stands for the Three Arts Ball to-morrow night, 12 tricks is twelve o'clock, and the Ace of Spades is the Ace of Spades."

"And what about its being necessary to finesse the King?"

"Well, that's what I thought we'd find out."

"I shouldn't wonder if you weren't right, Tuppence," said Tommy magnanimously. "But I don't quite see why you want to butt in upon other people's love affairs."

"I shan't butt in. What I'm proposing is an interesting experiment in detective work. We *need* practice."

"Business is certainly not too brisk," agreed Tommy. "All the same, Tuppence, what you want is to go to the Three Arts Ball and dance! Talk of red herrings."

Tuppence laughed shamelessly.

"Be a sport, Tommy. Try and forget you're thirty-two and have got one grey hair in your left eyebrow."

"I was always weak where women were concerned," murmured her husband. "Have I got to make an ass of myself in fancy dress?"

"Of course, but you can leave that to me. I've got a splendid idea."

Tommy looked at her with some misgiving. He was always profoundly mistrustful of Tuppence's brilliant ideas.

When he returned to the flat on the following evening, Tuppence came flying out of her bedroom to meet him.

"It's come," she announced.

"What's come?"

"The costume. Come and look at it."

Tommy followed her. Spread out on the bed was a complete fireman's kit with shining helmet.

"Good God!" groaned Tommy. "Have I joined the Wembley fire brigade?"

"Guess again," said Tuppence. "You haven't caught the idea yet. Use your little grey cells, mon ami. Scintillate, Watson. Be a bull that has been more than ten minutes in the arena."

"Wait a minute," said Tommy. "I begin to see. There is a dark purpose in this. What are you going to wear, Tuppence?"

"An old suit of your clothes, an American hat and some horn spectacles."

"Crude," said Tommy. "But I catch the idea. McCarty incog. And I am Riordan."

"That's it. I thought we ought to practise American detective methods as well as English ones. Just for once I am going to be the star, and you will be the humble assistant."

"Don't forget," said Tommy warningly, "that it's always an innocent remark by the simple Denny that puts McCarty on the right track."

But Tuppence only laughed. She was in high spirits.

It was a most successful evening. The crowds, the music, the fantastic dresses—everything conspired to make the young couple enjoy themselves. Tommy forgot his rôle of the bored husband dragged out against his will.

At ten minutes to twelve, they drove off in the car to the famous—or infamous—Ace of Spades. As Tuppence had said, it was an underground den, mean and tawdry in appearance, but it was nevertheless crowded with couples in fancy dress. There were closed in booths round the walls, and Tommy and Tuppence secured one of these. They left the doors purposely a little ajar so that they could see what was going on outside.

"I wonder which they are—our people, I mean," said Tuppence. "What about that Columbine over there with the red Mephistopheles?"

"I fancy the wicked Mandarin and the lady who calls herself a Battleship—more of a fast Cruiser, I should say."

"Isn't he witty?" said Tuppence. "All done on a little drop of drink! Who's this coming in dressed as the Queen of Hearts—rather a good get up, that."

The girl in question passed into the booth next to them accompanied by her escort who was "the gentleman dressed in newspaper" from Alice in Wonderland. They were both wearing masks—it seemed to be rather a common custom at the Ace of Spades.

"I'm sure we're in a real den of inquity," said Tuppence with a pleased face. "Scandals all round us. What a row everyone makes."

A cry, as of protest, rang out from the booth next door and was covered by a man's loud laugh. Everybody was laughing and singing. The shrill voices of the girls rose above the booming of their male escorts.

"What about that shepherdess?" demanded Tommy. "The one with the comic Frenchman. They might be our little lot."

"Anyone might be," confessed Tuppence. "I'm not going to bother. The great thing is that we are enjoying ourselves."

"I could have _enjoyed_ myself better in another costume," grumbled Tommy. "You've no idea of the heat of this one."

"Cheer up," said Tuppence. "You look lovely."

"I'm glad of that," said Tommy. "It's more than you do. You're the funniest little guy I've ever seen."

"Will you keep a civil tongue in your head, Denny, my boy. Hullo, the gentleman in newspaper is leaving his lady alone. Where's he going, do you think?"

"Going to hurry up the drinks, I expect," said Tommy.

"I wouldn't mind doing the same thing."

"He's a long time doing it," said Tuppence, when four or five minutes had passed. "Tommy, would you think me an awful ass—" She paused.

Suddenly she jumped up.

"Call me an ass if you like. I'm going in next door."

"Look here, Tuppence—you can't—"

"I've a feeling there's something wrong. I *know* there is. Don't try and stop me."

She passed quickly out of their own booth, and Tommy followed her. The doors of the one next door were closed. Tuppence pushed them apart and went in, Tommy on her heels.

The girl dressed as the Queen of Hearts sat in the corner leaning up against the wall in a queer huddled position. Her eyes regarded them steadily through her mask, but she did not move. Her dress was carried out in a bold design of red and white, but on the left hand side the pattern seemed to have got mixed. There was more red than should have been. . . .

With a cry Tuppence hurried forward. At the same time Tommy saw what she had seen, the hilt of a jewelled dagger just below the heart. Tuppence dropped on her knees by the girl's side.

"Quick, Tommy, she's still alive. Get hold of the Manager and make him get a doctor at once."

"Right. Mind you don't touch the handle of that dagger, Tuppence."

"I'll be careful. Go quickly."

Tommy hurried out, pulling the doors to behind him. Tuppence passed her arm round the girl. The latter made a faint gesture, and Tuppence realised that she wanted to get rid of the mask. Tuppence unfastened it gently. She saw a fresh flower like face, and wide starry eyes that were full of horror, suffering, and a kind of dazed bewilderment.

"My dear," said Tuppence, very gently. "Can you speak at all? Will you tell me, if you can, who did this?"

She felt the eyes fix themselves on her face. The girl was sighing, the deep palpitating sighs of a failing heart.

And still she looked steadily at Tuppence. Then her lips parted.

"Bingo did it—" she said in a strained whisper.

Then her hands relaxed, and she seemed to nestle down on Tuppence's shoulder.

Tommy came in, two men with him. The bigger of the two came forward with an air of authority, the word, doctor, written all over him.

Tuppence relinquished her burden.

"She's dead, I'm afraid," she said with a catch in her voice.

The doctor made a swift examination.

"Yes," he said. "Nothing to be done. We had better leave things as they are till the police come. How did the thing happen?"

Tuppence explained rather haltingly, slurring over her reasons for entering the booth.

"It's a curious business," said the doctor. "You heard nothing?"

"I heard her give a kind of cry, but then the man laughed. Naturally I didn't think—"

"Naturally not," agreed the doctor. "And the man wore a mask, you say. You wouldn't recognise him?"

"I'm afraid not. Would you, Tommy?"

"No. Still there in his costume."

"The first thing will be to identify this poor lady," said the doctor. "After that, well, I suppose the police will get down to things pretty quickly. It ought not to be a difficult case. Ah, here they come."

8

The Gentleman Dressed in Newspaper

It was after three o'clock when, weary and sick at heart, the husband and wife reached home. Several hours passed before Tuppence could sleep. She lay tossing from side to side, seeing always that flower-like face with the horror stricken eyes.

The dawn was coming in through the shutters when Tuppence finally dropped off to sleep. After the excitement, she slept heavily and dreamlessly. It was broad daylight when she awoke to find Tommy, up and dressed, standing by the bedside, shaking her gently by the arm.

"Wake up, old thing. Inspector Marriot and another man are here and want to see you."

"What time is it?"

"Just on eleven. I'll get Alice to bring you your tea right away."

"Yes, do. Tell Inspector Marriot I'll be there in ten minutes."

A quarter of an hour later, Tuppence came hurrying into the sitting room. Inspector Marriot who was sitting looking very straight and solemn, rose to greet her.

"Good morning, Mrs. Beresford. This is Sir Arthur Merivale."

Tuppence shook hands with a tall thin man with haggard eyes and greying hair.

"It's about this sad business last night," said Inspector Marriot. "I want Sir Arthur to hear from your own lips what you told me—the words the poor lady said before she died. Sir Arthur has been very hard to convince."

"I can't believe," said the other, "and I won't believe, that Bingo Hale ever hurt a hair on Vere's head."

Inspector Marriot went on.

"We've made some progress since last night, Mrs. Beresford," he said. "First of all we managed to identify the lady as Lady Merivale. We communicated with Sir Arthur here. He recognised the body at once, and was horrified beyond words, of course. Then I asked him if he knew anyone called Bingo."

"You must understand, Mrs. Beresford," said Sir Arthur, "that Captain Hale, who is known to all his friends as Bingo, is the dearest pal I have. He practically lives with us. He was staying at my house when they arrested him this morning. I cannot but believe that you have made a mistake—it was not his name that my wife uttered."

"There is no possibility of mistake," said Tuppence gently. "She said 'Bingo did it—'"

"You see, Sir Arthur," said Marriot.

The unhappy man sank into a chair and covered his face with his hands.

"It's incredible. What earthly motive could there be? Oh! I know your idea, Inspector Marriot. You think Hale was my wife's lover, but even if that were so—which I don't admit for a moment—what motive was there for killing her?"

Inspector Marriot coughed.

"It's not a very pleasant thing to say, sir. But Captain Hale has been paying a lot of attention to a certain young American lady of late—a young lady with a considerable amount of money. If Lady Merivale liked to turn nasty, she could probably stop his marriage."

"This is outrageous, Inspector."

Sir Arthur sprang angrily to his feet. The other calmed him with a soothing gesture.

"I beg your pardon, I'm sure, Sir Arthur. You say that you and Captain Hale both decided to attend this show. Your wife was away on a visit at the time, and you had no idea that she was to be there?"

"Not the least idea."

"Just show him that advertisement you told me about, Mrs. Beresford."

Tuppence complied.

"That seems to me clear enough. It was inserted by Captain Hale to catch your wife's eye. They had already arranged to meet there. But you only made up your mind to go the day before, hence it was necessary to warn her. That is the explanation of the phrase "Necessary to finesse the King." You ordered your costume from a theatrical firm at the last minute, but Captain Hale's was a home made affair. He went as the Gentleman Dressed in Newspaper. Do you know, Sir Arthur, what we found clasped in the dead lady's hand? A fragment torn from a newspaper. My men have orders to take Captain Hale's costume away with them from your house. I shall find it at the Yard when I get back. If there's a tear in it corresponding to the missing piece— well, it'll be the end of the case."

"You won't find it," said Sir Arthur. "I know Bingo Hale."

Apologising to Tuppence for disturbing her, they took their leave.

Late that evening, there was a ring at the bell, and somewhat to the astonishment of the young pair, Inspector Marriot once more walked in.

"I thought Blunt's Brilliant Detectives would like to hear the latest developments," he said, with a hint of a smile.

"They would," said Tommy. "Have a drink?"

He placed materials hospitably at Inspector Marriot's elbow.

"It's a clear case," said the latter, after a minute or two. "Dagger was the lady's own—the idea was to have made it look like suicide, evidently, but thanks to you two being on the spot, that didn't come off. We've found plenty of letters—they'd been carrying on together for some time, that's clear—without Sir Arthur tumbling to it. Then we found the last link—"

"The last what?" said Tuppence sharply.

"The last link in the chain—that fragment of the Daily Leader. It was torn from the dress he wore—fits exactly. Oh! yes, it's a perfectly clear case. By the way, I brought round a photograph of those two exhibits—I thought they might interest you. It's very seldom that you get such a perfectly clear case."

"Tommy," said Tuppence, when her husband returned from showing the Scotland Yard man out. "Why do you think Inspector Marriot keeps repeating that it's a perfectly clear case?"

"I don't know. Smug satisfaction, I suppose."

"Not a bit of it. He's trying to get us irritated. You know, Tommy, butchers, for instance, know something about meat, don't they?"

"I should say so, but what on earth—"

"And in the same way, greengrocers know all about vegetables, and fishermen about fish. Detectives, professional detectives, must know all about criminals. They know the real thing when they see it—and they know when it isn't the real thing. Marriot's expert knowledge tells him that Captain Hale isn't a criminal—but all the facts are dead against him. As a last resource Marriot is egging us on, hoping against hope that some little detail or other will come back to us—something that happened last night—which will throw a different light on things. Tommy, why shouldn't it be suicide, after all?"

"Remember what she said to you."

"I know—but take that a different way. It was Bingo's doing—his conduct that drove her to kill herself. It's just possible."

"Just. But it doesn't explain that fragment of newspaper."

"Let's have a look at Marriot's photographs. I forgot to ask him what Hale's account of the matter was."

"I asked him that in the hall just now. Hale declared he had never spoken to Lady Merivale at the show. Says somebody shoved a note into his hand which said: "Don't try and speak to me to-night. Arthur suspects." He couldn't produce the piece of paper, though, and it doesn't sound a very likely story. Anyway, you and I *know* he was with her at the Ace of Spades because we saw him."

Tuppence nodded and pored over the two photographs. One was a tiny fragment with the legend DAILY LE—and the rest torn off. The other was the front sheet of the Daily Leader with the small round tear at the top of it. There was no doubt about it. The two fitted together perfectly.

"What are all those marks down the side?" asked Tommy.

"Stitches," said Tuppence. "Where it was sewn to the others, you know."

"I thought it might be a new scheme of dots," said Tommy. Then he gave a slight shiver. "My word, Tuppence, how creepy it makes one feel. To think that you and I were discussing dots and puzzling over that advertisement—all as lighthearted as anything."

Tuppence did not answer. Tommy looked at her, and was startled to observe that she was staring ahead of her, her mouth slightly open, and a bewildered expression on her face.

"Tuppence," said Tommy gently, shaking her by the arm. "What's the matter with you? Are you just going to have a stroke or something?"

But Tuppence remained motionless. Presently she said in a far away voice.

"Denis Riordan."

"Eh?" said Tommy staring.

"It's just as you said. One simple innocent remark! Find me all this week's Daily Leaders."

"What are you up to?"

"I'm being McCarty. I've been worrying round, and thanks to you, I've got a notion at last. This is the front sheet of Tuesday's paper. I seem to remember that Tuesday's paper was the one with two dots in the L of LEADER. This has a dot in the D of DAILY—and one in the L too.

Get me the papers and let's make sure."

They compared them anxiously. Tuppence had been quite right in her remembrance.

"You see? This fragment wasn't torn from Tuesday's paper."

"But Tuppence, we can't be sure. It may merely be different editions."

"It may—but at any rate it's given me an idea. It can't be coincidence—that's certain. There's only one thing it can be if I'm right in my idea. Ring up Sir Arthur, Tommy. Ask him to come round here at once. Say I've got important news for him. Then get hold of Marriot. Scotland Yard will know his address if he's gone home."

Sir Arthur Merivale, very much intrigued by the summons, arrived at the flat in about half an hour's time. Tuppence came forward to greet him.

"I must apologise for sending for you in such a peremptory fashion," she said. "But my husband and I have discovered something that we think you ought to know at once. Do sit down."

Sir Arthur sat down, and Tuppence went on.

"You are, I know, very anxious to clear your friend."

Sir Arthur shook his head sadly.

"I was, but even I have had to give in to the overwhelming evidence."

"What would you say if I told you that chance has placed in my hands a piece of evidence that will certainly clear him of all complicity?"

"I should be overjoyed to hear it, Mrs. Beresford."

"Supposing," continued Tuppence, "that I had come across a girl who was actually dancing with Captain Hale last night at twelve o'clock—the hour when he was supposed to be at the Ace of Spades."

"Marvellous," cried Sir Arthur. "I knew there was some mistake. Poor Vere must have killed herself after all."

"Hardly that," said Tuppence. "You forget the other man."

"What other man?"

"The one my husband and I saw leave the booth. You see, Sir Arthur, there must have been a second man dressed in newspaper at the Ball. By the way, what was your own costume?"

"Mine? I went as a seventeenth century executioner."

"How very appropriate," said Tuppence softly.

"Appropriate, Mrs. Beresford? What do you mean by appropriate?"

"For the part you played. Shall I tell you my ideas on the subject, Sir Arthur? The newspaper dress is easily put on over that of an executioner. Previously a little note has been slipped into Captain Hale's hand, asking him not to speak to a certain lady. But the lady herself knows nothing of that note. She goes to the Ace of Spades at the appointed time, and sees the figure she expects to see. They go into the booth. He takes her in his arms, I think, and kisses her—the kiss of a Judas, and as he kisses he strikes with the dagger. She only utters one faint cry and he covers that with a laugh. Presently he goes away—and to the last, horrified and bewildered, she believes her lover is the man who killed her.

"But she has torn a small fragment from the costume. The murderer notices that—he is a man who pays great attention to detail. To make the case absolutely clear against his victim the fragment must seem to have been torn from Captain Hale's costume. That would present great difficulties unless the two men happened to be living in the same house. Then, of course, the thing would be simplicity itself. He makes an exact duplicate of the tear in Captain Hale's costume—then he burns his own and prepares to play the part of the loyal friend."

Tuppence paused.

"Well, Sir Arthur?"

Sir Arthur rose and made her a bow.

"The rather vivid imagination of a charming lady who reads too much fiction."

"You think so?" said Tommy.

"And a husband who is guided by his wife," said Sir Arthur. "I do not fancy you will find anybody to take the matter seriously."

He laughed out loud, and Tuppence stiffened in her chair.

"I would swear to that laugh anywhere," she said. "I heard it last in the Ace of Spades. And you are under a little misapprehension about us both. Beresford is our real name, but we have another."

She picked up a card from the table and handed it to him. Sir Arthur read it aloud.

"International Detective Agency . . ." He drew his breath sharply. "So that is what you really are! That was why Marriot brought me here this morning. It was a trap—"

He strolled to the window.

"A fine view you have from here," he said. "Right over London."

"Inspector Marriot," cried Tommy sharply.

In a flash the Inspector appeared from the communicating door in the opposite wall.

A little smile of amusement came to Sir Arthur's lips.

"I thought as much," he said. "But you won't get me this time, I'm afraid, Inspector. I prefer to take my own way out."

And, putting his hands on the sill, he vaulted clean through the window.

Tuppence shrieked and clapped her hands to her ears to shut out the sound she had already imagined—the sickening thud far beneath. Inspector Marriot uttered an oath.

"We should have thought of the window," he said. "Though, mind you, it would have been a difficult thing to prove. I'll go down and—and—see to things."

"Poor devil," said Tommy slowly. "If he was fond of his wife—"

But the Inspector interrupted him with a snort.

"Fond of her? That's as may be. He was at his wits' end where to turn for money. Lady Merivale had a large fortune of her own, and it all went to him. If she'd bolted with young Hale, he'd never have seen a penny of it."

"That was it, was it?"

"Of course, from the very start, I sensed that Sir Arthur was a bad lot, and that Captain Hale was all right. We know pretty well what's what at the Yard—but it's awkward when you're up against facts. I'll be going down now—I should give your wife a glass of brandy if I were you, Mr. Beresford—it's been upsetting like for her."

"Greengrocers," said Tuppence in a low voice as the door closed behind the imperturbable Inspector. "Butchers. Fishermen. Detectives. I was right, wasn't I? He knew."

Tommy, who had been busy at the sideboard, approached her with a large glass.

"Drink this."

"What is it? Brandy?"

"No, it's a large cocktail—suitable for a triumphant McCarty. Yes, Marriot's right all round—that was the way of it. A bold finesse for game and rubber."

Tuppence nodded.

"But he finessed the wrong way round."

"And so," said Tommy. "Exit the King."

9

The Case of
The Missing Lady

The buzzer on Mr. Blunt's desk—(International Detective Agency, Manager, Theodore Blunt) uttered its warning call. Tommy and Tuppence both flew to their respective peepholes which commanded a view of the outer office. There it was Albert's business to delay the prospective clients with various artistic devices.

"I will see, sir," he was saying. "But I'm afraid Mr. Blunt is very busy just at present. He is engaged with Scotland Yard on the phone just now."

"I'll wait," said the visitor. "I haven't got a card with me, but my name is Gabriel Stavansson."

The client was a magnificent specimen of manhood, standing over six feet high. His face was bronzed and weather beaten, and the extraordinary blue of his eyes made an almost startling contrast to the brown skin.

Tommy swiftly made up his mind. He put on his hat, picked up some gloves, and opened the door. He paused on the threshold.

"This gentleman is waiting to see you, Mr. Blunt," said Albert.

A quick frown passed over Tommy's face. He took out his watch.

"I am due at the Duke's at a quarter to eleven," he said. Then he looked keenly at the visitor. "I can give you a few minutes if you will come this way."

The latter followed him obediently into the inner office where Tuppence was sitting demurely with pad and pencil.

"My confidential secretary, Miss Robinson," said Tommy. "Now, sir, perhaps you will state your business? Beyond the fact that it is urgent, that you came here in a taxi, and that you have lately been in the Arctic—or possibly the Antarctic, I know nothing."

The visitor stared at him in amazement.

"But this is marvellous," he cried. "I thought detectives only did such things in books! Your office boy did not even give you my name!"

Tommy sighed deprecatingly.

"Tut tut, all that was very easy," he said. "The rays of the midnight sun within the Arctic circle have a peculiar action upon the skin—the actinic rays have certain properties. I am writing a little monograph on the subject shortly. But all this is wide of the point. What is it that has brought you to me in such distress of mind?"

"To begin with, Mr. Blunt, my name is Gabriel Stavansson—"

"Ah! of course," said Tommy. "The well known explorer. You have recently returned from the region of the North Pole, I believe?"

"I landed in England three days ago. A friend who was cruising in Northern waters brought me back on his yacht. Otherwise I should not have got back for another fortnight. Now I must tell you, Mr. Blunt, that before I started on this last expedition two years ago, I had the great good fortune to become engaged to Mrs. Maurice Leigh Gordon—"

Tommy interrupted.

"Mrs. Leigh Gordon was, before her marriage—"

"The Honorable Hermione Crane, second daughter of Lord Lanchester," reeled off Tuppence glibly.

Tommy threw her a glance of admiration.

"Her first husband was killed in the War," added Tuppence.

Gabriel Stavansson nodded.

"That is quite correct. As I was saying, Hermione and I became engaged. I offered, of course, to give up this expedition, but she wouldn't hear of such a thing—bless her! She's the right kind of woman for an explorer's wife. Well, my first thought on landing was to see Hermione. I sent a telegram from Southampton, and rushed up to town by the first train. I knew that she was living for the time being with an aunt of hers, Lady Susan Clonray, in Pont Street, and I went straight there. To my great disappointment, I found that Hermy was away visiting some friends in Northumberland. Lady Susan was quite nice about it, after getting over her first surprise at seeing me. As I told you, I wasn't expected for another fortnight. She said Hermy would be returning in a few days' time. Then I asked for her address, but the old woman hummed and hawed—said Hermy was staying at one or two different places, and that she wasn't quite sure what order she was taking them in. I may as well tell you, Mr. Blunt, that Lady Susan and I have never got on very well. She's one of those fat women with double chins. I loathe fat women—always have—fat women and fat dogs are an abomination unto the Lord—and unfortunately they so often go together! It's an idiosyncracy of mine, I know—but there it is—I never can get on with a fat woman."

"Fashion agrees with you, Mr. Stavansson," said Tommy drily. "And everyone has their own pet aversion—that of the late Lord Roberts was cats."

"Mind you, I'm not saying that Lady Susan isn't a perfectly charming woman—she may be, but I've never taken to her. I've always felt, deep down, that she disapproved of our engagement, and I feel sure that she would influence Hermy against me if that were possible. I'm telling you this for what it's worth. Count it out as prejudice, if you like. Well, to go on with my story, I'm the kind of obstinate brute who likes his own way. I didn't leave Pont Street until

I'd got out of her the names and addresses of the people Hermy was likely to be staying with. Then I took the mail train North."

"You are, I perceive, a man of action, Mr. Stavansson," said Tommy, smiling.

"The thing came upon me like a bombshell. Mr. Blunt, none of these people had seen a sign of Hermy—Of the three houses, only one had been expecting her—Lady Susan must have made a bloomer over the other two—and she had put off her visit there at the last moment by telegram. I returned post haste to London, of course, and went straight to Lady Susan. I will do her the justice to say that she seemed upset. She admitted that she had no idea where Hermy could be. All the same, she strongly negatived any idea of going to the police. She pointed out that Hermy was not a silly young girl, but an independent woman who had always been in the habit of making her own plans. She was probably carrying out some idea of her own.

"I thought it quite likely that Hermy didn't want to report all her movements to Lady Susan. But I was still worried. I had that queer feeling one gets when something is wrong. I was just leaving when a telegram was brought to Lady Susan. She read it with an expression of relief and handed it to me. It ran as follows. *Changed my plans Just off to Monte Carlo for a week Hermy.*"

Tommy held out his hand.

"You have got the telegram with you?"

"No, I haven't. But it was handed in at Maldon, Surrey. I noticed that at the time, because it struck me as odd. What should Hermy be doing at Maldon? She'd no friends there that I had ever heard of."

"You didn't think of rushing off to Monte Carlo in the same way that you had rushed North?"

"I thought of it, of course. But I decided against it. You see, Mr. Blunt, whilst Lady Susan seemed quite satisfied by that telegram, I wasn't. It struck me as odd that she should always telegraph, not write. A line or two in her own handwriting would have set all my fears at rest. But anyone can sign a telegram 'Hermy.' The more I thought it over, the more uneasy I got. In the end I went down to Maldon. That was yesterday afternoon. It's a fair sized place—good links there and all that—two hotels. I inquired everywhere I could think of, but there wasn't a sign that Hermy had ever been there. Coming back in the train I read your advertisement, and I thought I'd put it up to you. If Hermy has really gone off to Monte Carlo, I don't want to set the police on her track and make a scandal, but I'm not going to be sent off on a wild goose chase myself. I stay here in London, in case—in case there's been foul play of any kind."

Tommy nodded thoughtfully.

"What do you suspect exactly?"

"I don't know. But I feel there's something wrong."

With a quick movement, Stavansson took a case from his pocket and laid it open before them.

"That is Hermione," he said. "I will leave it with you."

The photograph represented a tall willowy woman, no longer in her first youth, but with a charming frank smile and lovely eyes.

"Now, Mr. Stavansson," said Tommy. "There is nothing you have omitted to tell me?"

"Nothing whatever."

"No detail, however small?"

"I don't think so."

Tommy sighed.

"That makes the task harder," he observed. "You must often have noticed, Mr. Stavansson, in reading of crime, how one small detail is all the great detective needs to set him on the track. I may say that this case presents some unusual features. I have, I think, practically solved it already, but time will show."

He picked up a violin which lay on the table, and drew the bow once or twice across the strings. Tuppence ground her teeth and even the explorer blenched. The performer laid the instrument down again.

"A few chords from Mosgovskensky," he murmured. "Leave me your address, Mr. Stavansson, and I will report progress to you."

As the visitor left the office, Tuppence grabbed the violin and putting it in the cupboard turned the key in the lock.

"If you must be Sherlock Holmes," she observed, "I'll get you a nice little syringe and a bottle labelled Cocaine, but for God's sake leave that violin alone. If that nice explorer man hadn't been as simple as a child, he'd have seen through you. Are you going on with the Sherlock Holmes touch?"

"I flatter myself that I have carried it through very well so far," said Tommy with some complacence. "The deductions were good, weren't they? I had to risk the taxi. After all, it's the only sensible way of getting to this place."

"It's lucky I had just read the bit about his engagement in this morning's Daily Mirror," remarked Tuppence.

"Yes, that looked well for the efficiency of Blunt's Brilliant Detectives. This is decidedly a Sherlock Holmes case. Even you cannot have failed to notice the similiarity between it and the disappearance of Lady Frances Carfax."

"Do you expect to find Mrs. Leigh Gordon's body in a coffin?"

"Logically, history should repeat itself. Actually—well, what do you think?"

"Well," said Tuppence. "The most obvious explanation seems to be that for some reason or other Hermy, as he calls her, is afraid to meet her fiancé, and that Lady Susan is backing her up. In fact, to put it bluntly, she's come a cropper of some kind, and has got the wind up about it."

"That occurred to me also," said Tommy. "But I thought we'd better make pretty certain before suggesting that explanation to a man like Stavansson. What about a run down to Maldon, old thing? And it would do no harm to take some golf clubs with us."

Tuppence agreeing, the International Detective Agency was left in the charge of Albert.

Maldon, though a well known residential place, did not cover a large area. Tommy and Tuppence, making every possible inquiry that ingenuity could suggest, nevertheless drew a complete blank. It was as they were returning to London that a brilliant idea occurred to Tuppence.

"Tommy, why did they put Maldon Surrey on the telegram?"

"Because Maldon is in Surrey, idiot."

"Idiot yourself—I don't mean that. If you get a telegram from—Hastings, say, or Torquay, they don't put the county after it. But from Richmond, they do put Richmond Surrey. That's because there are two Richmonds."

Tommy, who was driving, slowed up.

"Tuppence," he said affectionately. "Your idea is not so dusty. Let us make inquiries at yonder post office."

They drew up before a small building in the middle of a village street. A very few minutes sufficed to elicit the information that there were two Maldons. Maldon, Surrey, and Maldon, Sussex, the latter a tiny hamlet but possessed of a telegraph office.

"That's it," said Tuppence excitedly. "Stavansson knew Maldon was in Surrey, so he hardly looked at the word beginning with S. after Maldon."

"Tomorrow," said Tommy. "We'll have a look at Maldon, Sussex."

Maldon, Sussex, was a very different proposition to its Surrey namesake. It was four miles from a railway station, possessed two public houses, two small shops, a post and telegraph office combined with a sweet and picture postcard business, and about seven small cottages. Tuppence took on the shops whilst Tommy betook himself to the Cock and Sparrow. They met half an hour later.

"Well?" said Tuppence.

"Quite good beer," said Tommy, "but no information."

"You'd better try the King's Head," said Tuppence. "I'm going back to the post office. There's a sour old woman there, but I heard them yell to her that dinner was ready."

She returned to the place, and began examining postcards. A fresh faced girl, still munching, came out of the back room.

"I'd like these, please," said Tuppence. "And do you mind waiting whilst I just look over these comic ones?"

She sorted through a packet, talking as she did so.

"I'm ever so disappointed you couldn't tell me my sister's

address. She's staying near here and I've lost her letter. Leigh Wood, her name is."

The girl shook her head.

"I don't remember it. And we don't get many letters through here either—so I probably should if I'd seen it on a letter. Apart from the Grange, there isn't many big houses round about."

"What is the Grange?" asked Tuppence. "Who does it belong to?"

"Doctor Horriston has it. It's turned into a Nursing Home now. Nerve cases mostly, I believe. Ladies that come down for rest cures, and all that sort of thing. Well, it's quiet enough down here, Heaven knows." She giggled.

Tuppence hastily selected a few cards and paid for them.

"That's Doctor Horriston's car coming along now," exclaimed the girl.

Tuppence hurried to the shop door. A small two seater was passing. At the wheel was a tall dark man with a neat black beard and a powerful, unpleasant face. The car went straight on down the street. Tuppence saw Tommy crossing the road towards her.

"Tommy, I believe I've got it. Doctor Horriston's Nursing Home."

"I heard about it at the King's Head, and I thought there might be something in it. But if she's had a nervous breakdown or anything of that sort, her aunt and her friends would know about it surely."

"Ye-es. I didn't mean that. Tommy, did you see that man in the two seater?"

"Unpleasant looking brute, yes."

"That was Doctor Horriston."

Tommy whistled.

"Shifty looking beggar. What do you say about it, Tuppence? Shall we go and have a look at the Grange?"

They found the place at last, a big rambling house, surrounded by deserted grounds, with a swift mill stream running behind the house.

"Dismal sort of abode," said Tommy. "It gives me the creeps, Tuppence. You know, I've a feeling this is going to turn out a far more serious matter than we thought at first."

"Oh! don't. If only we are in time. That woman's in some awful danger, I feel it in my bones."

"Don't let your imagination run away with you."

"I can't help it. I mistrust that man. What shall we do? I think it would be a good plan if I went and rang the bell alone first, and asked boldly for Mrs. Leigh Gordon just to see what answer I get. Because, after all, it may be perfectly fair and above board."

Tuppence carried out her plan. The door was opened almost immediately by a man servant with an impassive face.

"I want to see Mrs. Leigh Gordon if she is well enough to see me."

She fancied that there was a momentary flicker of the man's eyelashes, but he answered readily enough.

"There is no one of that name here, Madam."

"Oh! surely. This is Doctor Horriston's place, The Grange, is it not?"

"Yes, Madam, but there is nobody of the name of Mrs. Leigh Gordon here."

Baffled, Tuppence was forced to withdraw and hold a further consultation with Tommy outside the gate.

"Perhaps he was speaking the truth. After all, we don't *know*."

"He wasn't. He was lying. I'm sure of it."

"Wait until the doctor comes back," said Tommy. "Then I'll pass myself off as a journalist anxious to discuss his new system of rest cure with him. That will give me a chance of getting inside and studying the geography of the place."

The doctor returned about half an hour later. Tommy gave him about five minutes, then he in turn marched up to the front door. But he too returned baffled.

"The doctor was engaged and couldn't be disturbed. And he never sees journalists. Tuppence, you're right. There's something fishy about this place. It's ideally situated— miles from anywhere. Any mortal thing could go on here, and no one would ever know."

"Come on," said Tuppence, with determination.

"What are you going to do?"

"I'm going to climb over the wall, and see if I can't get up to the house quietly without being seen."

"Right. I'm with you."

The garden was somewhat overgrown, and afforded a multitude of cover. Tommy and Tuppence managed to reach the back of the house unobserved.

Here there was a wide terrace, with some crumbling steps leading down from it. In the middle some French windows opened onto the terrace, but they dared not step out into the open, and the windows where they were crouching were too high for them to be able to look in. It did not seem as though their reconnaissance would be much use when suddenly Tuppence tightened her grasp of Tommy's arm.

Someone was speaking in the room close to them. The window was open and the fragment of conversation came clearly to their ears.

"Come in, come in, and shut the door," said a man's voice irritably. "A lady came about an hour ago, you said, and asked for Mrs. Leigh Gordon?"

Tuppence recognised the answering voice as that of the impassive man servant.

"Yes, sir."

"You said she wasn't here, of course?"

"Of course, sir."

"And now this journalist fellow," fumed the other.

He came suddenly to the window, throwing up the sash, and the two outside, peering through a screen of bushes, recognised Dr. Horriston.

"It's the woman I mind most about," continued the doctor. "What did she look like?"

"Young, good-looking, and very smartly dressed, sir."

Tommy nudged Tuppence in the ribs.

"Exactly," said the doctor between his teeth. "As I feared. Some friend of the Leigh Gordon woman's. It's getting very difficult. I shall have to take steps—"

He left the sentence unfinished. Tommy and Tuppence

heard the door close. There was silence.

Gingerly, Tommy led the retreat. When they had reached a little clearing not far away, but out of earshot from the house, he spoke.

"Tuppence, old thing, this is getting serious. They mean mischief. I think we ought to get back to town at once and see Stavansson."

To his surprise Tuppence shook her head.

"We must stay down here. Didn't you hear him say he was going to take steps—That might mean anything."

"The worst of it is we've hardly got a case to go to the police on."

"Listen, Tommy. Why not ring up Stavansson from the village? I'll stay around here."

"Perhaps that is the best plan," agreed her husband. "But, I say—Tuppence—"

"Well?"

"Take care of yourself—won't you?"

"Of course I shall, you silly old thing. Cut along."

It was some two hours later that Tommy returned. He found Tuppence awaiting him near the gate.

"Well?"

"I couldn't get on to Stavansson. Then I tried Lady Susan. She was out too. Then I thought of ringing up old Brady. I asked him to look up Horriston in the Medical Directory or whatever the thing calls itself."

"Well, what did Dr. Brady say?"

"Oh! he knew the name at once. Horriston was once a bona fide doctor, but he came a cropper of some kind. Brady called him a most unscrupulous quack, and said he, personally, wouldn't be surprised at anything. The question is, what are we to do now?"

"We must stay here," said Tuppence instantly. "I've a feeling they mean something to happen tonight. By the way, a gardener has been clipping ivy round the house. Tommy, *I saw where he put the ladder.*"

"Good for you, Tuppence," said her husband appreciatively. "Then tonight—"

"As soon as it's dark—"

"We shall see—"

"What we shall see."

Tommy took his turn at watching the house whilst Tuppence went to the village and had some food.

Then she returned and they took up the vigil together. At nine o'clock, they decided that it was dark enough to commence operations. They were now able to circle round the house in perfect freedom. Suddenly Tuppence clutched Tommy by the arm.

"Listen."

The sound she had heard came again, borne faintly on the night air. It was the moan of a woman in pain. Tuppence pointed upward to a window on the first floor.

"It came from that room," she whispered.

Again that low moan rent the stillness of the night.

The two listeners decided to put their original plan into action. Tuppence led the way to where she had seen the gardener put the ladder. Between them they carried it to the side of the house from which they had heard the moaning. All the blinds of the ground floor rooms were drawn, but this particular window upstairs was unshuttered.

Tommy put the ladder as noiselessly as possible against the side of the house.

"I'll go up," whispered Tuppence. "You stay below. I don't mind climbing ladders and you can steady it better than I could. And in case the doctor should come round the corner you'd be able to deal with him and I shouldn't."

Nimbly Tuppence swarmed up the ladder, and raised her head cautiously to look in at the window. Then she ducked it swiftly, but after a minute or two brought it very slowly up again. She stayed there for about five minutes. Then she descended again.

"It's her," she said breathlessly and ungrammatically, "But oh! Tommy, it's horrible. She's lying there in bed, moaning, and turning to and fro—and just as I got there a woman dressed as a nurse came in. She bent over her and injected something in her arm and then went away again. What shall we do?"

"Is she conscious?"

"I think so. I'm almost sure she is. I fancy she may be strapped to the bed. I'm going up again, and if I can, I'm going to get into that room."

"I say, Tuppence—"

"If I'm in any sort of danger I'll yell for you. So long."

Avoiding further argument Tuppence hurried up the ladder again. Tommy saw her try the window, then noiselessly push up the sash. Another second, and she had disappeared inside.

And now an agonising time came for Tommy. He could hear nothing at first. Tuppence and Mrs. Leigh Gordon must be talking in whispers if they were talking at all. Presently he did hear a low murmur of voices and drew a breath of relief. But suddenly the voices stopped. Dead silence.

Tommy strained his ears. Nothing. What could they be doing?

Suddenly a hand fell on his shoulder.

"Come on," said Tuppence's voice out of the darkness.

"Tuppence! How did you get here?"

"Through the front door. Let's get out of this."

"Get out of this?"

"That's what I said."

"But—Mrs. Leigh Gordon?"

In a tone of indescribable bitterness Tuppence replied.

"Getting thin!"

Tommy looked at her, suspecting irony.

"What do you mean?"

"What I say. Getting thin. Slinkiness. Reduction of weight. Didn't you hear Stavansson say he hated fat women? In the two years he's been away, his Hermy has put on weight. Got a panic when she knew he was coming back, and rushed off to do this new treatment of Dr. Horriston's. It's injections of some sort, and he makes a deadly secret of it, and charges through the nose. I daresay he *is* a quack—but he's a damned successful one! Stavansson comes home a fortnight too soon, when she's only beginning the treatment. Lady Susan has been sworn to secrecy, and plays up. And we come down here and make blithering idiots of ourselves!"

Tommy drew a deep breath.

"I believe, Watson," he said with dignity, "that there is a very good Concert at the Queen's Hall tomorrow. We shall be in plenty of time for it. And you will oblige me by not placing this case upon your records. It has absolutely *no* distinctive features."

10

Blindman's Buff

"Right," said Tommy, and replaced the receiver on its hook.

Then he turned to Tuppence.

"That was the Chief. Seems to have got the wind up about us. It appears that the parties we're after have got wise to the fact that I'm not the genuine Mr. Theodore Blunt. We're to expect excitements at any minute. The Chief begs you as a favor to go home and stay at home, and not mix yourself up in it any more. Apparently the hornet's nest we've stirred up is bigger than anyone imagined."

"All that about my going home is nonsense," said Tuppence decidedly. "Who is going to look after you if I go home? Besides, I like excitement. Business hasn't been very brisk just lately."

"Well, one can't have murders and robberies every day," said Tommy. "Be reasonable. Now my idea is this. When business is slack, we ought to do a certain amount of home exercises every day."

"Lie on our backs and wave our feet in the air? That sort of thing?"

"Don't be so literal in your interpretation. When I say exercises, I mean exercises in the detective art. Reproductions of the Great Masters. For instance—"

From the drawer beside him, Tommy took out a formidable dark green eyeshade covering both eyes. This he adjusted with some care. Then he drew a watch from his pocket.

"I broke the glass this morning," he remarked. "That paved the way for its being the crystalless watch which my sensitive fingers touch so lightly."

"Be careful," said Tuppence. "You nearly had the short hand off then."

"Give me your hand," said Tommy. He held it, one finger feeling for the pulse. "Ah! the keyboard of silence. This woman has *not* got heart disease."

"I suppose," said Tuppence, "that you are Thornley Colton?"

"Just so," said Tommy. "The blind Problemist. And you're thingummybob, the black-haired apple-cheeked secretary—"

"The bundle of baby clothes picked up on the banks of the English river," finished Tuppence.

"And Albert is the Fee, alias Shrimp."

"We must teach him to say 'Gee'," said Tuppence. "And his voice isn't shrill. It's dreadfully hoarse."

"Against the wall by the door," said Tommy, "you perceive the slim hollow cane which held in my sensitive hand tells me so much."

He rose and cannoned into a chair.

"Damn!" said Tommy. "I forgot that chair was there."

"It must be beastly to be blind," said Tuppence with feeling.

"Rather," agreed Tommy heartily. "I'm sorrier for all those poor devils who lost their eyesight in the War than for anyone else. But they say that when you live in the dark you really do develop special senses. That's what I want to try and see if one couldn't do. It would be jolly handy to train oneself to be some good in the dark. Now, Tuppence, be a good Sydney Thames. How many steps to that cane?"

Tuppence made a desperate guess.

"Three straight, five left," she hazarded.

Tommy paced it uncertainly, Tuppence interrupting with a cry of warning as she realised that the fourth step left would take him slap against the wall.

"There's a lot in this," said Tuppence. "You've no idea how difficult it is to judge how many steps are needed."

"It's jolly interesting," said Tommy. "Call Albert in. I'm going to shake hands with you both, and see if I know which is which."

"All right," said Tuppence, "but Albert must wash his hands first. They're sure to be sticky from those beastly acid drops he's always eating."

Albert, introduced to the game, was full of interest.

Tommy, the hand shakes completed, smiled complacently.

"The keyboard of silence cannot lie," he murmured. "The first was Albert, the second, you, Tuppence."

"Wrong!" shrieked Tuppence. "Keyboard of silence indeed! You went by my wedding ring. And I put that on Albert's finger."

Various other experiments were carried out, with indifferent success.

"But it's coming," declared Tommy. "One can't expect to be infallible straight away. I tell you what. It's just lunch time. You and I will go to the Blitz, Tuppence. Blind man and his keeper. Some jolly useful tips to be picked up there."

"I say, Tommy, we shall get into trouble."

"No, we shan't. I shall behave quite like the little gentleman. But I bet you that by the end of luncheon I shall be startling you."

All protests being thus overborne, a quarter of an hour later saw Tommy and Tuppence comfortably ensconced at a corner table in the Gold Room of the Blitz.

Tommy ran his fingers lightly over the Menu.

"Pilaff de Homard and Grilled Chicken for me," he murmured.

Tuppence also made her selection, and the waiter moved away.

"So far, so good," said Tommy. "Now for a more ambitious venture. What beautiful legs that girl in the short skirt has—the one who has just come in."

"How was that done, Thorn?"

"Beautiful legs impart a particular vibration to the floor which is received by my hollow cane. Or, to be honest, in a big Restaurant there is nearly always a girl with beautiful legs standing in the doorway looking for her friends, and with short skirts going around, she'd be sure to take advantage of them."

The meal proceeded.

"The man two tables from us is a very wealthy profiteer, I fancy," said Tommy carelessly. "Jew, isn't he?"

"Pretty good," said Tuppence appreciatively. "I don't follow that one."

"I shan't tell you how it's done every time. It spoils my show. The head waiter is serving champagne three tables off to the right. A stout woman in black is about to pass our table."

"Tommy, how can you—"

"Aha! You're beginning to see what I can do. That's a nice girl in brown just getting up at the table behind you."

"Snoo!" said Tuppence. "It's a young man in grey."

"Oh!" said Tommy, momentarily disconcerted.

And at that moment two men who had been sitting at a table not far away, and who had been watching the young pair with keen interest, got up and came across to the corner table.

"Excuse me," said the elder of the two, a tall well dressed man with an eyeglass and a small grey moustache. "But you have been pointed out to me as Mr. Theodore Blunt. May I ask if that is so?"

Tommy hesitated a minute, feeling somewhat at a disadvantage. Then he bowed his head.

"That is so. I am Mr. Blunt."

"What an unexpected piece of good fortune! Mr. Blunt, I was going to call at your offices after lunch. I am in trouble—very grave trouble. But—excuse me—you have had some accident to your eyes?"

"My dear sir," said Tommy in a melancholy voice. "I am blind—completely blind."

"What?"

"You are astonished. But surely you have heard of blind detectives?"

"In fiction. Never in real life. And I have certainly never heard that you were blind."

"Many people are not aware of the fact," murmured Tommy. "I am wearing an eyeshade today to save my eyeballs from glare. But without it, quite a host of people have never suspected my infirmity—if you call it that. You see, my eyes cannot mislead me. But enough of all this. Shall we go at once to my office, or will you give me the facts of the case here? The latter would be best, I think."

A waiter brought up two extra chairs, and the two men sat down. The second man, who had not yet spoken, was shorter, sturdy in build and very dark.

"It is a matter of great delicacy," said the older man dropping his voice confidentially. He looked uncertainly at Tuppence. Mr. Blunt seemed to feel the glance.

"Let me introduce my confidential secretary," he said. "Miss Ganges. Found on the banks of the Indian river—a mere bundle of baby clothes. Very sad history. Miss Ganges is my eyes. She accompanies me everywhere."

The stranger acknowledged the introduction with a bow.

"Then I can speak out. Mr. Blunt, my daughter, a girl of sixteen, has been abducted under somewhat peculiar circumstances. I discovered this half an hour ago. The circumstances of the case were such that I dared not call in the police. Instead I rang up your office. They told me you were out to lunch, but would be back by half past two. I came in here with my friend Captain Harker—"

The short man jerked his head and muttered something.

"By the greatest good fortune you happened to be lunching here also. We must lose no time. You must return with me to my house immediately."

Tommy demurred cautiously.

"I can be with you in half an hour. I must return to my office first."

Captain Harker, turning to glance at Tuppence, may have

been surprised to see a half smile lurking for a moment at
the corners of her mouth.

"No, no, that will not do. You must return with me."
The grey haired man took a card from his pocket and handed
it across the table. "That is my name."

Tommy fingered it.

"My fingers are hardly sensitive enough for that," he said
with a smile, and handed it to Tuppence, who read out in
a low voice: "The Duke of Blairgowrie."

She looked with great interest at their client. The Duke
of Blairgowrie was well known to be a most haughty and
inaccessible nobleman who had married as a wife the daughter of a Chicago pork butcher, many years younger than
himself, and of a lively temperament that augured ill for
their future together. There had been rumors of disaccord
lately.

"You will come at once, Mr. Blunt?" said the Duke,
with a tinge of acerbity in his manner.

Tommy yielded to the inevitable.

"Miss Ganges and I will come with you," he said quietly.
"You will excuse my just stopping to drink a large cup of
black coffee? They will serve it immediately. I am subject
to very distressing headaches, the result of my eye trouble,
and the coffee steadies my nerves."

He called a waiter and gave the order. Then he spoke to
Tuppence.

"Miss Ganges—I am lunching here tomorrow with the
French Prefect of Police. Just note down the luncheon, and
give it to the head waiter with instructions to reserve me
my usual table. I am assisting the French Police in an important case. *The fee—*" he paused—"is considerable. Are
you ready, Miss Ganges?"

"Quite ready," said Tuppence, her stylo poised.

"We will start with that special salad of Shrimps that
they have here. Then to follow—let me see, *to follow—*
Yes. Omelette Blitz, and perhaps a couple of *Tournedos á
l'Étranger.*"

He looked up, catching the Duke's eye.

"You will forgive me, I hope," he murmured. "Ah! yes, *Soufflé en surprise*. That will conclude the repast. A most interesting man, the French prefect. You know him, perhaps?"

The other replied in the negative, as Tuppence rose and went to speak to the head waiter. Presently she returned, just as the coffee was brought.

Tommy drank a large cup of it, sipping it slowly, then rose.

"My cane, Miss Ganges? Thank you. Directions, please?"

It was a moment of agony for Tuppence.

"One right, eighteen straight. About the fifth step, there is a waiter serving the table on your left."

Swinging his cane jauntily, Tommy set out. Tuppence kept close beside him, and endeavored unobtrusively to steer him. All went well until they were just passing out through the doorway. A man entered rather hurriedly, and before Tuppence could warn the blind Mr. Blunt, he had barged right into the newcomer. Explanations and apologies ensued.

At the door of the Blitz a smart laundalette was waiting. The Duke himself aided Mr. Blunt to get in.

"Your car here, Harker?" he asked over his shoulder.

"Yes. Just round the corner."

"Take Miss Ganges in it, will you."

Before another word could be said, he had jumped in beside Tommy, and the car rolled smoothly away.

"A very delicate matter," murmured the Duke. "I can soon acquaint you with all the details."

Tommy raised his hand to his head.

"I can remove my eyeshade now," he observed pleasantly. "It was only the glare of artificial light in the Restaurant necessitated its use."

But his arm was jerked down sharply. At the same time he felt something hard and round being poked between his ribs. "No, my dear Mr. Blunt," said the Duke's voice— but a voice that seemed suddenly different. "You will not remove that eyeshade. You will sit perfectly still and not move in any way. You understand? I don't want this pistol of mine to go off. You see, I happen not to be the Duke of Blairgowrie at all. I borrowed his name for the occasion, knowing that you would not refuse to accompany such a celebrated client. I am something much more prosaic—a ham merchant who has lost his wife."

He felt the start the other gave.

"That tells you something," he laughed. "My dear young man, you have been incredibly foolish. I'm afraid—I'm very much afraid that your activities will be curtailed in future."

He spoke the last words with a sinister relish.

Tommy sat motionless. He did not reply to the other's taunts.

Presently the car slackened its pace and drew up.

"Just a minute," said the pseudo Duke. He twisted a handkerchief deftly into Tommy's mouth, and drew up his scarf over it.

"In case you should be foolish enough to think of calling for help," he explained suavely.

The door of the car opened and the chauffeur stood ready. He and his master took Tommy between them and propelled him rapidly up some steps and in at the door of a house.

The door closed behind them. There was a rich oriental smell in the air. Tommy's feet sank deep into velvet pile. He was propelled in the same fashion up a flight of stairs and into a room which he judged to be at the back of the house. Here the two men bound his hands together. The chauffeur went out again, and the other removed the gag.

"You may speak freely now," he announced pleasantly. "What have you to say for yourself, young man?"

Tommy cleared his throat and eased the aching corners of his mouth.

"I hope you haven't lost my hollow cane," he said mildly. "It cost me a lot to have that made."

"You have nerve," said the other, after a minute's pause. "Or else you are just a fool. Don't you understand that I have got you—got you in the hollow of my hand? That you're absolutely in my power? That no one who knows you is ever likely to see you again?"

"Can't we cut out the melodrama?" asked Tommy plaintively. "Have I got to say 'You villain, I'll foil you yet?' That sort of thing is so very much out of date."

"What about the girl?" said the other, watching him. "Doesn't that move you?"

"Putting two and two together during my enforced silence just now," said Tommy, "I have come to the inevitable conclusion that that chatty lad Harker is another of the doers of desperate deeds, and that therefore my unfortunate secretary will shortly join this little tea party."

"Right as to one point, but wrong on the other. Mrs. Beresford—you see I know all about you—Mrs. Beresford will not be brought here. That is a little precaution I took. It occurred to me that just probably your friends in high places might be keeping you shadowed. In that case, by dividing the pursuit, you could not both be trailed. I should still keep one in my hands. I am waiting now—"

He broke off, as the door opened. The chauffeur spoke.

"We've not been followed, sir. It's all clear."

"Good. You can go, Gregory."

The door closed again.

"So far, so good," said the 'Duke'. "And now what are we to do with you, Mr. Beresford Blunt?"

"I wish you'd take this confounded eyeshade off me," said Tommy.

"I think not. With it on, you are truly blind—without it you would see as well as I do—and that would not suit my little plan. For I have a plan. You are fond of sensational fiction, Mr. Blunt. This little game that you and your wife were playing today proves that. Now I too have arranged a little game—something rather ingenious, as I am sure you will admit when I explain it to you.

"You see, this floor on which you are standing is made of metal, and here and there on its surface are little projections. I touch a switch—so." A sharp click sounded. "Now the electric current is switched on. To tread on one of those little knobs now means—death! You understand? If you could see . . . but you cannot see. You are in the dark. That is the game—Blindman's Bluff with death. If you can reach the door in safety—freedom! But I think that long before you reach it you will have trodden on one of the danger spots. And that will be very amusing—for me!"

He came forward and unbound Tommy's hands. Then he handed him his cane with a little ironical bow.

"The blind Problemist. Let us see if he will solve this problem. I shall stand here with my pistol ready. If you raise your hands to your head to remove that eyeshade, I shoot. Is that clear?"

"Perfectly clear," said Tommy. He was rather pale, but determined. "I haven't got a dog's chance, I suppose?"

"Oh! that—" the other shrugged his shoulders.

"Damned ingenious devil, aren't you?" said Tommy. "But you've forgotten one thing. May I light a cigarette, by the way? My poor little heart's going pit a pat."

"You may light a cigarette—but no tricks. I am watching you, remember, with the pistol ready."

"I'm not a performing dog," said Tommy. "I don't do tricks." He extracted a cigarette from his case, then felt for a match box. "It's all right. I'm not feeling for a revolver. But you know well enough that I'm not armed. All the same, as I said before, you've forgotten one thing."

"What is that?"

Tommy took a match from the box, and held it ready to strike.

"I'm blind and you can see. That's admitted. The advantage is with you. But supposing we were both in the dark—eh? Where's your advantage then?"

He struck the match.

The 'Duke' laughed contemptuously.

"Thinking of shooting at the switch of the lights? Plunging the room into darkness? It can't be done."

"Just so," said Tommy. "I can't give you darkness. But extremes meet, you know. What about *light?*"

As he spoke, he touched the match to something he held in his hand, and threw it down upon the table.

A blinding glare filled the room.

Just for a minute, blinded by the intense white light, the 'Duke' blinked and fell back, his pistol hand lowered.

He opened his eyes again to feel something sharp pricking his breast.

"Drop that pistol," ordered Tommy. "Drop it quick. I agree with you that a hollow cane is a pretty rotten affair. So I didn't get one. A good *sword stick* is a very useful weapon, though. Don't you think so? Almost as useful as magnesium wire. *Drop that pistol.*"

Obedient to the necessity of that sharp point, the man dropped it. Then, with a laugh, he sprang back.

"But I still have the advantage," he mocked. "For I can see, and you cannot."

"That's where you're wrong," said Tommy. "I can see perfectly. This eyeshade's a fake. I was going to put one over on Tuppence. Make one or two bloomers to begin with, and then put in some perfectly marvellous stuff towards the end of the lunch. Why, bless you, I could have walked to the door and avoided all the knobs with perfect ease. But I didn't trust you to play a sporting game. You'd never have let me get out of this alive. Careful now—"

For, with his face distorted with rage, the 'Duke' sprang forward, forgetting in his fury to look where he put his feet.

There was a sudden blue crackle of flame, and he swayed for a minute, then fell like a log. A faint odor of singed flesh filled the room, mingling with a stronger smell of ozone.

"Whew," said Tommy.

He wiped his face.

Then, moving gingerly, and with every precaution, he reached the wall, and touched the switch he had seen the other manipulate.

He crossed the room to the door, opened it carefully, and looked out. There was no one about. He went down the stairs and out through the front door.

Safe in the street, he looked up at the house with a shudder, noting the number. Then he hurried to the nearest telephone box.

There was a moment of agonising anxiety, and then a well known voice spoke.

"Tuppence, thank goodness!"

"Yes, I'm all right. I got all your points. The Fee, Shrimp Come to the Blitz and follow the two strangers. Albert got there in time, and when we went off in separate cars, followed me in a taxi, saw where they took me, and rang up the police."

"Albert's a good lad," said Tommy. "Chivalrous. I was pretty sure he'd choose to follow you. But I've been worried, all the same. I've got lots to tell you. I'm coming straight back now. And the first thing I shall do when I get back is to write a thumping big cheque for St. Dunstan's. Lord, it must be awful not to be able to see."

II

The Man in
The Mist

Tommy was not pleased with life. Blunt's Brilliant Detectives had met with a reverse, distressing to their pride if not to their pockets. Called in professionally to elucidate the mystery of a stolen pearl necklace at Adlington Hall, Adlington, Blunt's Brilliant Detectives had failed to make good. Whilst Tommy, hard on the track of a gambling Countess, was tracking her in the disguise of a Roman Catholic Priest, and Tuppence was 'getting off' with a nephew of the house on the golf links, the local Inspector of Police had unemotionally arrested the second footman who proved to be a thief well known at headquarters and who admitted his guilt without making any bones about it.

Tommy and Tuppence, therefore, had withdrawn with what dignity they could muster, and were at the present moment solacing themselves with cocktails at the Grand Adlington Hotel. Tommy still wore his clerical disguise.

"Hardly a Father Brown touch, that," he remarked gloomily. "And yet I've got just the right kind of umbrella."

"It wasn't a Father Brown problem," said Tuppence. "One needs a certain atmosphere from the start. One must be doing something quite ordinary, and then bizarre things

96

begin to happen. That's the idea."

"Unfortunately," said Tommy, "we have to return to town. Perhaps something bizarre will happen on the way to the station."

He raised the glass he was holding to his lips, but the liquid in it was suddenly spilled, as a heavy hand smacked him on the shoulder, and a voice to match the hand boomed out words of greeting.

"Upon my soul, it is! Old Tommy! And Mrs. Tommy too. Where did you blow in from? Haven't seen or heard anything of you for years."

"Why, it's Bulger!" said Tommy, setting down what was left of the cocktail, and turning to look at the intruder, a big square-shouldered man of thirty years of age, with a round red beaming face, and dressed in golfing kit. "Good old Bulger!"

"But I say, old chap," said Bulger (whose real name by the way, was Mervyn Estcourt), "I never knew you'd taken orders. Fancy you a blinking parson."

Tuppence burst out laughing, and Tommy looked embarrassed. And then they suddenly became conscious of a fourth person.

A tall slender creature, with very golden hair and very round blue eyes, almost impossibly beautiful, with an effect of really expensive black topped by wonderful ermines, and very large pearl earrings. She was smiling. And her smile said many things. It asserted, for instance, that she knew perfectly well that she herself was the thing best worth looking at certainly in England, and possibly in the whole world. She was not vain about it in any way, but she just knew, with certainty and confidence, that it was so.

Both Tommy and Tuppence recognised her immediately. They had seen her three times in "The Secret of the Heart," and an equal number of times in that other great success, "Pillars of Fire," and in innumerable other plays. There was, perhaps, no other actress in England who had so firm a hold on the British public, as Miss Gilda Glen. She was reported to be the most beautiful woman in England. It was also rumored that she was the stupidest.

"Old friends of mine, Miss Glen," said Estcourt, with a tinge of apology in his voice for having presumed, even for a moment, to forget such a radiant creature. "Tommy, and Mrs. Tommy, let me introduce you to Miss Gilda Glen."

The ring of pride in his voice was unmistakable. By merely being seen in his company, Miss Glen had conferred great glory upon him.

The actress was staring with frank interest at Tommy.

"Are you really a Priest?" she asked. "A Roman Catholic Priest, I mean? Because I thought they didn't have wives."

Estcourt went off in a boom of laughter again.

"That's good," he exploded. "You sly dog, Tommy. Glad he hasn't renounced you, Mrs. Tommy, with all the rest of the pomps and vanities."

Gilda Glen took not the faintest notice of him. She continued to stare at Tommy with puzzled eyes.

"Are you a Priest?" she demanded.

"Very few of us are what we seem to be," said Tommy gently. "My profession is not unlike that of a Priest. I don't give Absolution—but I listen to Confessions—I—"

"Don't you listen to him," interrupted Erstcourt. "He's pulling your leg."

"If you're not a clergyman, I don't see why you're dressed up like one," she puzzled. "That is, unless—"

"Not a criminal flying from justice," said Tommy. "The other thing."

"Oh!" she frowned, and looked at him with beautiful bewildered eyes.

"I wonder if she'll ever get that," thought Tommy to himself. "Not unless I put it in words of one syllable for her, I should say."

Aloud he said:

"Know anything about the trains back to town, Bulger? We've got to be pushing for home. How far is it to the station?"

"Ten minutes' walk. But no hurry. Next train up is the 6.35 and it's only about twenty to six now. You've just missed one."

"Which way is it to the station from here?"

"Sharp to the left when you turn out of the Hotel. Then—let me see—down Morgan's Avenue would be the best way, wouldn't it?"

"Morgan's Avenue?" Miss Glen started violently, and stared at him with startled eyes.

"I know what you're thinking of," said Estcourt, laughing. "The Ghost. Morgan's Avenue is bounded by the cemetery on one side, and tradition has it that a policeman who met his death by violence gets up and walks on his old beat up and down Morgan's Avenue. A spook policeman! Can you beat it? But lots of people swear to having seen him."

"A Policeman?" said Miss Glen. She shivered a little. "But there aren't really any ghosts, are there? I mean—there aren't such things?"

She got up, folding her wrap tighter round her.

"Good bye," she said vaguely.

She had ignored Tuppence completely throughout, and now she did not even glance in her direction. But over her shoulder she threw one puzzled questioning glance at Tommy.

Just as she got to the door, she encountered a tall man with grey hair and a puffy red face who uttered an exclamation of surprise. His hand on her arm, he led her through the doorway, talking in an animated fashion.

"Beautiful creature, isn't she?" said Estcourt. "Brains of a rabbit. Rumor has it that she's going to marry Lord Leconbury. That was Leconbury in the doorway."

"He doesn't look a very nice sort of man to marry," remarked Tuppence.

Estcourt shrugged his shoulders.

"A title has a kind of glamor still, I suppose," he said. "And Leconbury is not an impoverished peer by any means. She'll be in clover. Nobody knows where she sprang from. Pretty near the gutter, I daresay. There's something deuced mysterious about her being down here anyway. She's not staying at the Hotel. And when I tried to find out where she was staying, she snubbed me—snubbed me quite crudely, in the only way she knows. Blessed if I know what it's all about."

He glanced at his watch and uttered an exclamation.

"I must be off. Jolly glad to have seen you two again. We must have a bust in town together some night. So long."

He hurried away, and as he did so, a page approached with a note on a salver. The note was unaddressed.

"But it's for you, sir," he said to Tommy. "From Miss Gilda Glen."

Tommy tore it open and read it with some curiosity. Inside were a few lines written in a straggling untidy hand.

> I'm not sure, but I think you might be able to help me. And you'll be going that way to the station. Could you be at the White House, Morgan's Avenue, at ten minutes past six?
>
> > Yours sincerely,
> > Gilda Glen.

Tommy nodded to the page who departed, and then handed the note to Tuppence.

"Extraordinary," said Tuppence. "Is it because she still thinks you're a Priest?"

"No," said Tommy thoughtfully. "I should say it's because she's at last taken in that I'm not one. Hullo! what's this?"

"This" was a young man with flaming red hair, a pugnacious jaw and appallingly shabby clothes. He had walked into the room and was now striding up and down muttering to himself.

"Hell!" said the red haired man, loudly and forcibly. "That's what I say—Hell!"

He dropped into a chair near the young couple and stared at them moodily.

"Damn all women, that's what I say," said the young man, eyeing Tuppence ferociously. "Oh! all right, kick up a row if you like. Have me turned out of the Hotel. It won't be for the first time. Why shouldn't we say what we think? Why should we go about bottling up our feelings, and smirking, and saying things exactly like everyone else? I don't feel pleasant and polite. I feel like getting hold of someone round the throat and gradually choking them to death."

He paused.

"Any particular person?" asked Tuppence. "Or just anybody?"

"One particular person," said the young man grimly.

"This is very interesting," said Tuppence. "Won't you tell us some more?"

"My name's Reilly," said the red haired man. "James Reilly. You may have heard it. I wrote a little volume of Pacifist poems—good stuff, although I say so."

"Pacifist Poems?" said Tuppence.

"Yes—why not?" demanded Mr. Reilly belligerently.

"Oh! nothing," said Tuppence hastily.

"I'm for peace all the time," said Mr. Reilly fiercely. "To Hell with war. And women! Women! Did you see that creature who was trailing around here just now? Gilda Glen, she calls herself. Gilda Glen! God! how I've worshipped that woman. And I'll tell you this—if she's got a heart at all, it's on my side. She cared once for me, and I could make her care again. And if she sells herself to that muck heap Leconbury—well, God help her. I'd as soon kill her with my own hands."

And on this, suddenly, he rose and rushed from the room.

Tommy raised his eyebrows.

"A somewhat excitable gentleman," he murmured. "Well, Tuppence, shall we start?"

A fine mist was coming up as they emerged from the Hotel into the cool outer air. Obeying Estcourt's directions, they turned sharp to the left, and in a few minutes they came to a turning labelled Morgan's Avenue.

The mist had increased. It was soft and white, and hurried past them in little eddying drifts. To their left was the high wall of the Cemetery, on their right a row of small houses. Presently these ceased, and a high hedge took their place.

"Tommy," said Tuppence. "I'm beginning to feel jumpy. The mist—and the silence. As though we were miles from anywhere."

"One does feel like that," agreed Tommy. "All alone in the world. It's the effect of the mist, and not being able to see ahead of one."

Tuppence nodded.

"Just our footsteps echoing on the pavement. What's that?"

"What's what?"

"I thought I heard other footsteps behind us."

"You'll be seeing the ghost in a minute if you work yourself up like this," said Tommy kindly. "Don't be so nervy. Are you afraid the spook policeman will lay his hand on your shoulder?"

Tuppence emitted a shrill squeal.

"Don't, Tommy. Now you've put it into my head."

She craned her head back over her shoulder, trying to peer into the white veil that was wrapped all round them.

"There they are again," she whispered. "No, they're in front now. Oh! Tommy, don't say you can't hear them?"

"I do hear something. Yes, it's footsteps behind us. Somebody else walking this way to catch the train. I wonder—"

He stopped suddenly, and stood still, and Tuppence gave a gasp.

For the curtain of mist in front of them suddenly parted in the most artificial manner, and there, not twenty feet away a gigantic policeman suddenly appeared, as though materialised out of the fog. One minute he was not there, the next minute he was—so at least it seemed to the rather superheated imaginations of the two watchers. Then as the mist rolled back still more, a little scene appeared, as though set on a stage.

The big blue policeman, a scarlet pillar box, and on the right of the road the outlines of a white house.

"Red, white, and blue," said Tommy. "It's damned pictorial. Come on, Tuppence, there's nothing to be afraid of."

For, as he had already seen, the policeman was a real policeman. And moreover, he was not nearly so gigantic as he had at first seemed looming up out of the mist.

But as they started forward, footsteps came from behind

them. A man passed them, hurrying along. He turned in at the gate of the white house, ascended the steps, and beat a deafening tattoo upon the knocker. He was admitted just as they reached the spot where the policeman was standing staring after him.

"There's a gentleman seems to be in a hurry," commented the policeman.

He spoke in a slow reflective voice, as of one whose thoughts took some time to mature.

"He's the sort of gentleman always would be in a hurry," remarked Tommy.

The policeman's stare, slow and rather suspicious, came round to rest on his face.

"Friend of yours?" he demanded, and there was distinct suspicion now in his voice.

"No," said Tommy. "He's not a friend of mine, but I happen to know who he is. Name of Reilly."

"Ah!" said the policeman. "Well, I'd better be getting along."

"Can you tell me where the White House is?" asked Tommy.

The constable jerked his head sideways.

"This is it. Mrs. Honeycott's." He paused, and added evidently with the idea of giving them valuable information. "Nervous party. Always suspecting burglars is around. Always asking me to have a look around the place. Middle aged women get like that."

"Middle aged, eh?" said Tommy. "Do you happen to know if there's a young lady staying there?"

"A young lady," said the policeman, ruminating. "A young lady. No, I can't say I know anything about that."

"She mayn't be staying here, Tommy," said Tuppence. "And anyway, she mayn't be here yet. She could only have started just before we did."

"Ah!" said the policeman suddenly. "Now that I call it to mind, a young lady did go in at this gate. I saw her as I was coming up the road. About three or four minutes ago it might be."

"With ermine furs on?" asked Tuppence eagerly.

"She had some kind of white rabbit round her throat," admitted the policeman.

Tuppence smiled. The policeman went on in the direction from which they had just come, and they prepared to enter the gate of the White House.

Suddenly a faint muffled cry sounded from inside the house, and almost immediately afterwards the front door opened and James Reilly came rushing down the steps. His face was white and twisted, and his eyes glared in front of him unseeingly. He staggered like a drunken man.

He passed Tommy and Tuppence as though he did not see them, muttering to himself with a kind of dreadful repetition.

"My God! My God! Oh, my God!"

He clutched at the gate post, as though to steady himself, and then, as though animated by sudden panic, he raced off down the road as hard as he could go in the opposite direction to that taken by the policeman.

12

The Man in
The Mist (continued)

Tommy and Tuppence stared at each other in bewilderment.

"Well," said Tommy, "something's happened in that house to scare our friend Reilly pretty badly."

Tuppence drew her finger absently across the gate post.

"He must have put his hand on some wet red paint somewhere," she said idly.

"H'm," said Tommy. "I think we'd better go inside rather quickly. I don't understand this business."

In the doorway of the house a white capped maid servant was standing, almost speechless with indignation.

"Did you ever see the likes of that now, Father," she burst out, as Tommy ascended the steps. "That fellow comes here, asks for the young lady, rushes upstairs without how or by your leave. She lets out a screech like a wild cat— and what wonder, poor pretty dear, and straightway he comes rushing down again, with the white face on him, like one who's seen a ghost. What will be the meaning of it all?"

"Who are you talking with at the front door, Ellen?" demanded a sharp voice from the interior of the hall.

"Here's Missus," said Ellen, somewhat unnecessarily.

105

She drew back and Tommy found himself confronting a grey haired, middle aged woman, with frosty blue eyes imperfectly concealed by pince nez, and a spare figure clad in black with bugle trimming.

"Mrs. Honeycott?" said Tommy. "I came here to see Miss Glen."

Mrs. Honeycott gave him a sharp glance, then went on to Tuppence and took in every detail of her appearance.

"Oh! you did, did you?" she said. "Well, you'd better come inside."

She led the way into the hall and along it into a room at the back of the house facing on the garden. It was a fair sized room, but looked smaller than it was, owing to the large amount of chairs and tables crowded into it. A big fire burned in the grate, and a chintz covered sofa stood at one side of it. The wall paper was a small grey stripe with a festoon of roses round the top. Quantities of engravings and oil paintings covered the walls.

It was a room almost impossible to associate with the expensive personality of Miss Gilda Glen.

"Sit down," said Mrs. Honeycott. "To begin with, you'll excuse me if I say I don't hold with the Roman Catholic religion. Never did I think to see a Roman Catholic priest in my house. But if Gilda's gone over to the Scarlet Woman it's only what's to be expected in a life like hers—and I daresay it might be worse. She mightn't have any religion at all. I should think more of Roman Catholics if their priests were married—I always speak my mind. And to think of those convents—quantities of beautiful young girls shut up there, and no one knowing what becomes of them—well, it won't bear thinking about."

Mrs. Honeycott came to a full stop, and drew a deep breath.

Without entering upon a defence of the celibacy of the priesthood or the other controversial points touched upon, Tommy went straight to the point.

"I understand, Mrs. Honeycott, that Miss Glen is in this house."

"She is. Mind you, I don't approve. Marriage is marriage

and your husband's your husband. As you make your bed, so you must lie on it."

"I don't quite understand—" began Tommy, bewildered.

"I thought as much. That's the reason I brought you in here. You can go up to Gilda after I've spoken my mind. She came to me—after all these years, think of it!—and asked me to help her. Wanted me to see this man and persuade him to agree to a divorce. I told her straight out I'd have nothing whatever to do with it. Divorce is sinful. But I couldn't refuse my own sister shelter in my house, could I now?"

"Your sister?" exclaimed Tommy.

"Yes, Gilda's my sister. Didn't she tell you?"

Tommy stared at her open mouthed. The thing seemed fantastically impossible. Then he remembered that the angelic beauty of Gilda Glen had been in evidence for many years. He had been taken to see her act as quite a small boy. Yes, it was possible after all. But what a piquant contrast. So it was from this lower middle class respectability that Gilda Glen had sprung. How well she had guarded her secret!

"I am not yet quite clear," he said. "Your sister is married?"

"Ran away to be married as a girl of seventeen," said Mrs. Honeycott succinctly. "Some common fellow far below her in station. And our father a reverend. It was a disgrace. Then she left her husband and went on the stage. Play acting! I've never been inside a theatre in my life. I hold no truck with wickedness. Now, after all these years, she wants to divorce the man. Means to marry some big wig, I suppose. But her husband's standing firm—not to be bullied and not to be bribed— I admire him for it."

"What is his name?" asked Tommy suddenly.

"That's an extraordinary thing now, but I can't remember! It's nearly twenty years ago, remember, since I heard it. My father forbade it to be mentioned. And I've refused to discuss the matter with Gilda. She knows what I think, and that's enough for her."

"It wasn't Reilly, was it?"

"Might have been. I really can't say. It's gone clean out of my head."

"The man I mean was here just now."

"That man! I thought he was an escaped lunatic. I'd been in the kitchen giving orders to Ellen. I'd just got back into this room, and was wondering whether Gilda had come in yet (she has a latch key) when I heard her. She hesitated a minute or two in the hall and then went straight upstairs. About three minutes later, all this tremendous rat tatting began. I went out into the hall, and just saw a man rushing upstairs. Then there was a sort of cry upstairs and presently down he came again and rushed out like a madman. Pretty goings on."

Tommy rose.

"Mrs. Honeycott, let us go upstairs at once. I am afraid—"

"What of?"

"Afraid that you have no red wet paint in the house."

Mrs. Honeycott stared at him.

"Of course I haven't."

"That is what I feared," said Tommy gravely. "Please let us go to your sister's room at once."

Momentarily silenced, Mrs. Honeycott led the way. They caught a glimpse of Ellen in the hall, backing hastily into one of the rooms.

Mrs. Honeycott opened the first door at the top of the stairs. Tommy and Tuppence entered close behind her.

Suddenly she gave a gasp and fell back.

A motionless figure in black and ermine lay stretched on the sofa. The face was untouched, a beautiful soulless face like a mature child asleep. The wound was on the side of the head, a heavy blow with some blunt instrument had crushed in the skull. Blood was dripping slowly onto the floor, but the wound itself had long since ceased to bleed . . .

Tommy examined the prostrate figure, his face very white.

"So," he said at last, "he didn't strangle her after all."

"What do you mean? Who?" cried Mrs. Honeycott. "Is she dead?"

"Oh! yes, Mrs. Honeycott, she's dead. Murdered. The

question is—by whom? Not that it is much of a question. Funny—for all his ranting words, I didn't think the fellow had got it in him."

He paused a minute, then turned to Tuppence with decision.

"Will you go out and get a policeman, or ring up the police station from somewhere?"

Tuppence nodded. She, too, was very white. Tommy led Mrs. Honeycott downstairs again.

"I don't want there to be any mistake about this," he said. "Do you know exactly what time it was when your sister came in?"

"Yes, I do," said Mrs. Honeycott. "Because I was just setting the clock on five minutes as I have to do every evening. It gains just five minutes a day. It was exactly eight minutes past six by my watch, and that never loses or gains a second."

Tommy nodded. That agreed perfectly with the policeman's story. He had seen the woman with the white furs go in at the gate, probably three minutes had elapsed before he and Tuppence had reached the same spot. He had glanced at his own watch then and had noted that it was just one minute after the time of their appointment.

There was just the faint chance that someone might have been waiting for Gilda Glen in the room upstairs. But if so, he must still be hiding in the house. No one but James Reilly had left it.

He ran upstairs and made a quick but efficient search of the premises. But there was no one concealed anywhere.

Then he spoke to Ellen. After breaking the news to her, and waiting for her first lamentations and invocations to the Saints to have exhausted themselves, he asked a few questions.

Had anyone come to the house that afternoon asking for Miss Glen? No one whatsoever. Had she herself been upstairs at all that evening? Yes, she'd gone up at six o'clock as usual to draw the curtains—or it might have been a few minutes after six. Anyway it was just before that wild fellow come breaking the knocker down. She'd run downstairs to answer the door. And him a black hearted murderer all the time.

Tommy let it go at that. But he still felt a curious pity for Reilly, an unwillingness to believe the worst of him. And yet there was no one else who could have murdered Gilda Glen. Mrs. Honeycott and Ellen had been the only two people in the house.

He heard voices in the hall, and went out to find Tuppence and the policeman from the beat outside. The latter had produced a notebook, and a rather blunt pencil which he licked surreptitiously. He went upstairs and surveyed the victim stolidly, merely remarking that if he was to touch anything the Inspector would give him beans. He listened to all Mrs. Honeycott's hysterical outbursts and confused explanations, and occasionally he wrote something down. His presence was calming and soothing.

Tommy finally got him alone for a minute or two on the steps outside, ere he departed to telephone headquarters.

"Look here," said Tommy. "You saw the deceased turning in at the gate, you say. Are you sure she was alone?"

"Oh, she was alone all right. Nobody with her."

"And between that time and when you met us, nobody came out of the gate?"

"Not a soul."

"You'd have seen them if they had?"

"Of course I should. Nobody came out till that wild chap did."

The majesty of the law moved portentously down the steps and paused by the white gate post which bore the imprint of a hand in red.

"Kind of amateur he must have been," he said pityingly. "To leave a thing like that."

Then he swung out into the road.

It was the day after the crime. Tommy and Tuppence were still at the Grand Hotel, but Tommy had thought it prudent to discard his clerical disguise.

James Reilly had been apprehended, and was in custody.

His solicitor, Mr. Marvell, had just finished a lengthy conversation with Tommy on the subject of the crime.

"I never would have believed it of James Reilly," he said simply. "He's always been a man of violent speech, but that's all."

Tommy nodded.

"If you disperse energy in speech, it doesn't leave you too much over for action. What I realise is that I shall be one of the principal witnesses against him. That conversation he had with me just before the crime was particularly damning. And in spite of everything, I like the man, and if there was anyone else to suspect, I should believe him to be innocent. What's his own story?"

The solicitor pursed up his lips.

"He declares that he found her lying there dead. But that's impossible, of course. He's using the first lie that comes into his head."

"Because, if he happened to be speaking the truth, it would mean that our garrulous Mrs. Honeycott committed the crime—and that is fantastic. Yes, he must have done it."

"The maid heard her cry out, remember."

"The maid—yes—"

Tommy was silent a moment. Then he said thoughtfully.

"What credulous creatures we are, really. We believe evidence as though it were gospel truth. And what is it really? Only the impressions conveyed to the mind by the senses—and suppose they're the wrong impressions?"

The lawyer shrugged his shoulders.

"Oh! we all know that there are unreliable witnesses, witnesses who remember more and more as time goes on, with no real intention to deceive."

"I don't mean only that. I mean all of us—we say things that aren't really so, and never know that we've done so. For instance, both you and I, without doubt, have said some time or other 'There's the post,' when what we really meant was that we'd heard a double knock and the rattle of the letter box. Nine times out of ten we'd be right, and it would be the post, but just possibly the tenth time it might be only a little urchin playing a joke on us. See what I mean?"

"Ye-es," said Mr. Marvell slowly. "But I don't see what you're driving at?"

"Don't you? I'm not sure that I do myself. But I'm beginning to see. It's like the stick, Tuppence. You remember? One end of it pointed one way—but the other end always points the opposite way. It depends whether you get hold of it by the right end. Doors open—but they also shut. People go upstairs, but they also go downstairs. Boxes shut, but they also open."

"What *do* you mean?" demanded Tuppence.

"It's so ridiculously easy, really," said Tommy. "And yet it's only just come to me. How do you know when a person's come into the house? You hear the door open and bang to, and if you're expecting anyone to come in, you will be quite sure it is them. But it might just as easily be someone going *out*."

"But Miss Glen didn't go out?"

"No, I know *she* didn't. But someone else did—the murderer."

"But how did she get in, then?"

"She came in whilst Mrs. Honeycott was in the kitchen talking to Ellen. They didn't hear her. Mrs. Honeycott went back to the drawing-room, wondered if her sister had come in and began to put the clock right, and then, as she thought, she heard her come in and go upstairs."

"Well, what about that? The footsteps going upstairs?"

"That was Ellen, going up to draw the curtains. You remember, Mrs. Honeycott said her sister paused before going up. That pause was just the time needed for Ellen to come out from the kitchen into the hall. She just missed seeing the murderer."

"But Tommy," cried Tuppence. "The cry she gave?"

"That was James Reilly. Didn't you notice what a high pitched voice he has? In moments of great emotion, men often squeal just like a woman."

"But the murderer? We'd have seen him?"

"We *did* see him. We even stood talking to him. Do you remember the sudden way that policeman appeared? That was because he stepped out of the gate, just after the mist cleared from the road. It made us jump, don't you remember? After all, though we never think of them as that, policemen are men just like any other men. They love and they hate. They marry. . . .

"I think Gilda Glen met her husband suddenly just outside that gate, and took him in with her to thrash the matter out. He hadn't Reilly's relief of violent words, remember. He just saw red—and he had his truncheon handy. . . ."

13

The Crackler

"Tuppence," said Tommy, "we shall have to move into a much larger office."

"Nonsense," said Tuppence. "You mustn't get swollen headed and think you are a millionaire just because you solved two or three twopenny halfpenny cases with the aid of the most amazing luck."

"What some call luck, others call skill."

"Of course if you really think you are Sherlock Holmes, Thorndyke, McCarty and the Brothers Okewood all rolled into one there is no more to be said. Personally I would much rather have luck on my side than all the skill in the world."

"Perhaps there is something in that," conceded Tommy. "All the same, Tuppence, we do need a larger office."

"Why?"

"The Classics," said Tommy. "We need several hundreds of yards of extra book shelf if Edgar Wallace is to be properly represented."

"We haven't had an Edgar Wallace case yet."

"I am afraid we never shall," said Tommy. "If you notice he never does give the amateur sleuth much of a chance. It is all stern Scotland Yard kind of stuff—the real thing and no base counterfeit."

Albert, the office boy, appeared at the door.

"Inspector Marriot to see you," he announced.

"The mystery man of Scotland Yard," murmured Tommy.

"The busiest of the Busies," said Tuppence. "Or is it 'Noses'? I always get mixed between Busies and Noses."

The Inspector advanced upon them with a beaming smile of welcome.

"Well and how are things?" he asked breezily. "None the worse for our little adventure the other day?"

"Oh! rather not," said Tuppence. "Too, too marvelous, wasn't it?"

"Well, I don't know that I would describe it exactly that way myself," said Marriot cautiously.

"What has brought you here today, Marriot?" asked Tommy. "Not just solicitude for our nervous systems, is it?"

"No," said the Inspector. "It is work for the brilliant Mr. Blunt."

"Ha!" said Tommy. "Let me put my brilliant expression on."

"I have come to make you a proposition, Mr. Beresford. What would you say to rounding up a really big gang?"

"Is there such a thing?" asked Tommy.

"What do you mean, is there such a thing?"

"I always thought that gangs were confined to fiction—like master crooks, and super criminals."

"The master crook isn't very common," agreed the Inspector. "But Lord bless you, sir, there's any amount of gangs knocking about."

"I don't know that I should be at my best dealing with a gang," said Tommy. "The amateur crime, the crime of quiet family life—that is where I flatter myself that I shine. Drama of strong domestic interest. That's the thing—with Tuppence at hand to supply all those little feminine details which are so important, and so apt to be ignored by the denser male."

His eloquence was arrested abruptly, as Tuppence threw a cushion at him and requested him not to talk nonsense.

"Will have your little bit of fun, won't you, sir?" said Inspector Marriot, smiling paternally at them both. "If you'll not take offence at my saying so, it's a pleasure to see two young people enjoying life as much as you two do."

"Do we enjoy life?" said Tuppence, opening her eyes very wide. "I suppose we do. I've never thought about it before."

"To return to that gang you were talking about," said Tommy. "In spite of my extensive private practice, Duchesses, millionaires, and all the best charwomen—I might perhaps condescend to look into the matter for you. I don't like to see Scotland Yard at fault. You'll have the Daily Mail after you before you know where you are."

"As I said before, you must have your bit of fun. Well, it's like this." Again he hitched his chair forward. "There's any amount of forged notes going about just now—hundreds of 'em! The amount of counterfeit Treasury notes in circulation would surprise you. Most artistic bit of work it is. Here's one of 'em."

He took a one pound note from his pocket and handed it to Tommy.

"Looks all right, doesn't it?"

Tommy examined the note with great interest.

"By Jove, I'd never spot there was anything wrong with that."

"No more would most people. Now here's a genuine one. I'll show you the differences—very slight they are, but you'll soon learn to tell them apart. Take this magnifying glass."

At the end of five minutes' coaching, both Tommy and Tuppence were fairly expert.

"What do you want us to do, Inspector Marriot?" asked Tuppence. "Just keep our eyes open for these things?"

"A great deal more than that, Mrs. Beresford. I'm pinning my faith on you to get to the bottom of the matter. You see, we've discovered that the notes are being circulated from the West End. Somebody pretty high up in the social scale is doing the distributing. They're passing them the other side of the Channel as well. Now there's a certain person who is interesting us very much. A Major Laidlaw— perhaps you've heard the name?"

"I think I have," said Tommy. "Connected with racing, isn't that it?"

"Yes. Major Laidlaw is pretty well known in connection with the Turf. There's nothing actually against him, but there's a general impression that he's been a bit too smart over one or two rather shady transactions. Men in the know look queer when he's mentioned. Nobody knows much of his past or where he came from. He's got a very attractive French wife who's seen about everywhere with a train of admirers. They must spend a lot of money, the Laidlaws, and I'd like to know where it comes from."

"Possibly from the train of admirers," suggested Tommy.

"That's the general idea. But I'm not so sure. It may be coincidence, but a lot of notes have been forthcoming from a certain very smart little gambling club which is much frequented by the Laidlaws and their set. This racing, gambling set get rid of a lot of loose money in notes. There couldn't be a better way of getting it into circulation."

"And where do we come in?"

"This way. Young St. Vincent and his wife are friends of yours, I understand? They're in pretty thick with the Laidlaw set—though not as thick as they were. Through them it will be easy for you to get a footing in the same set in a way that none of our people could attempt. There's no likelihood of their spotting you. You'll have an ideal opportunity."

"What have we got to find out exactly?"

"Where they get the stuff from, if they *are* passing it."

"Quite so," said Tommy. "Major Laidlaw goes out with an empty suitcase. When he returns it is crammed to the bursting point with Treasury notes. How is it done? I sleuth him and find out. Is that the idea?"

"More or less. But don't neglect the lady, and her father,

M. Heroulade. Remember the notes are being passed on both sides of the Channel."

"My dear Marriot," exclaimed Tommy reproachfully. "Blunt's Brilliant Detectives do not know the meaning of the word neglect."

The Inspector rose.

"Well, good luck to you," he said, and departed.

"Slush," said Tuppence enthusiastically.

"Eh?" said Tommy perplexed.

"Counterfeit money," explained Tuppence. "It is always called Slush. I know I'm right. Oh, Tommy, we have got an Edgar Wallace case. At last we are Busies."

"We are," said Tommy, "and we are out to get The Crackler and we will get him good."

"Did you say The Cackler or The Crackler?"

"The Crackler."

"Oh, what is a Crackler?"

"A new word that I have coined," said Tommy. "Descriptive of one who passes false notes into circulation. Bank notes crackle; therefore he is called a Crackler. Nothing could be more simple."

"That is rather a good idea," said Tuppence, "it makes it seem more real. I like the Rustler myself. Much more descriptive and sinister."

"No," said Tommy, "I said the Crackler first and I stick to it."

"I shall enjoy this case," said Tuppence. "Lots of Night Clubs and cocktails in it. I shall buy some eyelash black to-morrow."

"Your eyelashes are black already," objected her husband.

"I could make them blacker," said Tuppence, "and cherry lip stick would be useful too. That ultra bright kind."

"Tuppence," said Tommy, "you're a real rake at heart. What a good thing it is that you are married to a sober steady middle aged man like myself."

"You wait," said Tuppence. "When you have been to the Python Club a bit you mayn't be so sober yourself."

Tommy produced from a cupboard various bottles, two glasses, and a cocktail shaker.

"Let's start now," he said. "We are after you, Crackler, and we mean to get you."

14

The Crackler (continued)

Making the acquaintance of the Laidlaws proved an easy affair. Tommy and Tuppence, young, well dressed, eager for life and with apparently money to burn, were soon made free of that particular coterie in which the Laidlaws had their being.

Major Laidlaw was a tall fair man, typically English in appearance, with a hearty sportsmanlike manner, slightly belied by the hard lines round his eyes and the occasional quick sideways glance that assorted oddly with his supposed character.

He was a very dexterous card player, and Tommy noticed that when the stakes were high he seldom rose from the table a loser.

Marguerite Laidlaw was quite a different proposition. She was a charming creature, with the slenderness of a wood nymph and the face of a Greuze picture. Her dainty broken English was fascinating, and Tommy felt that it was no wonder most men were her slaves. She seemed to take a great fancy to Tommy from the first, and playing his part, he allowed himself to be swept into her train.

"My Tommee," she would say. "But positively I cannot

120

go without my Tommee. His 'air, eet ees the color of the sunset, ees eet not?"

Her father was a more sinister figure. Very correct, very upright, with his little black beard and his watchful eyes.

Tuppence was the first to report progress. She came to Tommy with ten one pound notes.

"Have a look at these. They're wrong 'uns, aren't they?"

Tommy examined them and confirmed Tuppence's diagnosis.

"Where did you get them from?"

"That boy, Jimmy Faulkener. Marguerite Laidlaw gave them to him to put on a horse for her. I said I wanted small notes, and gave him a tenner in exchange."

"All new and crisp," said Tommy thoughtfully. "They can't have passed through many hands. I suppose young Faulkener is all right?"

"Jimmy? Oh! he's a dear. He and I are becoming great friends."

"So I have noticed," said Tommy coldly. "Do you really think it is necessary?"

"Oh! it isn't business," said Tuppence cheerily. "It's pleasure. He's such a nice boy. I'm glad to get him out of that woman's clutches. You've no idea of the amount of money she's cost him."

"It looks to me as though he were getting rather a pash for you, Tuppence."

"I've thought the same myself sometimes. It's nice to know one's still young and attractive, isn't it?"

"Your moral tone, Tuppence, is deplorably low. You look at these things from the wrong point of view."

"I haven't enjoyed myself so much for years," declared Tuppence shamelessly. "And anyway, what about you? Do I ever see you nowadays? Aren't you always living in Marguerite Laidlaw's pocket?"

"Business," said Tommy crisply.

"But she is attractive, isn't she?"

"Not my type," said Tommy. "I don't admire her."

"Liar," laughed Tuppence. "But I always did think I'd rather marry a liar than a fool."

"I suppose," said Tommy, "that there's no absolute necessity for a husband to be either?"

But Tuppence merely threw him a pitying glance and withdrew.

Amongst Mrs. Laidlaw's train of admirers was a simple but extremely wealthy gentleman of the name of Hank Ryder.

Mr. Ryder came from Alabama, and from the first he was disposed to make a friend and confidant of Tommy.

"That's a wonderful woman, sir," said Mr. Ryder, following the lovely Marguerite with reverential eyes. "Plumb full of civilisation. Can't beat *la gaie France*, can you? When I'm near her, I feel as though I was one of the Almighty's earliest experiments. I guess He'd got to get His hand in before He attempted anything so lovely as that perfectly lovely woman."

Tommy agreeing politely with these sentiments, Mr. Ryder unburdened himself still further.

"Seems kind of a shame a lovely creature like that should have money worries."

"Has she?" asked Tommy.

"You betcha life she has. Queer fish, Laidlaw. She's skeered of him. Told me so. Daren't tell him about her little bills."

"Are they *little* bills?" asked Tommy.

"Well—when I say little! After all, a woman's got to wear clothes, and the less there are of them the more they cost, the way I figure it out. And a pretty woman like that doesn't want to go about in last season's goods. Cards too, the poor little thing's been mighty unlucky at cards. Why, she lost fifty to me last night."

"She won two hundred from Jimmy Faulkener the night before," said Tommy drily.

"Did she indeed? That relieves my mind some. By the way, there seems to be a lot of dud notes floating around in your country just now. I paid in a bunch at my bank this morning, and twenty-five of them were down and outers, so the polite gentleman behind the counter informed me."

"That's rather a large proportion. Were they new looking?"

"New and crisp as they make 'em. Why, they were the ones Mrs. Laidlaw paid over to me, I reckon. Wonder where she got 'em from. One of these toughs on the race course as likely as not."

"Yes," said Tommy. "Very likely."

"You know, Mr. Beresford, I'm new to this sort of high life. All these swell dames, and the rest of the outfit. Only made my pile a short while back. Came right over to Yurrop to see life."

Tommy nodded. He made a mental note to the effect that with the aid of Marguerite Laidlaw Mr. Ryder would probably see a good deal of life and that the price charged would be heavy.

Meantime, for the second time, he had evidence that the forged notes were being distributed pretty near at hand, and that in all probability Marguerite Laidlaw had a hand in their distribution.

On the following night he himself was given a proof.

It was at that small select meeting place mentioned by Inspector Marriot. There was dancing there, but the real attraction of the place lay behind a pair of imposing folding doors. There were two rooms there with green baize covered tables, where vast sums changed hands nightly.

Marguerite Laidlaw, rising at last to go, thrust a quantity of small notes into Tommy's hands.

"They are so bulkee, Tommee—you will change them, yes? A beeg note. See my so sweet leetle bag, it bulges him to distraction."

Tommy brought her the hundred pound note she asked for. Then in a quiet corner, he examined the notes she had given him. At least a quarter of them were counterfeit.

But where did she get her supplies from? To that he had as yet no answer. By means of Albert's coöperation, he was almost sure that Laidlaw was not the man. His movements had been watched closely and had yielded no result.

Tommy suspected her father, the saturnine M. Heroulade. He went to and fro to France fairly often. What could be simpler than to bring the notes across with him? A false bottom to a trunk—something of that kind.

Tommy strolled slowly out of the Club, absorbed in these thoughts, but was suddenly recalled to immediate necessities. Outside in the street was Mr. Hank P. Ryder, and it was clear at once that Mr. Ryder was not strictly sober. At the moment he was trying to hang his hat on the radiator of a car, and missing it by some inches every time.

"This goddarned hatshtand, this goddarned hatshtand," said Mr. Ryder tearfully. "Not like that in the Shtates. Man can hang up hishhat every night—every night, sir. You're wearing two hatshs. Never sheen a man wearing two hatsh before. Mushtbe effectclimate."

"Perhaps I've got two heads," said Tommy gravely.

"Sho you have," said Mr. Ryder. "Thatsh odd. Thatsh remarkable fac. Letsh have a cocktail. Prohibition—probishun—thatsh whatsh done me in. I guess I'm drunk—constootionally drunk. Cocktailsh—mixed 'em—Angel's Kiss—that's Marguerite—lovely creature, fon' o' me too. Horshes Neck, two Martinis—three Road to Ruinsh—no, roadshto roon—mixed 'em all—in a beer tankard. Bet me I wouldn't—I shaid—to hell, I shayed—"

Tommy interrupted.

"That's all right," he said soothingly. "Now what about getting home?"

"No home to go to," said Mr. Ryder sadly; and wept.

"What Hotel are you staying at?" asked Tommy.

"Can't go home," said Mr. Ryder. "Treasurehunt. Swell thing to do. She did it. Whitechapel—White heartsh, white headsn shorrow to the grave—"

"Never mind that," said Tommy. "Where are you—"

But Mr. Ryder became suddenly dignified. He drew himself erect and attained a sudden miraculous command over his speech.

"Young man, I'm telling you. Margee took me. In her car. Treasure Hunting. Englisharishtocrashy all do it. Under the cobblestones. Five hundred poundsh. Solemn thought, *'tis* solemn thought. I'm *telling* you, young man. You've been kind to me. I've got your welfare at heart, sir, at heart. We Americans—"

Tommy interrupted him this time with even less ceremony.

"What's that you say? Mrs. Laidlaw took you in a car?"

The American nodded with a kind of owlish solemnity.

"To Whitechapel?" Again that owlish nod. "And you found five hundred pounds there?"

Mr. Ryder struggled for words.

"S-she did," he corrected his questioner. "Left me outside. Outside the door. Always left outside. It's kinder sad. Outside—always outside."

"Would you say you know your way there?"

"I guess so. Hank Ryder doesn't lose his bearings—"

Tommy hauled him along unceremoniously. He found his own car where it was waiting, and presently they were bowling eastward. The cool air revived Mr. Ryder. After slumping against Tommy's shoulder in a kind of stupor, he awoke clear headed and refreshed.

"Say, boy, where are we?" he demanded.

"Whitechapel," said Tommy crisply. "Is this where you came with Mrs. Laidlaw tonight?"

"It looks kinder familiar," admitted Mr. Ryder looking round. "Seems to me we turned off to the left somewhere down here. That's it—that street there."

Tommy turned off obediently. Mr. Ryder issued directions.

"That's it. Sure. And round to the right. Say, aren't the smells awful? Yes, past that pub at the corner—sharp round, and stop at the mouth of that little alley. But what's the big idea? Hand it to me. Some of the oof left behind? Are we going to put one over on them?"

"That's exactly it," said Tommy. "We're going to put one over on them. Rather a joke, isn't it?"

"I'll tell the world," assented Mr. Ryder. "Though I'm just a mite hazed about it all," he ended wistfully.

Tommy got out and assisted Mr. Ryder to alight also. They advanced into the alley way. On the left were the backs of a row of dilapidated houses, most of which had doors opening into the alley. Mr. Ryder came to a stop before one of these doors.

"In here she went," he declared. "It was this door—I'm plumb certain of it."

"They all look very alike," said Tommy. "Reminds me of the story of the soldier and the Princess. You remember, they made a cross on the door to show which one it was. Shall we do the same?"

Laughing, he drew a piece of white chalk from his pocket and made a rough cross low down on the door. Then he looked up at various dim shapes that prowled high on the walls of the alley, one of which was uttering a blood curdling yawl.

"Lots of cats about," he remarked cheerfully.

"What is the procedure?" asked Mr. Ryder. "Do we step inside?"

"Adopting due precautions we do," said Tommy.

He glanced up and down the alley way, then softly tried the door. It yielded. He pushed it open, and peered into a dim yard.

Noiselessly he passed through, Mr. Ryder on his heels.

"Gee!" said the latter. "There's someone coming down the alley."

He slipped outside again. Tommy stood still for a minute, then hearing nothing went on. He took a torch from his pocket and switched on the light for a brief second. That momentary flash enabled him to see his way ahead. He pushed forward and tried the closed door ahead of him. That too gave, and very softly he pushed it open and went in.

After standing still a second and listening, he again switched on the torch, and at that flash, as though at a given signal, the place seemed to rise round him. Two men were in front of him, two men were behind him. They closed in on him, and bore him down.

"Lights," growled a voice.

An incandescent gas burner was lit. By its light Tommy saw a circle of unpleasing faces. His eyes wandered gently round the room and noted some of the objects in it.

"Ah!" he said pleasantly. "The headquarters of the counterfeiting industry, if I am not mistaken."

"Shut your jaw," growled one of the men.

The door opened and shut behind Tommy, and a genial and well known voice spoke.

"Got him, boys. That's right. Now, Mr. Busy, let me tell you you're up against it."

"That dear old word," said Tommy. "How it thrills me. Yes. I am the Mystery Man of Scotland Yard. Why it's Mr. Hank Ryder. This *is* a surprise."

"I guess you mean that too. I've been laughing fit to bust all this evening—leading you here like a little child. And you so pleased with your cleverness. Why, sonny, I was on to you from the start. You weren't in with that crowd for your health. I let you play about for a while, and when you got real suspicious of the lovely Marguerite, I said to myself 'Now's the time to lead him to it.' I guess your friends won't be hearing of you for some time."

"Going to do me in? That's the correct expression, I believe. You have got it in for me."

"You've got a nerve all right. No, we shan't attempt violence. Just keep you under restraint, so to speak."

"I'm afraid you're backing the wrong horse," said Tommy. "I've no intention of being 'kept under restraint' as you call it."

Mr. Ryder smiled genially. From outside a cat uttered a melancholy cry to the moon.

"Banking on that cross you put on the door, eh Sonny?" said Mr. Ryder. "I shouldn't if I were you. Because I know that story you mentioned. Heard it when I was a little boy. I stepped back into the alleyway to enact the part of the dog with eyes as big as cart wheels. If you were in that alley now, you would observe that every door in the alley is marked with an identical cross."

Tommy drooped his head despondently.

"Thought you were mighty clever, didn't you?" said Ryder.

As the words left his lips a sharp rapping sounded on the door.

"What's that?" he cried, starting.

At the same time, an assault began on the front of the house. The door at the back was a flimsy affair. The lock gave almost immediately and Inspector Marriot showed in the doorway.

"Well done, Marriot," said Tommy. "You were quite right as to the district. I'd like you to make the acquaintance of Mr. Hank Ryder who knows all the best fairy tales.

"You see, Mr. Ryder," he added gently, "I've had my suspicions of you. Albert (that important looking boy with the big ears is Albert) had orders to follow on his motor cycle if you and I went off joy riding at any time. And whilst I was ostentatiously marking a chalk cross on the door to engage your attention, I almost emptied a little bottle of valerian on the ground. Nasty smell, but cats love it. All the cats in the neighborhood were assembled outside to mark the right house when Albert and the police arrived."

He looked at the dumbfounded Mr. Ryder with a smile. Then rose to his feet.

"I said I would get you, Crackler, and I have got you," he observed.

"What the Hell are you talking about?" asked Mr. Ryder. "What do you mean—Crackler?"

"You will find it in the glossary of the next criminal dictionary," said Tommy. "Etymology doubtful."

He looked round him with a happy smile.

"And all done without a Nose," he murmured brightly. "Good night, Marriot. I must go now to where the happy ending of the story awaits me. No reward like the love of a good woman—and the love of a good woman awaits me at home—that is I hope it does, but one never knows nowadays. This has been a very dangerous job, Marriot. Do you know Captain Jimmy Faulkener? His dancing is simply too marvellous and as for his taste in cocktails—! Yes, Marriot, it has been a very dangerous job."

15

The Sunningdale Mystery

"Do you know where we are going to lunch today, Tupence?"

Mrs. Beresford considered the question.

"The Ritz?" she suggested hopefully.

"Think again."

"That nice little place in Soho?"

"No." Tommy's tone was full of importance. "An A.B.C. shop. This one in fact."

He drew her deftly inside an establishment of the kind indicated, and steered her to a corner marble-topped table.

"Excellent," said Tommy with satisfaction, as he seated himself. "Couldn't be better."

"Why has this craze for the simple life come upon you?" demanded Tuppence.

"*You see, Watson, but you do not observe.* I wonder now whether one of these haughty damsels would condescend to notice us? Splendid, she drifts this way. It is true that she appears to be thinking of something else, but doubtless her subconscious mind is functioning busily with such matters as ham and eggs and pots of tea. Chop and fried potatoes, please, Miss, and a large coffee, a roll and butter, and a plate of tongue for the lady."

The waitress repeated the order in a scornful tone, but Tuppence leant forward suddenly and interrupted her.

"No, not a chop and fried potatoes. This gentleman will have a cheese cake and a glass of milk."

"A cheese cake and a milk," said the waitress with even deeper scorn if that were possible. Still thinking of something else, she drifted away again.

"That was uncalled for," said Tommy coldly.

"But I'm right, aren't I? You are the Old Man in the Corner? Where's your piece of string?"

Tommy drew a long twisted mesh of string from his pocket, and proceeded to tie a couple of knots in it.

"Complete to the smallest detail," he murmured.

"You made a small mistake in ordering your meal, though."

"Women are so literal minded," said Tommy. "If there's one thing I hate it's milk to drink, and cheese cakes are always so yellow and bilious looking."

"Be an artist," said Tuppence. "Watch me attack my cold tongue. Jolly good stuff, cold tongue. Now then, I'm all ready to be Miss Polly Burton. Tie a large knot and begin."

"First of all," said Tommy, "speaking in a strictly unofficial capacity, let me point out this. Business is not too brisk lately. If business does not come to us, we must go to business. Apply our minds to one of the great public mysteries of the moment. Which brings me to the point— the Sunningdale Mystery."

"Ah!" said Tuppence, with deep interest. "The Sunningdale Mystery!"

Tommy drew a crumpled piece of newspaper from his pocket and laid it on the table.

"That is the latest portrait of Captain Sessle as it appeared in the Daily Leader."

"Just so," said Tuppence. "I wonder someone doesn't sue these newspapers sometimes. You can see it's a man and that's all."

"When I said the Sunningdale Mystery, I should have said the so-called Sunningdale Mystery," went on Tommy rapidly. "A mystery to the police perhaps, but not to an intelligent mind."

"Tie another knot," said Tuppence.

"I don't know how much of the case you remember," continued Tommy quietly.

"All of it," said Tuppence, "but don't let me cramp your style."

"It was just over three weeks ago," said Tommy, "that that gruesome discovery was made on the famous golf links. Two members of the Club who were enjoying an early round were horrified to find the body of a man lying face downwards on the seventh tee. Even before they turned him over they had guessed him to be Captain Sessle, a well known figure on the links, and who always wore a golf coat of a peculiarly blue color.

"Captain Sessle was often seen out on the links early in the morning, practising, and it was thought at first that he had been suddenly overcome by some form of heart disease. But examination by a doctor revealed the sinister fact that he had been murdered, stabbed to the heart with a significant object, *a woman's hat pin*. He was also found to have been dead at least twelve hours.

"That put an entirely different complexion on the matter, and very soon some interesting facts came to light. Practically the last person to see Captain Sessle alive was his friend and partner Mr. Hollaby of the Porcupine Assurance Co., and he told his story as follows.

"Sessle and he had played a round earlier in the day. After tea the other suggested that they should play a few more holes before it got too dark to see. Hollaby assented. Sessle seemed in good spirits, and was in excellent form. There is a public footpath that crosses the links, and just as they were playing up to the sixth green Hollaby noticed a woman coming along it. She was very tall and dressed in brown, but he did not observe her particularly and Sessle he thought did not notice her at all.

"The footpath in question crosses in front of the seventh tee," continued Tommy. "The woman had passed along this, and was standing at the farther side, as though waiting.

Captain Sessle was the first to reach the tee, as Mr. Hollaby was replacing the pin in the hole. As the latter came towards the tee, he was astonished to see Sessle and the woman talking together. As he came nearer, they both turned abruptly, Sessle calling over his shoulder: 'Shan't be a minute.'

"The two of them walked off side by side, still deep in earnest conversation. The footpath there leaves the course, and passing between two narrow hedges of neighboring gardens comes out on the road to Windlesham.

"Captain Sessle was as good as his word. He reappeared within a minute or two, much to Hollaby's satisfaction, as two other players were coming up behind them, and the light was failing rapidly. They drove off, and at once Hollaby noticed that something had occurred to upset his companion. Not only did he foozle his drive badly, but his face was worried, and his forehead creased in a big frown. He hardly answered his companion's remarks, and his golf was atrocious. Evidently something had occurred to put him completely off his game.

"They played that hole and the eighth, and then Captain Sessle declared abruptly that the light was too bad and that he was off home. Just at that point there is another of those narrow 'slips' leading to the Windlesham road, and Captain Sessle departed that way which was a short cut to his home, a small bungalow on the road in question. The other two players came up, a Major Barnard and Mr. Lecky, and to them Hollaby mentioned Captain Sessle's sudden change of manner. They also had seen him speaking to the woman in brown, but had not been near enough to see her face. All three men wondered what she could have said to upset their friend to that extent.

"They returned to the Club House together, and as far as was known at the time, were the last people to see Captain Sessle alive. The day was a Wednesday and on Wednesdays cheap tickets to London are issued. The man and wife who ran Captain Sessle's small bungalow were up in town according to custom, and did not return until the late train. They entered the Bungalow as usual, and supposed their master to be in his room asleep. Mrs. Sessle, his wife, was away on a visit.

"The murder of the Captain was a nine days' wonder. Nobody could suggest a motive for it. The identity of the tall woman in brown was eagerly discussed, but without result. The police were, as usual, blamed for their supineness—most unjustly as time was to show. For a week later, a girl called Doris Evans was arrested and charged with the murder of Captain Anthony Sessle.

"The police had had little to work upon. A strand of fair hair caught in the dead man's fingers, and a few threads of flame colored wool caught on one of the buttons of his blue coat. Diligent inquiries at the Railway Station and elsewhere had elicited the following facts.

"A young girl dressed in a flame colored coat and skirt had arrived by train that evening about seven o'clock, and had asked the way to Captain Sessle's house. The same girl had reappeared again at the station, two hours later. Her hat was awry and her hair tousled, and she seemed in a state of great agitation. She inquired about the trains back to town, and was continually looking over her shoulder as though afraid of something.

"Our police force is in many ways very wonderful. With this slender evidence to go upon, they managed to track down the girl, and identify her as one Doris Evans. She was charged with murder, and cautioned that anything she might say would be used against her, but she nevertheless persisted in making a statement, and this statement she repeated again in detail, without any substantial variation, at the subsequent proceedings.

"Her story was this. She was a typist by profession, and had made friends one evening, in a Cinema, with a well dressed man who declared he had taken a fancy to her. His name, he told her, was Anthony, and he suggested that she should come down to his bungalow at Sunningdale. She had no idea then, or at any other time, that he had a wife. It was arranged between them that she should come down on the following Wednesday—the day, you will remember, when the servants would be absent and his wife away from home. In the end he told her his full name was Anthony Sessle, and gave her the name of his house.

"She duly arrived at the Bungalow on the evening in question, and was greeted by Sessle who had just come in from the links. Though he professed himself delighted to see her, the girl declared that from the first his manner was strange and different. A half acknowledged fear sprang up in her, and she wished fervently that she had not come.

"After a simple meal which was all ready and prepared, Sessle suggested going out for a stroll. The girl consenting, he took her out of the house, down the road, and along the 'slip' onto the golf course. And then suddenly, just as they were crossing the seventh tee, he seemed to go completely mad. Drawing a revolver from his pocket, he brandished it in the air, declaring that he had come to the end of his tether.

"'Everything must go! I'm ruined—done for. And you shall go with me. I shall shoot you first—then myself. They will find our bodies here in the morning side by side—together in death.'

"And so on—a lot more. He had hold of Doris Evans by the arm and she, realising she had to do with a madman, made frantic efforts to free herself, or failing that to get the revolver away from him. They struggled together, and in that struggle he must have torn out a piece of her hair and got the wool of her coat entangled on a button.

"Finally, with a desperate effort, she freed herself, and ran for her life across the golf links, expecting every minute to be shot down with a revolver bullet. She fell twice—tripping over the heather, but eventually regained the road to the station and realised that she was not being pursued.

"That is the story that Doris Evans tells—and from which she has never varied. She strenuously denies that she ever struck at him with a hat pin in self defence—a natural enough thing to do under the circumstances, though—and one which may well be the truth. In support of her story a revolver has been found in the furze bushes near where the body is lying. It had not been fired.

"Doris Evans has been sent for trial, but the mystery still

remains a mystery. If her story is to be believed, who was it who stabbed Captain Sessle? The other woman, the tall woman in brown whose appearance so upset him? So far no one has explained her connection with the case. She appears out of space suddenly on the footpath across the links, she disappears along the slip, and no one ever hears of her again. Who was she? A local resident? A visitor from London? If so, did she come by car or by train? There is nothing remarkable about her except her height, no one seems to be able to describe her appearance. She could not have been Doris Evans for Doris Evans is small and fair, and moreover was only just then arriving at the station."

"The wife?" suggested Tuppence. "What about the wife?"

"A very natural suggestion. But Mrs. Sessle is also a small woman, and besides Mr. Hollaby knows her well by sight, and there seems no doubt that she was really away from home. One further development has come to light. The Porcupine Assurance Co. is in liquidation. The accounts reveal the most daring misappropriation of funds. The reasons for Captain Sessle's wild words to Doris Evans are now quite apparent. For some years past, he must have been systematically embezzling money. Neither Mr. Hollaby, nor his son, had any idea of what was going on. They are practically ruined.

"The case stands like this. Captain Sessle was on the verge of discovery and ruin. Suicide would be a natural solution, but the nature of the wound rules that theory out. Who killed him? Was it Doris Evans? Was it the mysterious woman in brown?"

Tommy paused, took a sip of milk, made a wry face, and bit cautiously at the cheese cake.

16

The Sunningdale Mystery (continued)

"Of *course*," murmured Tommy, "I saw at once where the hitch in this particular case lay, and just where the police were going astray."

"Yes?" said Tuppence eagerly.

Tommy shook his head sadly.

"I wish I did. Tuppence, it's dead easy being the Old Man in the Corner up to a certain point. But the solution beats me. Who did murder the beggar? I don't know."

He took out some more newspaper cuttings out of his pocket.

"Further exhibits. Mr. Hollaby. His son. Mrs. Sessle. Doris Evans."

Tuppence pounced on the last, and looked at it for some time.

"She didn't murder him anyway," she remarked at last. "Not with a hat pin."

"Why this certainty?"

"A Lady Molly touch. She's got bobbed hair. Only one woman in twenty uses hat pins nowadays, anyway—long hair or short. Hats fit tight and pull on—there's no need for such a thing."

136

"Still, she might have had one by her."

"My dear boy, we don't keep them as heirlooms! What on earth should she have brought a hat pin down to Sunningdale for?"

"Then it must have been the other woman, the woman in brown."

"I wish she hadn't been tall. Then she could have been the wife. I always suspect wives who are away at the time and so couldn't have had anything to do with it. If she found her husband carrying on with that girl, it would be quite natural for her to go for him with a hat pin."

"I shall have to be careful, I see," remarked Tommy.

But Tuppence was deep in thought and refused to be drawn.

"What were the Sessles like?" she asked suddenly. "What sort of thing did people say about them?"

"As far as I can make out, they were very popular. He and his wife were supposed to be devoted to one another. That's what makes the business of the girl so odd. It's the last thing you'd have expected of a man like Sessle. He was an ex-soldier, you know. Came into a good bit of money, retired, and went into this Insurance business. The last man in the world, apparently, whom you would have suspected of being a crook."

"Is it absolutely certain that he was the crook? Couldn't it have been the other two who took the money?"

"The Hollabys? They say they're ruined."

"Oh! they say! Perhaps they've got it all in a Bank under another name. I put it foolishly, I daresay, but you know what I mean. Suppose they'd been speculating with the money for some time, unbeknownst to Sessle, and lost it all. It might be jolly convenient for them that Sessle died just when he did."

Tommy tapped the photograph of Mr. Hollaby senior with his finger nail.

"So you're accusing this respectable gentleman of murdering his friend and partner? You forget that he parted from Sessle on the links in full view of Barnard and Lecky, and spent the evening in the Dormy House. Besides, there's the hat pin."

"Bother the hat pin," said Tuppence impatiently. "That hat pin, you think, points to the crime having been committed by a woman?"

"Naturally. Don't you agree?"

"No. Men are notoriously old fashioned. It takes them ages to rid themselves of preconceived ideas. They associate hat pins and hairpins with the female sex, and call them 'women's weapons.' They may have been in the past, but they're both rather out of date now. Why, I haven't had a hat pin or hairpin for the last four years."

"Then you think—?"

"That it was a *man* killed Sessle. The hat pin was used to make it seem a woman's crime."

"There's something in what you say, Tuppence," said Tommy slowly. "It's extrordinary how things seem to straighten themselves out when you talk a thing over."

Tuppence nodded.

"Everything must be logical—if you look at it the right way. And remember what Marriot once said about the Amateur point of view—that it had the *intimacy*. We know something about people like Captain Sessle and his wife. We know what they're likely to do—and what they're not likely to do. And we've each got our special knowledge."

Tommy smiled.

"You mean," he said, "that you are an authority on what people with bobbed and shingled heads are likely to have in their possession, and that you have an intimate acquaintance with what wives are likely to feel and do?"

"Something of the sort."

"And what about me? What is my special knowledge? Do husbands pick up girls etc.?"

"No," said Tuppence gravely. "You know the course— you've been on it—not as a detective, searching for clues, but as a golfer. You know about golf, and what's likely to put a man off his game."

"It must have been something pretty serious to put Sessle off his game. His handicap's two, and from the seventh tee on he played like a child, so they say."

"Who say?"

"Barnard and Lecky. They were playing just behind him, you remember."

"That was after he met the woman—the tall woman in brown. They saw him speaking to her, didn't they?"

"Yes—at least—"

Tommy broke off. Tuppence looked up at him, and was puzzled. He was staring at the piece of string in his fingers, but staring with the eyes of one who sees something very different.

"Tommy—what is it?"

"Be quiet, Tuppence. I'm playing the sixth hole at Sunningdale. Sessle and old Hollaby are holding out on the sixth green ahead of me. It's getting dusk, but I can see that bright blue coat of Sessle's clearly enough. And on the footpath to the left of me there's a woman coming along. She hasn't crossed from the Ladies' Course—that's on the right—I should have seen her if she had done so. And it's odd I didn't see her on the footpath before—from the fifth tee, for instance."

He paused.

"You said just now I knew the course, Tuppence. Just behind the sixth tee, there's a little hut or shelter made of turf. Anyone could wait in there until—the right moment came. They could change their appearance there. I mean—tell me, Tuppence this is where your special knowledge comes in again—would it be very difficult for a man to look like a woman, and then change back to being a man again? Could he wear a skirt over plus fours, for instance?"

"Certainly he could. The woman would look a bit bulky, that would be all. A longish brown skirt, say, a brown sweater of the kind both men and women wear, and a woman's felt hat with a bunch of curls attached each side. That would be all that was needed—I'm speaking, of course, of what would pass at a distance, which I take to be what you are driving at. Switch off the skirt, take off the hat and curls, and put on a man's cap which you can carry rolled up in your hand, and there you'd be—back as a man again."

"And the time required for the transformation?"

"From woman to man, a minute and a half at the outside, probably a good deal less. The other way about would take longer, you'd have to arrange the hat and curls a bit, and the skirt would stick getting it on over the plus fours."

"That doesn't worry me. It's the time for the first that matters. As I tell you, I'm playing the sixth hole. The woman in brown has reached the seventh tee now. She crosses it and waits. Sessle in his blue coat goes towards her. They stand together a minute, and then they follow the path round the trees out of sight. Hollaby is on the tee alone. Two or three minutes pass. I'm on the green now. The man in the blue coat comes back and drives off, foozling badly. The light's getting worse. I and my partner go on. Ahead of us are those two, Sessle slicing and topping and doing everything he shouldn't do. At the eighth green, I see him stride off and vanish down the slip. What happened to him to make him play like a different man?"

"The woman in brown—or the man, if you think it was a man."

"Exactly, and where they were standing—out of sight, remember, of those coming after them—there's a deep tangle of furze bushes. You could thrust a body in there, and it would be pretty certain to lie hidden until the morning."

"Tommy! You think it was *then*—But someone would have heard—"

"Heard what? The doctors agreed death must have been instantaneous. I've seen men killed instantaneously in the War. They don't cry out as a rule—just a gurgle, or a moan—perhaps just a sigh, or a funny little cough. Sessle comes towards the seventh tee, and the woman comes forward and speaks to him. He recognises her perhaps, as a man he knows masquerading. Curious to learn the why and wherefore, he allows himself to be drawn along the footpath out of sight. One stab with the deadly hat pin as they walk along. Sessle falls—dead. The other man drags his body into the furze bushes, strips off the blue coat, then sheds his own skirt and the hat and curls. He puts on Sessle's well known blue coat and cap, and strides back to the tee.

Three minutes would do it. The others behind can't see his
face, only the peculiar blue coat they know so well. They
never doubt that it's Sessle—*but he doesn't play Sessle's
brand of golf*. They all say he played like a different man.
Of course he did. He *was* a different man."

"But—"

"Point No. 2. His action in bringing the girl down there
was the action of *a different man*. It wasn't Sessle who met
Doris Evans at a Cinema, and induced her to come down
to Sunningdale. It was a man *calling* himself Sessle. Remember, Doris Evans wasn't arrested until a fortnight after
the crime. *She never saw the body*. If she had, she might
have bewildered everyone by declaring that that wasn't the
man who took her out on the golf links that night, and spoke
so wildly of suicide. It was a carefully laid plot. The girl
invited down for Wednesday when Sessle's house would be
empty, then the hat pin which pointed to its being a woman's
doing. The murderer meets the girl, takes her into the Bungalow and gives her supper, then takes her out on the links,
and when he gets to the scene of the crime, brandishes his
revolver and scares the life out of her. Once she has taken
to her heels, all he has to do is to pull out the body and
leave it lying on the tee. The revolver he chucks into the
bushes. Then he makes a neat parcel of the skirt and hat
and—now I admit I'm guessing—in all probability walks
to Woking which is only about six or seven miles away,
and goes back to town from there."

"Wait a minute," said Tuppence. "There's one thing you
haven't explained. What about Hollaby?"

"Hollaby?"

"Yes. I admit that the people behind couldn't have seen
whether it was really Sessle or not. But you can't tell me
that the man who was playing with him was so hypnotised
by the blue coat that he never looked at his face."

"My dear old thing," said Tommy. "That's just the point.
Hollaby knew all right. You see, I'm adopting your
theory—that Hollaby and his son were the real embezzlers.
The murderer's got to be a man who knew Sessle pretty
well—knew, for instance, about the servants being always

out on a Wednesday, and that his wife was away. And also someone who was able to get an impression of Sessle's latch key. I think Hollaby Junior would fulfil all these requirements. He's about the same age and height as Sessle, and they were both clean shaven men. Doris Evans probably saw several photographs of the murdered man reproduced in the papers, but as you yourself observed—one can just see that it's a man and that's about all."

"Didn't she ever see Hollaby in Court?"

"The son never appeared in the case at all. Why should he? He had no evidence to give. It was old Hollaby, with his irreproachable alibi, who stood in the limelight throughout. Nobody has even bothered to inquire what the son was doing that particular evening."

"It all fits in," admitted Tuppence. She paused a minute, and then asked: "Are you going to tell all this to the police?"

"I don't know if they'd listen."

"They'd listen all right," said an unexpected voice behind him.

Tommy swung round to confront Inspector Marriot. The Inspector was sitting at the next table. In front of him was a poached egg.

"Often drop in here to lunch," said Inspector Marriot. "As I was saying, we'll listen all right—in fact I've been listening. I don't mind telling you that we've not been quite satisfied all along over those Porcupine figures. You see, we've had our suspicions of those Hollabys. But nothing to go upon. Too sharp for us. Then this murder came, and that seemed to upset all our ideas. But thanks to you and the lady, sir, we'll confront young Hollaby and Doris Evans and see if she recognises him. I rather fancy she will. That's a very ingenious idea of yours about the blue coat. I'll see that Blunt's Brilliant Detectives get the credit for it."

"You *are* a nice man, Inspector Marriot," said Tuppence gratefully.

"We think a lot of you two at the Yard," replied that stolid gentleman. "You'd be surprised. If I may ask you, sir, what's the meaning of that piece of string?"

"Nothing," said Tommy, stuffing it into his pocket. "A

bad habit of mine. As to the cheese cake and the milk—
I'm on a diet. Nervous dyspepsia. Busy men are always
martyrs to it."

"Ah!" said the detective. "I thought perhaps you'd been
reading—well, it's of no consequence."

But the Inspector's eyes twinkled.

17

The House of Lurking Death

"What—" began Tuppence, and then stopped.

She had just entered the private office of Mr. Blunt from the adjoining one marked "Clerks", and was surprised to behold her lord and master with his eye riveted to the private peep hole into the outer office.

"Ssh," said Tommy, warningly. "Didn't you hear the buzzer? It's a girl—rather a nice girl—in fact she looks to me a frightfully nice girl. Albert is telling her all that tosh about my being engaged with Scotland Yard."

"Let *me* see," demanded Tuppence.

Somewhat unwillingly, Tommy moved aside. Tuppence in her turn glued her eye to the peep hole.

"She's not bad," admitted Tuppence. "And her clothes are simply the latest shout."

"She's perfectly lovely," said Tommy. "She's like those girls Mason writes about—you know, frightfully sympathetic, and beautiful, and distinctly intelligent without being too saucy. I think, yes—I certainly think—I shall be the great Hanaud this morning."

"Hm," said Tuppence. "If there is one detective out of all the others whom you are most unlike—I should say it was Hanaud. Can you do the lightning changes of personality? Can you be the great comedian, the little gutter boy, the serious and sympathetic friend—all in five minutes?"

"I know this," said Tommy, rapping sharply on the desk, "I am the Captain of the Ship—and don't you forget it, Tuppence. I'm going to have her in."

He pressed the buzzer on his desk. Albert appeared ushering in the client.

The girl stopped in the doorway as though undecided. Tommy came forward.

"Come in, Mademoiselle," he said kindly, "and seat yourself here."

Tuppence choked audibly, and Tommy turned upon her with a swift change of manner. His tone was menacing.

"You spoke, Miss Robinson? Ah! no, I thought not."

He turned back to the girl.

"We will not be serious or formal," he said. "You will just tell me all about it, and then we will discuss the best way to help you."

"You are very kind," said the girl. "Excuse me, but are you a foreigner?"

A fresh choke from Tuppence. Tommy glared in her direction out of the corner of his eye.

"Not exactly," he said with difficulty. "But of late years I have worked a good deal abroad. My methods are the methods of the Sûreté."

"Oh!" The girl seemed impressed.

She was, as Tommy had indicated, a very charming girl. Young and slim, with a trace of golden hair peeping out from under her little brown felt hat, and big serious eyes.

That she was nervous could be plainly seen. Her little hands were twisting themselves together, and she kept clasping and unclasping the catch of her lacquer red handbag.

"First of all, Mr. Blunt, I must tell you that my name is Lois Hargreaves. I live in a great rambling old fashioned house called Thurnly Grange. It is in the heart of the country. There is the village of Thurnly near by, but it is very small and insignificant. There is plenty of hunting in winter, and we get tennis in summer, and I have never felt lonely there.

Indeed I much prefer country to town life.

"I tell you this so that you may realise that in a country village like ours, everything that happens is of supreme importance. About a week ago, I got a box of chocolates sent through the post. There was nothing inside to indicate who they came from. Now I myself am not particularly fond of choclates, but the others in the house are, and the box was passed round. As a result, everyone who had eaten any chocolates was taken ill. We sent for the doctor, and after various inquiries as to what other things had been eaten, he took the remains of the chocolates away with him, and had them analysed. Mr. Blunt, those chocolates contained arsenic! Not enough to kill anyone, but enough to make anyone quite ill."

"Extraordinary," commented Tommy.

"Dr. Burton was very excited over the matter. It seems that this was the third occurrence of the kind in the neighborhood. In each case a big house was selected, and the inmates were taken ill after eating the mysterious chocolates. It looked as though some local person of weak intellect was playing a particularly fiendish practical joke."

"Quite so, Miss Hargreaves."

"Dr. Burton put it down to Socialist agitation—rather absurdly, I thought. But there are one or two malcontents in Thurnly village, and it seemed possible that they might have had something to do with it. Dr. Burton was very keen that I should put the whole thing in the hands of the police."

"A very natural suggestion," said Tommy. "But you have not done so, I gather, Miss Hargreaves?"

"No," admitted the girl. "I hate the fuss and the publicity that would ensue—and you see, I know our local Inspector. I can never imagine him finding out anything! I have often seen your advertisements, and I told Dr. Burton that it would be much better to call in a private detective."

"I see."

"You say a great deal about discretion in your advertisement. I take that to mean—that—that—well, that you would not make anything public without my consent?"

Tommy looked at her curiously, but it was Tuppence who spoke.

"I think," she said quietly, "that it would be as well if Miss Hargreaves told us *everything*."

She laid especial stress upon the last word, and Lois Hargreaves flushed nervously.

"Yes," said Tommy quickly. "Miss Robinson is right. You must tell us everything."

"You will not—" she hesitated.

"Everything you say is understood to be strictly in confidence."

"Thank you. I know that I ought to have been quite frank with you. I have a reason for not going to the police. Mr. Blunt, that box of chocolates was sent by someone in our house!"

"How do you know that, Mademoiselle?"

"It's very simple. I've got a habit of drawing a little silly thing—three fish intertwined—whenever I have a pencil in my hand. A parcel of silk stockings arrived from a certain shop in London not long ago. We were at the breakfast table. I'd just been marking something in the newspaper, and without thinking, I began to draw my silly little fish on the label of the parcel before cutting the string and opening it. I thought no more about the matter, but when I was examining the piece of brown paper in which the chocolates had been sent, I caught sight of the corner of the original label—most of which had been torn off. My silly little drawing was on it."

Tommy drew his chair forward.

"That is very serious. It creates, as you say, a very strong presumption that the sender of the chocolates is a member of your household. But you will forgive me if I say that I still do not see why that fact should render you indisposed to call in the police?"

Lois Hargreaves looked him squarely in the face.

"I will tell you, Mr. Blunt. I may want the whole thing hushed up."

Tommy retired gracefully from the position.

"In that case," he murmured, "we know where we are.
I see, Miss Hargreaves, that you are not disposed to tell me
who it is you suspect?"

"I suspect no one—but there are possibilities."

"Quite so. Now will you describe the household to me
in detail?"

"The servants, with the exception of the parlormaid, are
all old ones who have been with us many years. I must
explain to you, Mr. Blunt, that I was brought up by my
Aunt, Lady Radclyffe, who was extremely wealthy. Her
husband made a big fortune, and was knighted. It was he
who bought Thurnly Grange, but he died two years after
going there, and it was then that Lady Radclyffe sent for
me to come and make my home with her. I was her only
living relation. The other inmate of the house was Dennis
Radclyffe, her husband's nephew. I have always called him
cousin, but of course he is really nothing of the kind. Aunt
Lucy always said openly that she intended to leave her
money, with the exception of a small provision for me, to
Dennis. It was Radclyffe money, she said, and ought to go
to a Radclyffe. However, when Dennis was twenty-two,
she quarrelled violently with him—over some debts that he
had run up, I think. When she died, a year later, I was
astonished to find that she had made a will leaving all her
money to me. It was, I know, a great blow to Dennis, and
I felt very badly about it. I would have given him the money
if he would have taken it, but it seems that that kind of
thing can't be done. However, as soon as I was twenty-
one, I made a will leaving it all to him. That's the least I
can do. So if I'm run over by a motor, Dennis will come
into his own."

"Exactly," said Tommy. "And when were you twenty-
one, if I may ask the question?"

"Just three weeks ago."

"Ah!" said Tommy. "Now will you give me fuller particulars of the members of your household at this minute?"

"Servants—or—others?"

"Both."

"The servants, as I say, have been with us some time.

There is old Mrs. Holloway, the cook, and her niece Rose, the kitchenmaid. Then there are two elderly housemaids, and Hannah who was my aunt's maid and who has always been devoted to me. The parlormaid is called Esther Quant, and seems a very nice quiet girl. As for ourselves, there is Miss Logan who was Aunt Lucy's companion and who runs the house for me, and Captain Radclyffe—Dennis, you know, whom I told you about, and there is a girl called Mary Chilcott, an old school friend of mine who is staying with us."

Tommy thought for a moment.

"That all seems fairly clear and straightforward, Miss Hargreaves," he said after a minute or two. "I take it that you have no special reason for attaching suspicion more to one person than another? You are only afraid it might prove to be—well—not a servant, shall we say?"

"That's it exactly, Mr. Blunt. I have honestly no idea who used that piece of brown paper. The handwriting was printed."

"There seems only one thing to be done," said Tommy. "I must be on the spot."

The girl looked at him inquiringly.

Tommy went on after a moment's thought.

"I suggest that you prepare the way for the arrival of— say, Mr. and Miss Van Dusen—American friends of yours. Will you be able to do that quite naturally?"

"Oh! yes. There will be no difficulty at all. When will you come down—to-morrow—or the day after?"

"To-morrow, if you please. There is no time to waste."

"That is settled, then."

The girl rose, and held out her hand.

"One thing, Miss Hargreaves, not a word, mind, to any-one—anyone at all, that we are not what we seem."

"What do you think of it, Tuppence?" he asked, when he returned from showing the visitor out.

"I don't like it," said Tuppence decidedly. "Especially I don't like the chocolates having so little arsenic in them."

"What *do* you mean?"

"Don't you see? All those chocolates being sent round

the neighborhood were a blind. To establish the idea of a local maniac. Then, when the girl was really poisoned, it would be thought to be the same thing. You see, but for a stroke of luck, no one would ever have guessed that the chocolates were actually sent by someone in the house itself."

"That was a stroke of luck. You're right. You think it's a deliberate plot against the girl herself?"

"I'm afraid so. I remember reading about old Lady Radclyffe's will. That girl has come into a terrific lot of money."

"Yes, and she came of age and made a will three weeks ago. It looks bad—for Dennis Radclyffe. He gains by her death."

Tuppence nodded.

"The worst of it is—that she thinks so too! That's why she won't have the police called in. Already she suspects him. And she must be more than half in love with him to act as she has done."

"In that case," said Tommy thoughtfully, "why the devil doesn't he marry her? Much simpler and safer."

Tuppence stared at him.

"You've said a mouthful," she observed. "Oh! boy. I'm getting ready to be Miss Van Dusen, you observe."

"Why rush to crime, where there is a lawful means near at hand?"

Tuppence reflected for a minute or two.

"I've got it," she announced. "Clearly he must have married a barmaid whilst at Oxford. Origin of the quarrel with his aunt. That explains everything."

"Then why not send poisoned sweets to the barmaid?" suggested Tommy. "Much more practical. I wish you wouldn't jump to these wild conclusions, Tuppence."

"They're deductions," said Tuppence, with a good deal of dignity. "This is your first *corrida*, my friend, but when you have been twenty minutes in the arena—"

Tommy flung the office cushion at her.

18

The House of Lurking Death
(continued)

"Tuppence, I say, Tuppence, come here."

It was breakfast time the next morning. Tuppence hurried out of her bedroom and into the dining room. Tommy was striding up and down, the open newspaper in his hand.

"What's the matter?"

Tommy wheeled round, and shoved the paper into her hand, pointing to the headlines.

MYSTERIOUS POISONING CASE
DEATHS FROM FIG SANDWICHES

Tuppence read on. This mysterious outbreak of ptomaine poisoning had occurred at Thurnly Grange. The deaths so far reported were those of Miss Lois Hargreaves, the owner of the house, and the parlormaid, Esther Quant. A Captain Radclyffe and a Miss Logan were reported to be still seriously ill. The cause of the outbreak was supposed to be some fig paste used in sandwiches, since another lady, a Miss Chilcott, who had not partaken of these, was reported to be quite well.

"We must get down there at once," said Tommy. "That

151

girl! That perfectly ripping girl! Why the devil didn't I go straight down there with her yesterday?"

"If you had," said Tuppence, "you'd probably have eaten fig sandwiches too for tea, and then you'd have been dead. Come on, let's start at once. I see it says that Dennis Radclyffe is seriously ill also."

"Probably shamming, the dirty blackguard."

They arrived at the small village of Thurnly about mid day. An elderly woman with red eyes opened the door to them when they arrived at Thurnly Grange.

"Look here," said Tommy quickly before she could speak. "I'm not a reporter or anything like that. Miss Hargreaves came to see me yesterday, and asked me to come down here. Is there anyone I can see?"

"Dr. Burton is here now if you'd like to speak to him," said the woman doubtfully. "Or Miss Chilcott. She's making all the arrangements."

But Tommy had caught at the first suggestion.

"Dr. Burton," he said authoritatively. "I should like to see him at once if he is here."

The woman showed them into a small morning room. Five minutes later the door opened, and a tall elderly man with bent shoulders and a kind but worried face, came in.

"Dr. Burton?" said Tommy. He produced his professional card. "Miss Hargreaves called on me yesterday with reference to those poisoned chocolates. I came down to investigate the matter at her request—alas! too late."

The doctor looked at him keenly.

"You are Mr. Blunt himself?"

"Yes. This is my assistant, Miss Robinson."

The doctor bowed to Tuppence.

"Under the circumstances, there is no need for reticence. But for the episode of the chocolates, I might have believed these deaths to be the result of severe ptomaine poisoning— but ptomaine poisoning of an unusually virulent kind. There is gastro-intestinal inflammation and hæmorrhage. As it is, I am taking the fig paste to be analysed."

"You suspect arsenic poisoning?"

"No. The poison, if a poison has been employed, is

something far more potent and swift in its action. It looks more like some powerful vegetable toxin."

"I see. I should like to ask you, Dr. Burton, whether you are thoroughly convinced that Captain Radclyffe is suffering from the same form of poisoning?"

The doctor looked at him.

"Captain Radclyffe is not suffering from any sort of poisoning now."

"Aha," said Tommy. "I—"

"Captain Radclyffe died at five o'clock this morning."

Tommy was utterly taken aback. The doctor prepared to depart.

"And the other victim, Miss Logan?" asked Tuppence.

"I have every reason to hope that she will recover since she has survived so far. Being an older woman, the poison seems to have had less effect on her. I will let you know the result of the analysis, Mr. Blunt. In the meantime, Miss Chilcott will, I am sure, tell you anything you want to know."

As he spoke, the door opened, and a girl appeared. She was tall, with a tanned face, and steady blue eyes.

Dr. Burton performed the necessary introductions.

"I am glad you have come, Mr. Blunt," said Mary Chilcott. "This affair seems too terrible. Is there anything you want to know that I can tell you?"

"Where did the fig paste come from?"

"It is a special kind that comes from London. We often have it. No one suspected that this particular pot differed from any of the others. Personally I dislike the flavor of figs. That explains my immunity. I cannot understand how Dennis was affected, since he was out for tea. He must have picked up a sandwich when he came home, I suppose."

Tommy felt Tuppence's hand press his arm ever so slightly.

"What time did he come in?" he asked.

"I don't really know. I could find out."

"Thank you, Miss Chilcott. It doesn't matter. You have no objection, I hope, to my questioning the servants?"

"Please do anything you like, Mr. Blunt. I am nearly

distraught. Tell me—you don't think there has been—foul play?"

Her eyes were very anxious as she put the question.

"I don't know what to think. We shall soon know."

"Yes, I suppose Dr. Burton will have the paste analysed."

Quickly excusing herself, she went out by the window to speak to one of the gardeners.

"You take the housemaids, Tuppence," said Tommy, "and I'll find my way to the kitchen. I say, Miss Chilcott may feel very distraught, but she doesn't look it."

Tuppence nodded assent without replying.

Husband and wife met half an hour later.

"Now to pool results," said Tommy. "The sandwiches came out from tea, and the parlormaid ate one—that's how she got it in the neck. Cook is positive Dennis Radclyffe hadn't returned when tea was cleared away. Query—how did *he* get poisioned?"

"He came in at a quarter to seven," said Tuppence. "Housemaid saw him from one of the windows. He had a cocktail before dinner—in the library. She was just clearing away the glass now, and luckily I got it from her before she washed it. It was after that that he complained of feeling ill."

"Good," said Tommy. "I'll take that glass along to Burton presently. Anything else?"

"I'd like you to see Hannah, the maid. She's—she's queer."

"How do you mean—queer?"

"She looks to me as though she were going off her head."

"Let me see her."

Tuppence led the way upstairs. Hannah had a small sitting-room of her own. The maid sat upright on a high chair. On her knees was an open Bible. She did not look towards the two strangers as they entered. Instead she continued to read aloud to herself.

"Let hot burning coals fall upon them, let them be cast into the fire and into the pit, that they never rise up again."

"May I speak to you a minute?" asked Tommy.

Hannah made an impatient gesture with her hand.

"This is no time. The time is running short, I say. *I will follow upon mine enemies and overtake them, neither will I turn again till I have destroyed them.* So it is written. The word of the Lord has come to me. I am the scourge of the Lord."

"Mad as a hatter," murmured Tommy.

"She's been going on like that all the time," whispered Tuppence.

Tommy picked up a book that was lying open, face downwards on the table. He glanced at the title and slipped it into his pocket.

Suddenly the old woman rose and turned towards them menacingly.

"Go out from here. The time is at hand! I am the flail of the Lord. The wind bloweth where it listeth—so do I destroy. The ungodly shall perish. This is a house of evil—of evil, I tell you! Beware of the wrath of the Lord whose handmaiden I am."

She advanced upon them fiercely. Tommy thought it best to humor her and withdrew. As he closed the door, he saw her pick up the Bible again.

"I wonder if she's always been like that," he muttered.

He drew from his pocket the book he had picked up off the table.

"Look at that. Funny reading for an ignorant maid."

Tuppence took the book.

"Materia Medica," she murmured. She looked at the fly leaf. "Edward Logan. It's an old book. Tommy, I wonder if we could see Miss Logan? Dr. Burton said she was better."

"Shall we ask Miss Chilcott?"

"No. Let's get hold of a housemaid, and send her in to ask."

After a brief delay, they were informed that Miss Logan would see them. They were taken into a big bedroom facing over the lawn. In the bed was an old lady with white hair, her delicate old face drawn by suffering.

"I have been very ill," she said faintly. "And I can't talk

much, but Ellen tells me you are detectives. Lois went to consult you then? She spoke of doing so."

"Yes, Miss Logan," said Tommy. "We don't want to tire you, but perhaps you can answer a few questions. The maid, Hannah, is she quite right in her head?"

Miss Logan looked at them with obvious surprise.

"Oh! yes. She is very religious—but there is nothing wrong with her."

Tommy held out the book he had taken from the table.

"Is this yours, Miss Logan?"

"Yes. It was one of my father's books. He was a great doctor, one of the pioneers of serum therapeutics."

The old lady's voice rang with pride.

"Quite so," said Tommy. "I thought I knew his name," he added mendaciously. "This book now, did you lend it to Hannah?"

"To Hannah?" Miss Logan raised herself in bed with indignation. "No, indeed. She wouldn't understand the first word of it. It is a highly technical book."

"Yes. I see that. Yet I found it in Hannah's room."

"Disgraceful," said Miss Logan. "I will not have the servants touching my things."

"Where ought it to be?"

"In the bookshelf in my sitting-room—or—stay, I lent it to Mary. The dear girl is very interested in herbs. She has made one or two experiments in my little kitchen. I have a little place of my own, you know, where I brew liqueurs and make preserves in the old fashioned way. Dear Lucy, Lady Radclyffe, you know, used to swear by my tansy tea—a wonderful thing for a cold in the head. Poor Lucy, she was subject to colds. So is Dennis. Dear boy, his father was my first cousin."

Tommy interrupted these reminiscences.

"This kitchen of yours? Does anyone else use it except you and Miss Chilcott?"

"Hannah clears up there. And she boils the kettle there for our early morning tea."

"Thank you, Miss Logan," said Tommy. "There is nothing more I want to ask you at present. I hope we haven't tired you too much."

He left the room and went down the stairs, frowning to himself.

"There is something here, my dear Mr. Ricardo, that I do not understand."

"I hate this house," said Tuppence with a shiver. "Let's go for a good long walk and try to think things out."

Tommy complied and they set out. First they left the cocktail glass at the doctor's house and then set off for a good tramp across country discussing the case as they did so.

"It makes it easier somehow if one plays the fool," said Tommy. "All this Hanaud business. I suppose some people would think I didn't care. But I do, most awfully. I feel that somehow or other we ought to have prevented this."

"I think that's foolish of you," said Tuppence. "It is not as though we had advised Lois Hargreaves not to go to Scotland Yard or anything like that. Nothing would have induced her to bring the police into the matter. If she hadn't come to us, she would have done nothing at all."

"And the result would have been the same. Yes, you are right, Tuppence. It's morbid to reproach oneself over something one couldn't help. What I would like to do is to make good now."

"And that's not going to be easy."

"No, it isn't. There are so many possibilities, and yet all of them seem wild and improbable. Supposing Dennis Radclyffe put the poison in the sandwiches. He knew he would be out to tea. That seems fairly plain sailing."

"Yes," said Tuppence, "that's all right so far. Then we can put against that the fact that he was poisoned himself so that seems to rule him out. There is one person we mustn't forget—and that is Hannah."

"Hannah?"

"People do all sorts of queer things when they have religious mania."

"She is pretty far gone with it too," said Tommy. "You

ought to drop a word to Dr. Burton about it."

"It must have come on very rapidly," said Tuppence. "That is if we go by what Miss Logan said."

"I believe religious mania does," said Tommy. "I mean, you go on singing hymns in your bedroom with the door open for years, and then you go suddenly right over the line and become violent."

"There is certainly more evidence against Hannah than against anybody else," said Tuppence thoughtfully, "and yet I have an idea—" She stopped.

"Yes?" said Tommy encouragingly.

"It is not really an idea. I suppose it is just a prejudice."

"A prejudice against someone?"

Tuppence nodded.

"Tommy—did *you* like Mary Chilcott?"

Tommy considered.

"Yes, I think I did. She struck me as extremely capable and businesslike—perhaps a shade too much so—but very reliable."

"You didn't think it was odd that she didn't seem more upset?"

"Well, in a way that is a point in her favor. I mean, if she had done anything, she would make a point of being upset—lay it on rather thick."

"I suppose so," said Tuppence. "And anyway there doesn't seem to be any motive in her case. One doesn't see what good this wholesale slaughter can do her."

"I suppose none of the servants are concerned?"

"It doesn't seem likely. They seem a quiet reliable lot. I wonder what Esther Quant, the parlormaid, was like."

"You mean, that if she was young and good-looking there was a chance that she was mixed up in it in some way."

"That is what I mean." Tuppence sighed. "It is all very discouraging."

"Well, I suppose the police will get down to it all right," said Tommy.

"Probably. I should like it to be us. By the way, did you notice a lot of small red dots on Miss Logan's arm?"

"I don't think I did. What about them?"

"They looked as though they were made by a hypodermic syringe," said Tuppence.

"Probably Dr. Burton gave her a hypodermic injection of some kind."

"Oh, very likely. But he wouldn't give her about forty."

"The cocaine habit," suggested Tommy helpfully.

"I thought of that," said Tuppence, "but her eyes were all right. You would see at once if it was cocaine or morphia. Besides she doesn't look that sort of old lady."

"Most respectable and God fearing," agreed Tommy.

"It is all very difficult," said Tuppence. "We have talked and talked and we don't seem any nearer now than we were. Don't let's forget to call at the doctor's on our way home."

The doctor's door was opened by a lanky boy of about fifteen.

"Mr. Blunt?" he inquired. "Yes, the doctor is out but he left a note for you in case you should call."

He handed them the note in question and Tommy tore it open.

> "*Dear Mr. Blunt,*
>   *There is reason to believe that the poison employed was Ricin, a vegetable toxalbumose of tremendous potency. Please keep this to yourself for the present.*"

Tommy let the note drop, but picked it up quickly.

"Ricin," he murmured. "Know anything about it, Tuppence? You used to be rather well up in these things."

"Ricin," said Tuppence, thoughtfully. "You get it out of Castor Oil, I believe."

"I never did take kindly to Castor Oil," said Tommy. "I am more set against it than ever now."

"The oil's all right. You get Ricin from the seeds of the Castor Oil plants. I believe I saw some Castor Oil plants in the garden this morning—big things with glossy leaves."

"You mean that someone extracted the stuff on the premises. Could Hannah do such a thing?"

Tuppence shook her head.

"Doesn't seem likely. She wouldn't know enough."

Suddenly Tommy gave an exclamation.

"That book. Have I got it in my pocket still? Yes." He took it out, and turned over the leaves vehemently. "I thought so. Here's the page it was open at this morning. Do you see, Tuppence? Ricin!"

Tuppence seized the book from him.

"Can you make head or tail of it? I can't."

"It's clear enough to me," said Tuppence. She walked along, reading busily, with one hand on Tommy's arm to steer herself. Presently she shut the book with a bang. They were just approaching the house again.

"Tommy, will you leave this to me? Just for once, you see, I am the bull that has been more than twenty minutes in the arena."

Tommy nodded.

"You shall be the Captain of the Ship, Tuppence," he said gravely. "We've got to get to the bottom of this."

"First of all," said Tuppence as they entered the house, "I must ask Miss Logan one more question."

She ran upstairs. Tommy followed her. She rapped sharply on the old lady's door, and went in.

"Is that you, my dear?" said Miss Logan. "You know you are much too young and pretty to be a detective. Have you found out anything?"

"Yes," said Tuppence. "I have."

Miss Logan looked at her questioningly.

"I don't know about being pretty," went on Tuppence, "but being young, I happened to work in a hospital during the War. I know something about serum therapeutics. I happen to know that when Ricin is injected in small doses hypodermically immunity is produced, antiricin is formed. That fact paved the way for the foundation of serum therapeutics. You knew that, Miss Logan. You injected Ricin for some time hypodermically into yourself. Then you let yourself be poisoned with the rest. You helped your father in his work, and you knew all about Ricin and how to obtain it and extract it from the seeds. You chose a day when Dennis Radclyffe was out for tea. It wouldn't do for him to be poisoned at the same time—he might die before Lois

Hargreaves. So long as she died first, he inherited her money, and at his death it passes to you, his next of kin. You remember, you told us this morning that his father was your first cousin."

The old lady stared at Tuppence with baleful eyes.

Suddenly a wild figure burst in from the adjoining room. It was Hannah. In her hand she held a lighted torch which she waved frantically.

"Truth has been spoken. That is the wicked one. I saw her reading the book, and smiling to herself and I knew. I found the book and the page—but it said nothing to me. But the voice of the Lord spoke to me. She hated my mistress, her ladyship. She was always jealous and envious. She hated my own sweet Miss Lois. But the wicked shall perish, the fire of the Lord shall consume them."

Waving her torch she sprang forward to the bed.

A cry arose from the old lady.

"Take her away—take her away. It's true—but take her away."

Tuppence flung herself upon Hannah, but the woman managed to set fire to the curtains of the bed before Tuppence could get the torch from her and stamp on it. Tommy, however, had rushed in from the landing outside. He tore down the bed hangings and managed to stifle the flames with a rug. Then he rushed to Tuppence's assistance and between them they subdued Hannah just as Dr. Burton came hurrying in.

A very few words sufficed to put him *au courant* of the situation.

He hurried to the bedside, lifted Miss Logan's hand, then uttered a sharp exclamation.

"The shock of fire has been too much for her. She's dead. Perhaps it is as well under the circumstances."

He paused and then added, "There was Ricin in the cocktail glass as well."

"It's the best thing that could have happened," said Tommy when they had relinquished Hannah to the doctor's care, and were alone together. "Tuppence, you were simply marvellous."

"There wasn't much Hanaud about it," said Tuppence.

"It was too serious for play acting. I still can't bear to think of that girl. I won't think of her. But, as I said before, you were marvellous. The honors are with you. To use a familiar quotation, 'It is a great advantage to be intelligent and not to look it.'"

"Tommy," said Tuppence. "You're a beast."

19

The Unbreakable Alibi

Tommy and Tuppence were busy sorting correspondence. Tuppence gave an exclamation and handed a letter across to Tommy.

"A new client," she said importantly.

"Ha!" said Tommy. "What do we deduce from this letter, Watson? Nothing much, except the somewhat obvious fact that Mr.—er—Montgomery Jones is not one of the world's best spellers, thereby proving that he has been expensively educated."

"Montgomery Jones?" said Tuppence. "Now what do I know about a Montgomery Jones? Oh, yes, I have got it now. I think Janet St. Vincent mentioned him. His mother was Lady Aileen Montgomery, very crusty and high church with gold crosses and things, and she married a man called Jones who is immensely rich."

"In fact the same old story," said Tommy. "Let me see, what time does this Mr. M. J. wish to see us? Ah, eleven thirty."

At eleven thirty precisely a very tall young man with an amiable and ingenuous countenance entered the outer office and addressed himself to Albert, the office boy.

"Look here—I say. Can I see Mr.—er—Blunt?"

"Have you an appointment, sir?" said Albert.

"I don't quite know. Yes, I suppose I have. What I mean is I wrote a letter—"

"What name, sir?"

"Mr. Montgomery Jones."

"I will take your name in to Mr. Blunt."

He returned after a brief interval.

"Will you wait a few minutes please, sir. Mr. Blunt is engaged on a very important conference at present."

"Oh—er—yes—certainly," said Mr. Montgomery Jones.

Having, he hoped, impressed his client sufficiently Tommy rang the buzzer on his desk, and Mr. Montgomery Jones was ushered into the inner office by Albert.

Tommy rose to greet him, and shaking him warmly by the hand motioned towards the vacant chair.

"Now, Mr. Montgomery Jones," he said briskly, "what can we have the pleasure of doing for you?"

Mr. Montgomery Jones looked uncertainly at the third occupant of the office.

"My confidential secretary, Miss Robinson," said Tommy. "You can speak quite freely before her. I take it that this is some family matter of a delicate kind?"

"Well—not exactly," said Mr. Montgomery Jones.

"You surprise me," said Tommy. "You are not in trouble of any kind yourself, I hope?"

"Oh rather not," said Mr. Montgomery Jones.

"Well," said Tommy, "perhaps you will—er—state the facts plainly."

That, however, seemed to be the one thing that Mr. Montgomery Jones could not do.

"It's a dashed odd sort of thing I have got to ask you," he said hesitatingly. "I—er—I really don't know how to set about it."

"We never touch divorce cases," said Tommy.

"Oh Lord no," said Mr. Montgomery Jones. "I don't mean that. It is just, well—it's a deuced silly sort of a joke. That's all."

"Someone has played a practical joke on you of a mysterious nature?" suggested Tommy.

But Mr. Montgomery Jones once more shook his head.

"Well," said Tommy retiring gracefully from the position, "take your own time and let us have it in your own words."

There was a pause.

"You see," said Mr. Jones at last, "it was at dinner. I sat next to a girl."

"Yes?" said Tommy encouragingly.

"She was a—oh, well, I really can't describe her, but she was simply one of the most sporting girls I ever met. She's an Australian over here with another girl, sharing a flat with her in Clarges Street. She's simply game for anything. I absolutely can't tell you the effect that girl had on me."

"We can quite imagine it, Mr. Jones," said Tuppence.

She saw clearly that if Mr. Montgomery Jones' troubles were ever to be extracted a sympathetic feminine touch was needed, as distinct from the business like methods of Mr. Blunt.

"We can understand," said Tuppence encouragingly.

"Well, the whole thing came as an absolute shock to me," said Mr. Montgomery Jones, "that a girl could, well— knock you over like that. There had been another girl—in fact two other girls. One was awfully jolly and all that but I didn't much like her chin. She danced marvellously though and I have known her all my life which makes a fellow feel kind of safe, you know. And then there was one of the girls at the 'Frivolity'. Frightfully amusing, but of course there would be a lot of ructions with the mater over that, and anyway I really didn't want to marry either of them, but I was thinking about things you know and then—slap out of the blue—I sat next to this girl and—"

"The whole world was changed," said Tuppence in a feeling voice.

Tommy moved impatiently in his chair. He was by now somewhat bored by the recital of Mr. Montgomery Jones' love affairs.

"You put it awfully well," said Mr. Montgomery Jones. "That is absolutely what it was like. Only, you know, I fancy she didn't think much of me. You mayn't think it but I am not terribly clever."

"Oh, you mustn't be too modest," said Tuppence.

"Oh, I do realize that I am not much of a chap," said Mr. Jones with an engaging smile. "Not for a perfectly marvellous girl like that. That is why I just feel I have got to put this thing through. It's my only chance. She's such a sporting girl that she would never go back on her word."

"Well I am sure we wish you luck and all that," said Tuppence kindly. "But I don't exactly see what you want us to do."

"Oh Lord!" said Mr. Montgomery Jones. "Haven't I explained?"

"No," said Tommy. "You haven't."

"Well, it was like this. We were talking about detective stories. Una—that's her name—is just as keen about them as I am. We got talking about one in particular. It all hinges on an alibi. Then we got talking about alibis and faking them. Then I said—no, she said—now which of us was it that said it?"

"Never mind which of you it was," said Tuppence.

"I said it would be a jolly difficult thing to do. She disagreed—said it only wanted a bit of brain work. We got all hot and excited about it and in the end she said 'I will make you a sporting offer. What do you bet that I can produce an alibi that nobody can shake?'

"Anything you like, I said, and we settled it then and there. She was frightfully cocksure about the whole thing. 'It's an odds on chance for me,' she said. 'Don't be so sure of that,' I said. 'Supposing you lose and I ask you for anything I like?' She laughed and said she came of a gambling family and I could."

"Well?" said Tuppence as Mr. Jones came to a pause and looked at her appealingly.

"Well, don't you see? It is up to me. It is the only chance I have got of getting a girl like that to look at me. You have no idea how sporting she is. Last summer she was out in a boat and someone bet her she wouldn't jump overboard and swim ashore in her clothes, and she did it."

"It is a very curious proposition," said Tommy. "I am not quite sure I yet understand it."

"It is perfectly simple," said Mr. Montgomery Jones. "You must be doing this sort of thing all the time. Investigating fake alibis and seeing where they fall down."

"Oh—er—yes, of course," said Tommy. "We do a lot of that sort of work."

"Someone has got to do it for me," said Montgomery Jones. "I shouldn't be any good at that sort of thing myself. You have only got to catch her out and everything is all right. I daresay it seems rather a futile business to you but it means a lot to me and I am prepared to pay—er—all necessary whatnots you know."

"That will be all right," said Tuppence. "I am sure Mr. Blunt will take the case on for you."

"Certainly, certainly," said Tommy. "A most refreshing case, most refreshing indeed."

Mr. Montgomery Jones heaved a sigh of relief and pulled a mass of papers from his pocket and selected one of them. "Here it is," he said. "She says, 'I am sending you proof I was in two distinct places at one and the same time. According to one story I dined at the Bon Temps Restaurant in Soho by myself, went to the Duke's Theatre and had supper with a friend, Mr. le Marchant, at the Savoy—but I was also staying at the Castle Hotel, Torquay, and only returned to London on the following morning. You have got to find out which of the two stories is the true one and how I managed the other."

"There," said Mr. Montgomery Jones. "Now you see what it is that I want you to do."

"A most refreshing little problem," said Tommy. "Very naïve."

"Here is Una's photograph," said Mr. Montgomery Jones. "You will want that."

"What is the lady's full name?" inquired Tommy.

"Miss Una Drake. And her address is 180 Clarges Street."

"Thank you," said Tommy. "Well, we will look into the

matter for you, Mr. Montgomery Jones. I hope we shall have good news for you very shortly."

"I say you know, I am no end grateful," said Mr. Jones rising to his feet and shaking Tommy by the hand. "It has taken an awful load off my mind."

Having seen his client out, Tommy returned to the inner office. Tuppence was at the cupboard that contained the Classic library.

"Inspector French," said Tuppence.

"Eh?" said Tommy.

"Inspector French of course," said Tuppence. "He always does alibis. I know the exact procedure. We have to go over everything and check it. At first it will seem all right and then when we examine it more closely we shall find the flaw."

"There ought not to be much difficulty about that," agreed Tommy. "I mean, knowing that one of them is a fake to start with makes the thing almost a certainty I should say. That is what worries me."

"I don't see anything to worry about in that."

"I am worrying about the girl," said Tommy. "She will probably be let in to marry that young man whether she wants to or not."

"Darling," said Tuppence, "don't be foolish. Women are never the wild gamblers they appear. Unless that girl was already perfectly prepared to marry that pleasant but rather empty-headed young man, she would never have let herself in for a wager of this kind. But, Tommy, believe me, she will marry him with more enthusiasm and respect if he wins the wager than if she has to make it easy for him some other way."

"You do think you know about everything," said her husband.

"I do," said Tuppence.

"And now to examine our data," said Tommy drawing the papers towards him. "First the photograph—hm—quite a nice looking girl—and quite a good photograph I should say. Clear and easily recognizable."

"We must get some other girls' photographs," said Tuppence.

"Why?"

"They always do," said Tuppence. "You show four or five to waiters and they pick out the right one."

"Do you think they do?" said Tommy—"pick out the right one I mean."

"Well, they do in books," said Tuppence.

"It is a pity that real life is so different from fiction," said Tommy. "Now then what have we here? Yes, this is the London lot. Dined at the Bon Temps seven thirty. Went to Duke's Theatre and saw Delphiniums Blue. Counterfoil of theatre ticket enclosed. Supper at the Savoy with Mr. le Marchant. We can, I suppose, interview Mr. le Marchant."

"That tells us nothing at all," said Tuppence, "because if he is helping her to do it he naturally won't give the show away. We can wash out anything he says now."

"Well, here is the Torquay end," went on Tommy. "Twelve o'clock train from Paddington, had lunch in the Restaurant Car, receipted bill enclosed. Stayed at Castle Hotel for one night. Again receipted bill."

"I think this is all rather weak," said Tuppence. "Anyone can buy a theatre ticket, you need never go near the theatre. The girl just went to Torquay and the London thing is a fake."

"If so, it is rather a sitter for us," said Tommy. "Well, I suppose we might as well go and interview Mr. le Marchant."

Mr. le Marchant proved to be a breezy youth who betrayed no great surprise on seeing them.

"Una has got some little game on, hasn't she?" he asked. "You never know what that kid is up to."

"I understand, Mr. le Marchant," said Tommy, "that Miss Drake had supper with you at the Savoy last Tuesday evening."

"That's right," said Mr. le Marchant. "I know it was Tuesday because Una impressed it on me at the time and what's more she made me write it down in a little book."

With some pride he showed an entry faintly pencilled: "Having supper with Una. Savoy. Tuesday 19th."

"Where had Miss Drake been earlier in the evening? Do you know?"

"She had been to some rotten show called Pink Peonies or something like that. Absolute slosh so she told me."

"You are quite sure Miss Drake was with you that evening?"

Mr. le Marchant stared at him.

"Why, of course. Haven't I been telling you?"

"Perhaps she asked you to tell us," said Tuppence.

"Well, for a matter of fact she did say something that was rather dashed odd. She said, what was it now? 'You think you are sitting here having supper with me, Jimmy, but really I am having supper two hundred miles away in Devonshire.' Now that was a dashed odd thing to say, don't you think so? Sort of astral-body stuff. The funny thing is that a pal of mine, Dicky Rice, thought he saw her there."

"Who is this Mr. Rice?"

"Oh, just a friend of mine. He had been down in Torquay staying with an aunt. Sort of old bean who is always going to die and never does. Dicky had been down doing the dutiful nephew. He said, 'I saw that Australian girl one day—Una something or other. Wanted to go and talk to her but my aunt carried me off to chat with an old Pussy in a bath chair.' I said, "When was this?' and he said, 'Oh, Tuesday about tea time.' I told him of course that he had made a mistake, but it was odd, wasn't it? With Una saying that about Devonshire that evening."

"Very odd," said Tommy. "Tell me, Mr. le Marchant, did anyone you know have supper near you at the Savoy?"

"Some people called Oglander were at the next table."

"Do they know Miss Drake?"

"Oh yes, they know her. They are not frightful friends or anything of that kind."

"Well, if there's nothing more you can tell us, Mr. le Marchant, I think we will wish you good morning."

"Either that chap is an extraordinary good liar," said

Tommy as they reached the street, "or else he is speaking the truth."

"Yes," said Tuppence. "I have changed my opinion. I have a sort of feeling now that Una Drake was at the Savoy for supper that night."

"We will now go to the Bon Temps," said Tommy. "A little food for starving sleuths is clearly indicated. Let's just get a few girls' photographs first."

This proved rather more difficult than was expected. Turning into a photographer's and demanding a few assorted photographs, they were met with a cold rebuff.

"Why are all the things that are so easy and simple in books so difficult in real life?" wailed Tuppence. "How horribly suspicious they looked. What do you think they thought we wanted to do with the photographs? We had better go and raid Jane's flat."

Tuppence's friend Jane proved of an accommodating disposition and permitted Tuppence to rummage in a drawer and select four specimens of former friends of Jane's who had been shoved hastily in to be out of sight and mind.

Armed with this galaxy of feminine beauty they proceeded to the Bon Temps where fresh difficulties and much expense awaited them. Tommy had to get hold of each waiter in turn, tip him and then produce the assorted photographs. The result was unsatisfactory. At least three of the photographs were promising starters as having dined there last Tuesday. They then returned to the office where Tuppence immersed herself in an A.B.C.

"Paddington twelve o'clock. Torquay three thirty-five. That's the train and le Marchant's friend, Mr. Sago or Tapioca or something, saw her there about tea time."

"We haven't checked his statement, remember," said Tommy. "If, as you said to begin with, le Marchant is a friend of Una Drake's, he may have invented this story."

"Oh, we'll hunt up Mr. Rice," said Tuppence. "I have a kind of hunch that Mr. le Marchant was speaking the truth. No, what I am trying to get at now is this. Una Drake leaves London by the twelve o'clock train, possibly takes

a room at a hotel and unpacks. Then she takes a train back
to town arriving in time to get to the Savoy. There is one
at four forty gets up to Paddington at nine ten."

"And then?" said Tommy.

"And then," said Tuppence, frowning, it is rather more
difficult. There is a midnight train from Paddington down
again but she could hardly take that, that would be too
early."

"A fast car," suggested Tommy.

"H'm," said Tuppence. "It is just on two hundred miles."

"Australians, I have always been told, drive very reck-
lessly."

"Oh, I suppose it could be done," said Tuppence, "she
would arrive there about seven."

"Are you supposing her to have nipped into her bed at
the Castle Hotel without being seen? Or arriving there explaining that she had been out all night and could she have
her bill, please?"

"Tommy," said Tuppence. "We are idiots. She needn't
have gone back to Torquay at all. She has only got to get
a friend to go to the Hotel and collect her luggage and pay
her bill. Then you get the receipted bill with the proper date
on it."

"I think on the whole we have worked out a very sound
hypothesis," said Tommy. "The next thing to do is to catch
the twelve o'clock train to Torquay tomorrow and verify
our brilliant conclusions."

Armed with a portfolio of photographs, Tommy and
Tuppence duly established themselves in a first class car-
riage the following morning, and booked seats for the second
lunch.

"It probably won't be the same dining car attendants,"
said Tommy. "That would be too much luck to expect. I
expect we shall have to travel up and down to Torquay for
days before we strike the right ones."

"This alibi business is very trying," said Tuppence. "In
books it is all passed over in two or three paragraphs. Inspector Something then boarded the train to Torquay and

questioned the dining car attendants and so ended the story."

For once, however, the young couple's luck was in. In answer to their question the attendant who brought their bill for lunch proved to be the same one who had been on duty the preceding Tuesday. What Tommy called the ten shilling note touch then came into action and Tuppence produced the portfolio.

"I want to know," said Tommy, "if any of these ladies had lunch on this train on Tuesday last?"

In a gratifying manner worthy of the best detective fiction the man at once indicated the photograph of Una Drake.

"Yes sir, I remember that lady, and I remember that it was Tuesday, because the lady herself drew attention to the fact saying it was always the luckiest day in the week for her."

"So far, so good," said Tuppence as they returned to their compartment. "And we will probably find that she booked at the Hotel all right. It is going to be more difficult to prove that she travelled back to London, but perhaps one of the porters at the station may remember."

Here, however, they drew a blank and crossing to the up platform Tommy made inquiries of the ticket collector and of various porters. After the distribution of half crowns as a preliminary to inquiring, two of the porters picked out one of the other photographs with a vague remembrance that someone like that travelled to town by the four forty that afternoon, but there was no identification of Una Drake.

"But that doesn't prove anything," said Tuppence as they left the station. "She may have travelled by that train and no one noticed her."

"She may have gone from the other station, from Torre."

"That's quite likely," said Tuppence, "however, we can see to that after we have been to the hotel."

The Castle Hotel was a big one overlooking the sea. After booking a room for the night and signing the register, Tommy observed pleasantly:

"I believe you had a friend of ours staying here last Tuesday. Miss Una Drake."

The young lady in the bureau beamed at him.

"Oh yes, I remember quite well. An Australian young lady I believe."

At a sign from Tommy Tuppence produced the photograph.

"That is rather a charming photograph of her, isn't it?" said Tuppence.

"Oh very nice, very nice indeed, quite stylish."

"Did she stay here long?" inquired Tommy.

"Only the one night. She went away by the Express the next morning back to London. It seemed a long way to come for one night but of course I suppose Australian ladies don't think anything of travelling."

"She is a very sporting girl," said Tommy, "always having adventures. It wasn't here, was it, that she went out to dine with some friends, went for a drive in their car afterwards, ran the car into a ditch and wasn't able to get home till morning?"

"Oh, no," said the young lady. "Miss Drake had dinner here in the Hotel."

"Really," said Tommy, "are you sure of that? I mean—how do you know?"

"Oh, I saw her."

"I asked because I understood she was dining with some friends in Torquay," explained Tommy.

"Oh, no sir, she dined here." The young lady laughed and blushed a little. "I remember she had on a most sweetly pretty frock. One of those new flowered chiffons all over pansies."

"Tuppence, this tears it," said Tommy when they had been shown upstairs to their room.

"It does rather," said Tuppence. "Of course that woman may be mistaken. We will ask the waiter at dinner. There can't be very many people here just at this time of year."

This time it was Tuppence who opened the attack.

"Can you tell me if a friend of mine was here last Tuesday?" she asked the waiter with an engaging smile. "A Miss Drake, wearing a frock all over pansies I believe." She produced a photograph. "This lady."

The waiter broke into immediate smiles of recognition.

"Yes, yes, Miss Drake. I remember her very well. She told me she came from Australia."

"She dined here?"

"Yes. It was last Tuesday. She asked me if there was anything to do afterwards in the town."

"Yes?"

"I told her the theatre, the Pavilion, but in the end she decided not to go and she stayed here listening to our orchestra."

"Oh damn," said Tommy under his breath.

"You don't remember what time she had dinner, do you?" said Tuppence.

"She came down a little late. It must have been about eight o'clock."

"Damn, Blast, and Curse," said Tuppence as she and Tommy left the dining-room. "Tommy, this is all going wrong. It seemed so clear and lovely."

"Well, I suppose we ought to have known it wouldn't all be plain sailing."

"Is there any train she could have taken after that I wonder?"

"Not one that would have landed her in London in time to go to the Savoy."

"Well," said Tuppence, "as a last hope I am going to talk to the chambermaid. Una Drake had a room on the same floor as ours."

The chambermaid was a voluble and informative woman. Yes, she remembered the young lady quite well. That was her picture right enough. A very nice young lady, very merry and talkative. Had told her a lot about Australia and the kangaroos.

The young lady rang the bell about half past nine and asked for her bottle to be filled and put in her bed and also to be called the next morning at half past seven — with coffee instead of tea.

"You did call her and she was in her bed?" asked Tuppence.

The chambermaid stared at her.

"Why, yes Ma'am, of course."

"Oh, I only wondered if she was doing exercises or anything," said Tuppence, wildly. "So many people do in the early morning."

"Well, that seems cast iron enough," said Tommy, when the chambermaid had departed. "There is only one conclusion to be drawn from it. It is the London side of the thing that *must* be faked."

"Mr. le Marchant must be a more accomplished liar than we thought," said Tuppence.

"We have a way of checking his statements," said Tommy. "He said there were people sitting at the next table whom Una knew slightly. What was their name—Oglander, that was it. We must hunt up these Oglanders and we ought also to make inquiries at Miss Drake's flat in Clarges Street."

The following morning they paid their bill and departed somewhat crestfallen.

Hunting out the Oglanders was fairly easy with the aid of the telephone book. Tuppence this time took the offensive and assumed the character of a representative of a new illustrated paper. She called on Mrs. Oglander asking for a few details of their "smart" supper party at the Savoy on Tuesday evening. These details Mrs. Oglander was only too willing to supply. Just as she was leaving Tuppence added carelessly: "Let me see, wasn't Miss Una Drake sitting at the table next you? Is it really true that she is engaged to the Duke of Perth? You know her, of course."

"I know her slightly," said Mrs. Oglander. "A very charming girl I believe. Yes, she was sitting at the next table to ours with Mr. le Marchant. My girls know her better than I do."

Tuppence's next port of call was the flat in Clarges Street. Here she was greeted by Miss Marjory Leicester, the friend with whom Miss Drake shared a flat.

"Do tell me what all this is about?" asked Miss Leicester plaintively. "Una has some deep game on and I don't know what it is. Of course she slept here on Tuesday night."

"Did you see her when she came in?"

"No, I had gone to bed. She has got her own latch key,

of course. She came in about one o'clock, I believe."

"When did you see her?"

"Oh, the next morning about nine—or perhaps it was nearer ten."

As Tuppence left the flat she almost collided with a tall, gaunt female who was entering.

"Excuse me, Miss, I'm sure," said the gaunt female.

"Do you work here?" asked Tuppence.

"Yes, Miss, I come daily."

"What time do you get here in the morning?"

"Nine o'clock is my time, Miss."

Tuppence slipped a hurried half crown into the gaunt female's hand.

"Was Miss Drake here last Tuesday morning when you arrived?"

"Why yes, Miss, indeed she was. Fast asleep in her bed and hardly woke up when I brought her in her tea."

"Oh, thank you," said Tuppence and went disconsolately down the stairs.

She had arranged to meet Tommy for lunch in a small Restaurant in Soho and there they compared notes.

"I have seen that fellow, Rice. It is quite true he did see Una Drake in the distance at Torquay."

"Well," said Tuppence, "we have checked these alibis all right. Here, give me a bit of paper and a pencil, Tommy. Let us put it down neatly like all detectives do."

1.30	Una Drake seen in Luncheon Car of train.
4 o'clock	Arrives at Castle Hotel.
5 o'clock	Seen by Mr. Rice.
8 o'clock	Seen dining at Hotel.
9.30	Asks for hot water bottle.
11.30	Seen at Savoy with Mr. le Marchant.
7.30 a.m.	Called by chambermaid at Castle Hotel.
9 o'clock	Called by charwoman at flat at Clarges Street.

They looked at each other.

"Well, it looks to me as if Blunt's Brilliant Detectives are beat," said Tommy.

"Oh, we mustn't give up," said Tuppence. "Somebody *must* be lying!"

"The queer thing is that it strikes me nobody was lying. They all seemed perfectly truthful and straightforward."

"Yet there must be a flaw. We know there is. I think of all sorts of things like private aeroplanes but that doesn't really get us any forwarder."

"I am inclined to the theory of an astral body."

"Well," said Tuppence, "the only thing to do is to sleep on it. Your subconscious works in your sleep."

"H'm," said Tommy. "If your subconscious provides you with a perfectly good answer to this riddle by tomorrow morning, I take off my hat to it."

They were very silent all that evening. Again and again Tuppence reverted to the paper of times. She wrote things on bits of paper. She murmured to herself, she sought perplexedly through Rail Guides. But in the end they both rose to go to bed with no faint glimmer of light on the problem.

"This is very disheartening," said Tommy.

"One of the most miserable evenings I have ever spent," said Tuppence.

"We ought to have gone to a Music Hall," said Tommy. "A few good jokes about mothers-in-law and twins and bottles of beer would have done us no end of good."

"No, you will see this concentration will work in the end," said Tuppence. "How busy our subconscious will have to be in the next eight hours!" And on this hopeful note they went to bed.

"Well," said Tommy next morning, "has the subconscious worked?"

"I have got an idea," said Tuppence.

"You have. What sort of an idea?"

"Well, rather a funny idea. Not at all like anything I have ever read in detective stories. As a matter of fact it is an idea that *you* put into my head."

"Then it must be a good idea," said Tommy firmly.

"Come on, Tuppence, out with it."

"I shall have to send a cable to verify it," said Tuppence. "No, I am not going to tell you. It's a perfectly wild idea but it's the only thing that fits the facts."

"Well," said Tommy, "I must away to the office. A roomful of disappointed clients must not wait in vain. I leave this case in the hands of my promising subordinate."

Tuppence nodded cheerfully.

She did not put in an appearance at the office all day. When Tommy returned that evening about half past five it was to find a wildly exultant Tuppence awaiting him.

"I have done it, Tommy. I have solved the mystery of the alibi. We can charge up all these half crowns and ten shilling notes and demand a substantial fee of our own from Mr. Montgomery Jones and he can go right off and collect his girl."

"What is the solution?" cried Tommy.

"A perfectly simple one," said Tuppence. *"Twins."*

"What do you mean?—Twins?"

"Why just that. Of course it is the only solution. I will say you put it into my head last night talking about mothers-in-law, twins, and bottles of beer. I cabled to Australia and got back the information I wanted. Una has a twin sister, Vera, who arrived in England last Monday. That is why she was able to make this bet so spontaneously. She thought it would be a frightful rag on poor Montgomery Jones. The sister went to Torquay and she stayed in London."

"Do you think she'll be terribly despondent that she's lost?" asked Tommy.

"No," said Tuppence. "I don't. I gave you my views about that before. She will put all the kudos down to Montgomery Jones. I always think respect for your husband's abilities should be the foundation of married life."

"I am glad to have inspired these sentiments in you, Tuppence."

"It is not a really satisfactory solution," said Tuppence. "Not the ingenious sort of flaw that Inspector French would have detected."

"Nonsense," said Tommy. "I think the way I showed

these photographs to the waiter in the Restaurant was exactly like Inspector French."

"He didn't have to use nearly so many half crowns and ten shilling notes as we seem to have done," said Tuppence.

"Never mind," said Tommy. "We can charge them all up with additions to Mr. Montgomery Jones. He will be in such a state of idiotic bliss that he would probably pay the most enormous bill without jibbing at it."

"So he should," said Tuppence. "Haven't Blunt's Brilliant Detectives been brilliantly successful? Oh, Tommy, I do think we are extraordinarily clever. It quite frightens me sometimes."

"The next case we have shall be a Roger Sheringham case and you, Tuppence, shall be Roger Sheringham."

"I shall have to talk a lot," said Tuppence.

"You do that naturally," said Tommy. "And now I suggest that we carry out my programme of last night and seek out a Music Hall where they have plenty of jokes about mothers-in-law, bottles of beer, *and Twins*."

20

The Clergyman's Daughter

"I wish," said Tuppence, roaming moodily round the office, "that we could befriend a clergyman's daughter."

"Why?" asked Tommy.

"You may have forgotten the fact, but I was once a clergyman's daughter myself. I remember what it was like. Hence this altruistic urge—this spirit of thoughtful consideration of others—this—"

"You are getting ready to be Roger Sheringham, I see," said Tommy. "If you will allow me to make a criticism, you talk quite as much as he does, but not nearly so well."

"On the contrary," said Tuppence, "there is a feminine subtlety about my conversation, a *je ne sais quoi*, that no gross male could ever attain to. I have, moreover, powers unknown to my prototype—do I mean prototype? Words are such uncertain things, they so often sound well but mean the opposite of what one thinks they do."

"Go on," said Tommy kindly.

"I was. I was only pausing to take breath. Touching these powers, it is my wish to-day to assist a clergyman's daughter. You will see, Tommy, the first person to enlist the aid of Blunt's Brilliant Detectives will be a clergyman's daughter."

"I'll bet you it isn't," said Tommy.

"Done," said Tuppence. "Hist! To your typewriters Oh! Israel. One comes."

Mr. Blunt's office was humming with industry as Albert opened the door and announced:

"Miss Monica Deane."

A slender brown haired girl, rather shabbily dressed, entered and stood hesitating. Tommy came forward.

"Good-morning, Miss Deane. Won't you sit down and tell us what we can do for you? By the way, let me introduce my confidential secretary, Miss Sheringham."

"I am delighted to make your acquaintance, Miss Deane," said Tuppence. "Your father was in the Church, I think."

"Yes, he was. But how *did* you know that?"

"Oh! we have our methods," said Tuppence. "You mustn't mind me rattling on. Mr. Blunt likes to hear me talk. He always says it gives him ideas."

The girl stared at him. She was a slender creature, not beautiful, but possessing a wistful prettiness. She had a quantity of soft mouse colored hair, and her eyes were dark blue and very lovely, though the dark shadows round them spoke of trouble and anxiety.

"Will you tell me your story, Miss Deane?" said Tommy.

The girl turned to him gratefully.

"It's such a long, rambling story," said the girl. "My name is Monica Deane. My father was the rector of Little Hampsley in Suffolk. He died three years ago, and my mother and I were left very badly off. I went out as a governess, but my mother became a confirmed invalid and I had to come home to look after her. We were desperately poor, but one day we received a lawyer's letter telling us that an aunt of my father's had died and had left everything to me. I had often heard of this aunt who had quarreled with my father many years ago, and I knew that she was very well off, so it really seemed that our troubles were at an end. But matters did not turn out quite as well as we had hoped. I inherited the house she had lived in, but after

paying one or two small legacies, there was no money left.
I suppose she must have lost it during the war, or perhaps
she had been living on her capital. Still, we had the house,
and almost at once we had a chance of selling it at quite an
advantageous price. But, foolishly perhaps, I refused the
offer. We were in tiny, but expensive lodgings, and I thought
it would be much nicer to live in the Red House where my
mother could have comfortable rooms and take in paying
guests to cover our expenses.

"I adhered to this plan, notwithstanding a further tempting offer from the gentlemen who wanted to buy. We moved
in, and I advertised for paying guests. For a time, all went
well, we have several answers to our advertisement, my
aunt's old servant remained on with us and she and I between
us did the work of the house. And then these unaccountable
things began to happen."

"What things?"

"The queerest things. The whole place seemed be-
witched. Pictures fell down, crockery flew across the room
and broke, one morning we came down to find all the
furniture moved round. At first we thought someone was
playing a practical joke, but we had to give up that explanation. Sometimes when we were all sitting down to dinner,
a terrific crash would be heard overhead. We would go up
and find no one there, but a piece of furniture thrown violently to the ground."

"A *poltergeist*," cried Tuppence, much interested.

"Yes, that's what Dr. O'Neill said—though I don't know
what it means."

"It's a sort of evil spirit that plays tricks," explained
Tuppence who in reality knew very little of the subject, and
was not even sure that she had got the word *poltergeist*
right.

"Well, at any rate, the effect was disastrous. Our visitors
were frightened to death, and left as soon as possible. We
got new ones, and they too left hurriedly. I was in despair,
and, to crown all, our own tiny income ceased suddenly—
the Company in which it was invested failed."

"You poor dear," said Tuppence sympathetically. "What

a time you have had. Did you want Mr. Blunt to investigate this 'haunting' business?"

"Not exactly. You see, three days ago, a gentleman called upon us. His name was Dr. O'Neill. He told us that he was a member of the Society for Psychical Research, and that he had heard about the curious manifestations that had taken place in our house and was much interested. So much so, that he was prepared to buy it from us, and conduct a series of experiments there."

"Well?"

"Of course, at first, I was overcome with joy. It seemed the way out of all our difficulties. But—"

"Yes?"

"Perhaps you will think me fanciful. Perhaps I am. But—oh! I'm sure I haven't made a mistake. It was the same man!"

"What same man?"

"The same man who wanted to buy it before. Oh! I'm sure I'm right."

"But why shouldn't it be?"

"You don't understand. The two men were quite different, different name and everything. The first man was quite young, a spruce dark young man of thirty odd. Dr. O'Neill is about fifty, he has a grey beard and wears glasses and stoops. But when he talked I saw a gold tooth one side of his mouth. It only shows when he laughs. The other man had a tooth in just the same position, and then I looked at his ears. I had noticed the other man's ears, because they were a peculiar shape with hardly any lobe. Dr. O'Neill's were just the same. Both things couldn't be a coincidence, could they? I thought and thought and finally I wrote and said I would let him know in a week. I had noticed Mr. Blunt's advertisement some time ago—as a matter of fact in an old paper that lined one of the kitchen drawers. I cut it out and came up to town."

"You were quite right," said Tuppence, nodding her head with vigor. "This needs looking into."

"A very interesting case, Miss Deane," observed Tommy.

"We shall be pleased to look into this for you—eh, Miss Sheringham?"

"Rather," said Tuppence, "and we'll get to the bottom of it too."

"I understand, Miss Deane," went on Tommy, "that the household consists of you and your mother and a servant. Can you give me any particulars about the servant?"

"Her name is Crockett. She was with my aunt about eight or ten years. She is an elderly woman, not very pleasant in manner, but a good servant. She is inclined to give herself airs because her sister married out of her station. Crockett has a nephew whom she is always telling us is 'quite the gentleman'."

"H'm," said Tommy, rather at a loss how to proceed.

Tuppence had been eyeing Monica keenly, now she spoke with sudden decision.

"I think the best plan would be for Miss Deane to come out and lunch with me. It's just on one o'clock. I can get full details from her."

"Certainly, Miss Sheringham," said Tommy. "An excellent plan."

"Look here," said Tuppence when they were comfortably ensconced at a little table in a neighboring restaurant, "I want to know. Is there any special reason why you want to find out about all this?"

Monica blushed.

"Well, you see—"

"Out with it," said Tuppence encouragingly.

"Well—there are two men who—who—want to marry me."

"The usual story, I suppose? One rich, one poor, and the poor one is the one you like!"

"I don't know how you know all these things," murmured the girl.

"That's a sort of law of Nature," explained Tuppence. "It happens to everybody. It happened to me."

"You see, even if I sell the house, it won't bring us in enough to live on. Gerald is a dear, but he's desperately poor—though he's a very clever engineer and if only he had a little capital, his firm would take him into partnership. The other, Mr. Partridge, is a very good man, I am sure— and well off, and if I married him it would be an end of all our troubles. But—but—"

"I know," said Tuppence sympathetically. "It isn't the same thing at all. You can go on telling yourself how good and worthy he is, and adding up his qualities as though they were an addition sum—and it all has a simply refrigerating effect."

Monica nodded.

"Well," said Tuppence, "I think it would be as well if we went down to the neighborhood and studied matters upon the spot. What is the address?"

"The Red House, Stourton in the Marsh."

Tuppence wrote down the address in her note book.

"I didn't ask you," Monica began—"about terms—" she ended, blushing a little.

"Our payments are strictly by results," said Tuppence gravely. "If the secret of the Red House is a profitable one, as seems possible from the anxiety displayed to acquire the property, we should expect a small percentage, otherwise— nothing!"

"Thank you very much," said the girl gratefully.

"And now," said Tuppence, "don't worry. Everything's going to be all right. Let's enjoy lunch and talk of interesting things."

21

The Red House

"Well," said Tommy, looking out of the window of the Crown and Anchor, "here we are at Toad in the Hole—or whatever this blasted village is called."

"Let us review the case," said Tuppence.

"By all means," said Tommy. "To begin with, getting my say in first, *I* suspect the invalid mother!"

"Why?"

"My dear Tuppence, grant that this *poltergeist* business is all a put up job, got up in order to persuade the girl to sell the house, someone must have thrown the things about. Now the girl said everyone was at dinner—but if the mother is a thoroughgoing invalid, she'd be upstairs in her room."

"If she was an invalid she could hardly throw furniture about."

"Ah! but she wouldn't be a real invalid. She'd be shamming."

"Why?"

"There you have me," confessed her husband. "I was really going on the well known principle of suspecting the most unlikely person."

"You always make fun of everything," said Tuppence

187

severely. "There must be *something* that makes these people so anxious to get hold of the house. And if you don't care about getting to the bottom of this matter, I do. I like that girl. She's a dear."

Tommy nodded seriously enough.

"I quite agree. But I never can resist ragging you, Tuppence. Of course there's something queer about the house, and whatever it is, it's something that's difficult to get at. Otherwise a mere burglary would do the trick. But to be willing to buy the house means either that you've got to take up floors or pull down walls, or else that there's a coal mine under the back garden!"

"I don't want it to be a coal mine. Buried treasure is much more romantic."

"H'm," said Tommy. "In that case I think I shall pay a visit to the local Bank Manager, explain that I am staying here over Christmas and probably buying the Red House, and discuss the question of opening an account."

"But why—?"

"Wait and see."

Tommy returned at the end of half an hour. His eyes were twinkling.

"We advance, Tuppence. Our interview proceeded on the lines indicated. I then asked casually whether he had had much gold paid in, as is often the case nowadays in these small country banks—small farmers who hoarded it during the war, you understand. From that we proceeded quite naturally to the extraordinary vagaries of old ladies. I invented an aunt who, on the outbreak of the war, drove to the Army and Navy Stores in a four wheeler, and returned with sixteen hams. He immediately mentioned a client of his own who had insisted on drawing out every penny of money she had—in gold as far as possible, and who also insisted on having her securities, bearer bonds and such things, given into her own custody. I exclaimed on such an act of folly, and he mentioned casually that she was the former owner of the Red House. You see, Tuppence? She drew out all this money, and she hid it somewhere. You remember that Monica Deane mentioned that they were astonished at the small amount of her estate? Yes, she hid it in the Red House, and someone knows about it. I can make a pretty good guess who that someone is too."

"Who?"

"What about the faithful Crockett? She would know all about her mistress's peculiarities."

"And that gold toothed Dr. O'Neill?"

"The gentlemanly nephew, of course! That's it. But whereabouts did she hide it? You know more about old ladies than I do, Tuppence. Where do they hide things?"

"Wrapped up in stockings and petticoats, under mat-tresses."

Tommy nodded.

"I expect you're right. All the same, she can't have done that because it would have been found when her things were turned over. It worries me—you see, an old lady like that can't have taken up floors or dug holes in the garden. All the same it's there in the Red House somewhere. Crockett hasn't found it, but she knows it's there, and once they get the house to themselves, she and her precious nephew, they can turn it upside down until they find what they're after. We've got to get ahead of them. Come on, Tuppence. We'll go to the Red House."

Monica Deane received them. To her mother and Crock-ett they were represented as would be purchasers of the Red House which would account for their being taken all over the house and grounds. Tommy did not tell Monica of the conclusions he had come to, but he asked her various search-ing questions. Of the garments and personal belongings of the dead woman, some had been given to Crockett and the others sent to various poor families. Everything had been gone through and turned out.

"Did your aunt leave any papers?"

"The desk was full, and there were some in a drawer in her bedroom, but there was nothing of importance amongst them."

"Have they been thrown away?"

"No, my mother is always very loath to throw away old papers. There were some old fashioned recipes among them which she intends to go through one day."

"Good," said Tommy approvingly. Then, indicating an old man who was at work upon one of the flower beds in the garden, he asked: "Was that old man the gardener here in your aunt's time?"

"Yes, he used to come three days a week. He lives in the village. Poor old fellow, he is past doing any really useful work. We have him just once a week to keep things tidied up. We can't afford more."

Tommy winked at Tuppence to indicate that she was to keep Monica with her, and he himself stepped across to where the gardener was working. He spoke a few pleasant words to the old man, asked him if he had been there in the old lady's time, and then said casually:

"You buried a box for her once, didn't you?"

"No, sir, I never buried naught for her. What should she want to bury a box for?"

Tommy shook his head. He strolled back to the house frowning. It was to be hoped that a study of the old lady's papers would yield some clue—otherwise the problem was a hard one to solve. The house itself was old fashioned, but not old enough to contain a secret room or passage.

Before leaving, Monica brought them down a big card-board box, tied with string.

"I've collected all the papers," she whispered. "And they're in here. I thought you could take it away with you, and then you'll have plenty of time to go over them—but I'm sure you won't find anything to throw light on the mysterious happenings in this house—"

Her words were interrupted by a terrific crash overhead. Tommy ran quickly up the stairs. A jug and basin in one of the front rooms was lying on the ground broken to pieces. There was no one in the room.

"The ghost up to its tricks again," he murmured with a grin.

He went down stairs again thoughtfully.

"I wonder, Miss Deane, if I might speak to the maid, Crockett, for a minute."

"Certainly. I will ask her to come to you."

Monica went off to the kitchen. She returned with the elderly maid who had opened the door to them earlier.

"We are thinking of buying this house," said Tommy pleasantly, "and my wife was wondering whether, in that case, you would care to remain on with us?"

Crockett's respectable face displayed no emotion of any kind.

"Thank you, sir," she said. "I should like to think it over if I may."

Tommy turned to Monica.

"I am delighted with the house, Miss Deane. I understand that there is another buyer in the market. I know what he has offered for the house, and I will willingly give a hundred more. And mind you, that is a good price I am offering."

Monica murmured something noncommittal, and the Beresfords took their leave.

"I was right," said Tommy, as they went down the drive. "Crockett's in it. Did you notice that she was out of breath? That was from running down the back stairs after smashing the jug and basin. Sometimes, very likely, she has admitted her nephew secretly, and he has done a little poltergeisting, or whatever you call it, whilst she has been innocently with the family. You'll see, Dr. O'Neill will make a further offer before the day is out."

True enough, after dinner a note was brought. It was from Monica.

"I have just heard from Dr. O'Neill. He raises his previous offer by £150."

"The nephew must be a man of means," said Tommy thoughtfully. "And I tell you what, Tuppence, the prize he's after must be well worth while."

"Oh! Oh! Oh! if only we could find it!"

"Well, let's get on with the spade work."

They were sorting through the big box of papers, a wearisome affair, as they were all jumbled up pell mell without any kind of order or method. Every few minutes they compared notes.

"What's the latest, Tuppence?"

"Two old receipted bills, three unimportant letters, a

recipe for preserving new potatoes and one for making lemon cheesecake. What's yours?"

"One bill, a poem on Spring, two newspaper cuttings: 'Why Women buy Pearls—a sound investment' and 'Man with Four Wives—Extraordinary Story,' and a recipe for Jugged Hare."

"It's heart breaking," said Tuppence, and they fell to once more. At last the box was empty. They looked at each other.

"I put this aside," said Tommy, picking up a half sheet of notepaper, "because it struck me as peculiar. But I don't suppose it's got anything to do with what we're looking for."

"Let's see it. Oh! it's one of those funny things, what do they call them? Anagrams, charades or something." She read it:

> "My *first* you put on glowing coal
> And into it you put my *whole*
> My *second* really is the first
> My third mislikes the winter blast."

"H'm," said Tommy critically. "I don't think much of the poet's rhymes."

"I don't see what you find peculiar about it, though," said Tuppence. "Everybody used to have a collection of these sort of things about fifty years ago. You saved them up for winter evenings round the fire."

"I wasn't referring to the verse. It's the words written below it that strike me as peculiar.

"St. Luke XI.9," she read. "It's a text."

"Yes. Doesn't that strike you as odd? Would an old lady of a religious persuasion write a text just under a charade?"

"It is rather odd," agreed Tuppence thoughtfully.

"I presume that you, being a clergyman's daughter, have got your Bible with you?"

"As a matter of fact I have. Aha, you didn't expect that. Wait a sec."

Tuppence ran to her suit case, extracted a small red

volume and returned to the table. She turned the leaves rapidly. "Here we are. Luke, Chapter XI, Verse 9. Oh! Tommy, look."

Tommy bent over and looked where Tuppence's small finger pointed to a portion of the verse in question.

"Seek, and ye shall find."

"That's it," cried Tuppence. "We've got it! Solve the cryptogram and the treasure is ours—or rather Monica's."

"Well, let's get to work on the cryptogram, as you call it. 'My *first* you put on glowing coal'. What does that mean, I wonder? Then—'My *second* really is the first.' That's pure gibberish."

"It's quite simple really," said Tuppence kindly. "It's just a sort of knack. Let *me* have it."

Tommy surrendered it willingly. Tuppence ensconced herself in an arm chair, and began muttering to herself with bent brows.

"It's quite simple really," murmured Tommy when half an hour had elapsed.

"Don't crow! We're the wrong generation for this. I've a good mind to go back to town tomorrow and call on some old pussy who would probably read it as easy as winking. It's a knack, that's all."

"Well, let's have one more try."

"There aren't many things you can put on glowing coal," said Tuppence thoughtfully. "There's water, to put it out, or wood, or a kettle."

"It must be one syllable, I suppose? What about *wood*, then?"

"You couldn't put anything *into* wood, though."

"There's no one syllable word instead of *water*, but there must be one syllable things you can put on a fire in the kettle line."

"Saucepans," mused Tuppence. "Frying pans. How about *pan*? Or *pot*? What's a word beginning pan or pot that is something you cook?"

"Pottery," suggested Tommy. "You bake that in the fire. Wouldn't that be near enough?"

"The rest of it doesn't fit. Pancakes? No. Oh! bother."

They were interrupted by the little serving maid, who told them that dinner would be ready in a few minutes.

"Only Mrs. Lumley, she wanted to know if you'd like your potatoes fried, or boiled in their jackets? She's got some of each."

"Boiled in their jackets," said Tuppence promptly. "I love potatoes—" She stopped dead with her mouth open.

"What's the matter, Tuppence? Have you seen a ghost?"

"Tommy," cried Tuppence. "Don't you see? That's it! The word, I mean. *Potatoes!* 'My first you put on glowing coal'—that's *pot*. 'And into it you put my whole'. 'My *second* really is the first' That's A, the first letter of the alphabet. 'My *third* mislikes the wintry blast"—cold *toes* of course!"

"You're right, Tuppence. Very clever of you. But I'm afraid we've wasted an awful lot of time over nothing. Potatoes don't fit in at all with missing treasure. Half a sec., though. What did you read out just now, when we were going through the box? Something about a recipe for New Potatoes. I wonder whether there's anything in that."

He rummaged hastily through the pile of recipes.

"Here it is. 'TO KEEP NEW POTATOES. Put the new potatoes into tins and bury them in the garden. Even in the middle of winter, they will taste as though freshly dug.'"

"We've got it," screamed Tuppence. "That's it. The treasure is in the garden, buried in a tin."

"But I asked the gardener. He said he'd never buried anything."

"Yes, I know, but that's because people never really answer what you say, they answer what they think you mean. He knew he'd never buried anything out of the common. We'll go to-morrow and ask him where he buried the potatoes."

The following morning was Christmas Eve. By dint of inquiry they found the old gardener's cottage. Tuppence broached the subject after some minutes' conversation.

"I wish one could have new potatoes at Christmas time," she remarked. "Wouldn't they be good with turkey? Do people round here ever bury them in tins? I've heard that keeps them fresh."

"Ay, that they do," declared the old man. "Old Miss Deane, up to the Red House, she allus had three tins buried every summer, and as often as not forgot to have 'em dug up again!"

"In the bed by the house, as a rule, didn't she?"

"No, over against the wall by the fir tree."

Having got the information they wanted, they soon took their leave of the old man, presenting him with five shillings as a Christmas box.

"And now for Monica," said Tommy.

"Tommy! You have no sense of the dramatic. Leave it to me. I've got a beautiful plan. Do you think you could manage to beg, borrow, or steal a spade?"

Somehow or other, a spade was duly produced, and that night, late, two figures might have been seen stealing into the grounds of the Red House. The place indicated by the gardener was easily found, and Tommy set to work. Presently his spade rang on metal, and a few seconds later he had unearthed a big biscuit tin. It was sealed round with adhesive plaster and firmly fastened down, but Tuppence, by the aid of Tommy's knife, soon managed to open it. Then she gave a groan. The tin was full of potatoes. She poured them out so that the tin was completely empty, but there were no other contents.

"Go on digging, Tommy."

It was some time before a second tin rewarded their search. As before Tuppence unsealed it.

"Well?" demanded Tommy anxiously.

"Potatoes again!"

"Damn!" said Tommy and set to once more.

"The third time is lucky," said Tuppence consolingly.

"I believe the whole thing's a mare's nest," said Tommy gloomily, but he continued to dig.

At last a third tin was brought to light.

"Potatoes aga—" began Tuppence, then stopped. "Oh! Tommy, we've got it. It's only potatoes on top. Look!"

She held up a big old fashioned velvet bag.

"Cut along home," cried Tommy. "It's icy cold. Take the bag with you. I must just shovel back the earth. And may a thousand curses light upon your head, Tuppence, if you open that bag before I come!"

"I'll play fair. Ouch! I'm frozen." She beat a speedy retreat.

On arrival at the Inn she had not long to wait. Tommy was hard upon her heels, perspiring freely after his digging and the final brisk run.

"Now then," said Tommy. "The private inquiry agents make good! Open the loot, Mrs. Beresford."

Inside the bag was a package done up in oil silk and a heavy chamois leather bag. They opened the latter first. It was full of gold sovereigns. Tommy counted them.

"Two hundred pounds. That was all they would let her have, I suppose. Cut open the package."

Tuppence did so. It was full of closely folded banknotes. Tommy and Tuppence counted them carefully. They amounted to exactly twenty thousand pounds!

"Whew!" said Tommy. "Isn't it lucky for Monica that we're both rich and honest? What's that done up in tissue paper?"

Tuppence unrolled the little parcel and drew out a magnificent string of pearls, exquisitely matched.

"I don't know much about these things," said Tommy slowly, "But I'm pretty sure that those pearls are worth another five thousand pounds at least. Look at the size of them. Now I see why the old lady kept that cutting about pearls being a good investment. She must have realized all her securities and turned them into notes and jewels."

"Oh! Tommy, isn't it wonderful? Darling Monica. Now she can marry her nice young man and live happily ever afterwards, like me."

"That's rather sweet of you, Tuppence. So you *are* happy with me?"

"As a matter of fact," said Tuppence, "I am. But I didn't mean to say so. It slipped out. What with being excited, and Christmas Eve, and one thing and another—"

"If you really love me," said Tommy, "will you answer me one question?"

"I hate these catches," said Tuppence. "But—well—all right."

"Then how did you know that Monica was a clergyman's daughter?"

"Oh, that was just cheating," said Tuppence happily. "I opened her letter making an appointment, and a Mr. Deane was Father's curate once and he had a little girl called Monica, about four or five years younger than me. So I put two and two together."

"You are a shameless creature," said Tommy. "Hullo, there's twelve o'clock. Happy Christmas, Tuppence."

"Happy Christmas, Tommy. It'll be a Happy Christmas for Monica too—and all owing to US. I am glad. Poor thing, she has been so miserable. Do you know, Tommy, I feel all queer and choky about the throat when I think of it."

"Darling Tuppence," said Tommy.

"Darling Tommy," said Tuppence. "How awfully sentimental we are getting."

"Christmas comes but once a year," said Tommy sententiously. "That's what our great grandmothers said and I expect there's a lot of truth in it still."

22

The Ambassador's Boots

"My dear fellow, my dear fellow," said Tuppence and waved a heavily buttered muffin.

Tommy looked at her for a minute or two, then a broad grin spread over his face and he murmured:

"We do have to be so very careful."

"That's right," said Tuppence delighted. "You guessed. I am the famous Dr. Fortune and you are Superintendent Bell."

"Why are you being Reginald Fortune?"

"Well really because I feel like a lot of hot butter."

"That is the pleasant side of it," said Tommy. "But there is another. You will have to examine horribly smashed faces and very extra dead bodies a good deal."

In answer Tuppence threw across a letter. Tommy's eyebrows rose in astonishment.

"Randolph Wilmott, the American Ambassador. I wonder what he wants."

"We shall know to-morrow at eleven o'clock."

Punctually to the time named, Mr. Randolph Wilmott, United States Ambassador to the Court of St. James, was ushered into Mr. Blunt's office. He cleared his throat and commenced speaking in a deliberate and characteristic manner.

"I have come to you, Mr. Blunt—By the way, it is Mr. Blunt himself to whom I am speaking, is it not?"

"Certainly," said Tommy. "I am Theodore Blunt, the head of the firm."

"I always prefer to deal with heads of de-partments," said Mr. Wilmott. "It is more satisfactory in every way. As I was about to say, Mr. Blunt, this business gets my goat. There's nothing in it to trouble Scotland Yard about—I'm not a penny the worse in any way, and it's probably all due to a simple mistake. But all the same, I don't see just how that mistake arose. There's nothing criminal in it, I daresay, but I'd like just to get the thing straightened out. It makes me mad not to see the why and wherefore of a thing."

"Absolutely," said Tommy.

Mr. Wilmott went on. He was slow and given to much detail. At last Tommy managed to get a word in.

"Quite so," he said, "the position is this. You arrived by the liner Nomadic a week ago. In some way your kitbag and the kitbag of another gentleman, Mr. Ralph Westerham whose initials are the same as yours, got mixed up. You took Mr. Westerham's kitbag, and he took yours. Mr. Westerham discovered the mistake immediately, sent round your kitbag to the Embassy, and took away his own. Am I right so far?"

"That is precisely what occurred. The two bags must have been practically identical, and with the initials R. W. being the same in both cases, it is not difficult to understand that an error might have been made. I myself was not aware of what had happened until my valet informed me of the mistake, and that Mr. Westerham—he is a Senator, and a man for whom I have a great admiration—had sent round for his bag and returned mine."

"Then I don't see—"

"But you will see. That's only the beginning of the story. Yesterday, as it chanced, I ran up against Senator Westerham, and I happened to mention the matter to him jestingly. To my great surprise, he did not seem to know what I was talking about, and when I explained, he denied the story absolutely. He had not taken my bag off the ship in mistake for his own—in fact, he had not travelled with such an article amongst his luggage."

"What an extraordinary thing!"

"Mr. Blunt, it *is* an extraordinary thing. There seems no rhyme or reason in it. Why, if anyone wanted to steal my kitbag, he could do so easily enough without resorting to all this round about business! And anyway, it was *not* stolen, but returned to me. On the other hand, if it were taken by mistake, why use Senator Westerham's name? It's a crazy business—but just for curiosity I mean to get to the bottom of it. I hope the case is not too trivial for you to undertake?"

"Not at all. It is a very intriguing little problem, capable as you say, of many simple explanations, but nevertheless baffling on the face of it. The first thing, of course, is the *reason* of the substitution, if substitution it was. You say nothing was missing from your bag when it came back into your possession?"

"My man says not. He would know."

"What was in it, if I may ask?"

"Mostly boots."

"Boots," said Tommy discouraged.

"Yes," said Mr. Wilmott. "Boots. Odd, isn't it?"

"You'll forgive my asking you," said Tommy, "but you didn't carry any secret papers, or anything of that sort sewn in the lining of a boot or screwed into a false heel?"

The Ambassador seemed amused by the question.

"Secret diplomacy hasn't got to that pitch, I hope."

"Only in fiction," said Tommy with an answering smile, and a slightly apologetic manner. "But you see, we've got to account for the thing somehow. Who came for the bag—the other bag, I mean?"

"Supposed to be one of Westerham's servants. Quite a quiet ordinary man, so I understand. My valet saw nothing wrong with him."

"Had it been unpacked, do you know?"

"That I can't say. I presume not. But perhaps you'd like

to ask the valet a few questions? He can tell you more than I can about the business."

"I think that would be the best plan, Mr. Wilmott."

The Ambassador scribbled a few words on a card and handed it to Tommy.

"I opine that you would prefer to go round to the Embassy and make your inquiries there? If not, I will have the man,— his name is Richards, by the way—sent round here."

"No, thank you, Mr. Wilmott. I should prefer to go to the Embassy."

The Ambassador rose, glancing at his watch.

"Dear me, I shall be late for an appointment. Well, good bye, Mr. Blunt. I leave the matter in your hands."

He hurried away. Tommy looked at Tuppence who had been scribbling demurely on her pad in the character of the efficient Miss Robinson.

"What about it, old thing?" he asked. "Do you see, as the old bird put it, any rhyme or reason in the proceeding?"

"None whatever," replied Tuppence cheerily.

"Well, that's a start anyway! It shows that there is really something very deep at the back of it."

"You think so?"

"It's a generally accepted hypothesis. Remember Sherlock Holmes and the depth the butter had sunk into the parsley—I mean the other way round. I've always had a devouring wish to know all about that case. Perhaps Watson will disinter it from his notebook one of these days. Then I shall die happy. But we must get busy."

"Quite so," said Tuppence. "Not a quick man, the esteemed Wilmott, but sure."

"She knows men," said Tommy. "Or do I say *he* knows men. It is so confusing when you assume the character of a male detective."

"Oh! my dear fellow, my dear fellow!"

"A little more action, Tuppence, and a little less repetition."

"A classic phrase cannot be repeated too often," said Tuppence with dignity.

"Have a muffin," said Tommy kindly.

"Not at eleven o'clock in the morning, thank you. Silly case, this. Boots—you know—Why boots?"

"Well," said Tommy, "why not?"

"It doesn't fit. Boots." She shook her head. "All wrong. Who wants other people's boots? The whole thing's mad."

"Perhaps they got hold of the wrong bag?" suggested Tommy.

"That's possible. But if they were after papers, a despatch case would be more likely. Papers are the only things one thinks of in connection with ambassadors."

"Boots suggest footprints," said Tommy thoughtfully. "Do you think they wanted to lay a trail of Wilmott's footsteps somewhere?"

Tuppence considered the suggestion, abandoning her rôle, then shook her head.

"It seems wildly impossible," she said. "No, I believe we shall have to resign ourselves to the fact that the boots have nothing to do with it."

"Well," said Tommy with a sigh. "The next step is to interview friend Richards. He may be able to throw some light on the mystery."

On production of the Ambassador's card, Tommy was admitted to the Embassy, and presently a pale young man, with a respectful manner, and a subdued voice, presented himself to undergo examination.

"I am Richards, sir, Mr. Wilmott's valet. I understood you wished to see me?"

"Yes, Richards. Mr. Wilmott called on me this morning, and suggested that I should come round and ask you a few questions. It is this matter of the kitbag."

"Mr. Wilmott was rather upset over the affair, I know, sir. I can hardly see why, since no harm was done. I certainly understood from the man who called for the other bag that it belonged to Senator Westerham, but of course I may have been mistaken."

"What kind of a man was he?"

"Middle-aged. Grey hair. Very good class, I should say— most respectable. I understood he was Senator Westerham's valet. He left Mr. Wilmott's bag and took away the other."

"Had it been unpacked at all?"

"Which one, sir?"

"Well, I meant the one you brought from the boat. But I should like to know about the other as well—Mr. Wilmott's own. Had that been unpacked, do you fancy?"

"I should say not, sir. It was just as I strapped it up on the boat. I should say the gentleman—whoever he was—just opened it—realized it wasn't his, and shut it up again."

"Nothing missing? No small article?"

"I don't think so, sir. In fact, I'm quite sure."

"And now the other one. Had you started to unpack that?"

"As a matter of fact, sir, I was just opening it at the very moment Senator Westerham's man arrived. I'd just undone the straps."

"Did you open it at all?"

"We just unfastened it together, sir, to be sure no mistake had been made this time. The man said it was all right, and he strapped it up again and took it away."

"What was inside? Boots also?"

"No, sir, mostly toilet things, I fancy. I know I saw a tin of bath salts."

Tommy abandoned that line of research.

"You never saw anyone tampering with anything in your master's cabin on board ship, I suppose?"

"Oh, no, sir."

"Never anything suspicious of any kind?"

"And what do I mean by that, I wonder," he thought to himself with a trace of amusement. "Anything suspicious—just words!"

But the man in front of him hesitated.

"Now that I remember it—"

"Yes," said Tommy eagerly. "What?"

"I don't think it could have anything to do with it. But there was a young lady."

"Yes? A young lady, you say, what was she doing?"

"She was taken faint, sir. A very pleasant young lady. Miss Eileen O'Hara, her name was. A dainty looking lady, not tall, with black hair. Just a little foreign looking."

"Yes?" said Tommy, with even greater eagerness.

"As I was saying, she was taken queer. Just outside Mr. Wilmott's cabin. She asked me to fetch the doctor. I helped her to the sofa, and then went off for the doctor. I was some time finding him, and when I found him and brought him back, the young lady was nearly all right again."

"Oh!" said Tommy.

"You don't think, sir—"

"It's difficult to know what to think," said Tommy noncommittally. "Was this Miss O'Hara travelling alone?"

"Yes, I think so, sir."

"You haven't seen her since you landed?"

"No, sir."

"Well," said Tommy, after a minute or two spent in reflection. "I think that's all. Thank you, Richards."

"Thank *you*, sir."

Back at the office of the Detective Agency, Tommy retailed his conversation with Richards to Tuppence who listened attentively.

"What do you think of it, Tuppence?"

"Oh! my dear fellow, we doctors are always sceptical of a sudden faintness! So very convenient. And Eileen as well as O'Hara. Almost too impossibly Irish, don't you think?"

"It's something to go upon at last. Do you know what I am going to do, Tuppence? Advertise for the lady."

"What?"

"Yes. Any information respecting Miss Eileen O'Hara, known to have travelled such and such a ship and such and such a date. Either she'll answer it herself if she's genuine, or someone may come forward to give up information about her. So far, it's the only hope of a clue."

"You'll also put her on her guard, remember."

"Well," said Tommy. "One's got to risk something."

"I still can't seen any sense in the thing," said Tuppence, frowning. "If a gang of crooks get hold of the Ambassador's bag for an hour or two, and then send it back, what possible good can it do them? Unless there are papers in it they want to copy, and Mr. Wilmott swears there was nothing of the kind."

Tommy stared at her thoughtfully.

"You put these things rather well, Tuppence," he said at last. "You've given me an idea."

.• • •

It was two days later. Tuppence was out to lunch. Tommy, alone in the austere office of Mr. Theodore Blunt, was improving his mind by reading the latest sensational thriller.

The door of the office opened and Albert appeared.

"A young lady to see you, sir. Miss Cicely March. She says she has called in answer to an advertisement."

"Show her in at once," cried Tommy, thrusting his novel into a convenient drawer.

In another minute Albert had ushered in the young lady. Tommy had just time to see that she was fair haired and extremely pretty when the amazing occurrence happened.

The door through which Albert had just passed out was rudely burst open. In the doorway stood a picturesque figure—a big dark man, Spanish in appearance, with a flaming red tie. His features were distorted with rage, and in his hand was a gleaming pistol.

"So this is the office of Mr. Busybody Blunt," he said in perfect English. His voice was low and venomous. "Hands up at once—or I shoot."

It sounded no idle threat. Tommy's hands went up obediently. The girl, crouched against the wall, gave a gasp of terror.

"This young lady will come with me," said the man. "Yes, you will, my dear. You have never seen me before, but that doesn't matter. I can't have my plans ruined by a silly little chit like you. I seem to remember that you were one of the passengers on the Nomadic. You must have been peering into things that didn't concern you—but I've no intention of letting you blab any secrets to Mr. Blunt here. A very clever gentleman, Mr. Blunt, with his fancy advertisements. But as it happens, I keep an eye on the advertisement columns. That's how I got wise to his little game."

"You interest me exceedingly," said Tommy. "Won't you go on?"

"Cheek won't help you, Mr. Blunt. From now on, you're a marked man. Give up this investigation, and we'll leave you alone. Otherwise—God help you! Death comes swiftly to those who thwart our plans."

Tommy did not reply. He was staring over the intruder's shoulder as though he saw a ghost.

As a matter of fact he was seeing something that caused him far more apprehension than any ghost could have done. Up to now, he had not given a thought to Albert as a factor in the game. He had taken for granted that Albert had already been dealt with by the mysterious stranger. If he had thought of him at all, it was as one lying stunned on the carpet in the outer office.

He now saw that Albert had miraculously escaped the stranger's attention. But instead of rushing out to fetch a policeman in good sound British fashion, Albert had elected to play a lone hand. The door behind the stranger had opened noiselessly, and Albert stood in the aperture enveloped in a coil of rope.

An agonized yelp of protest burst from Tommy, but too late. Fired with enthusiasm, Albert flung a loop of rope over the intruder's head, and jerked him backwards off his feet.

The inevitable happened. The pistol went off with a roar and Tommy felt the bullet scorch his ear in passing, ere it buried itself in the plaster behind him.

"I've got him, sir," cried Albert, flushed with triumph. "I've lassoed him. I've been practising with a lasso in my spare time, sir. Can you give me a hand? He's very violent."

Tommy hastened to his faithful henchman's assistance, mentally determining that Albert should have no further spare time.

"You damned idiot," he said. "Why didn't you go for a policeman? Owing to this fool's play of yours, he as near as anything plugged me through the head. Whew! I've never had such a near escape."

"Lassoed him in the nick of time, I did," said Albert, his ardor quite undamped. "It's wonderful what those chaps can do on the prairies, sir."

"Quite so," said Tommy, "but we're not on the prairies. We happen to be in a highly civilized city. And now, my dear sir," he added to his prostrate foe. "What are we going to do with you?"

A stream of oaths in a foreign language was his only reply.

"Hush," said Tommy. "I don't understand a word of what you're saying, but I've got a shrewd idea it's not the kind of language to use before a lady. You'll excuse him, won't you, Miss—do you know, in the excitement of this little, upset, I've quite forgotten your name?"

"March," said the girl. She was still white and shaken. But she came forward now and stood by Tommy looking down on the recumbent figure of the discomfited stranger. "What are you going to do with him?"

"I could fetch a bobby now," said Albert helpfully.

But Tommy, looking up, caught a very faint negative movement of the girl's head, and took his cue accordingly.

"We'll let him off this time," he remarked. "Nevertheless I shall give myself the pleasure of kicking him downstairs—if it's only to teach him manners to a lady."

He removed the rope, hauled the victim to his feet, and propelled him briskly through the outer office.

A series of shrill yelps was heard and then a thud. Tommy came back, flushed but smiling.

The girl was staring at him with round eyes.

"Did you—hurt him?"

"I hope so," said Tommy. "But these foreigners make a practise of crying out before they're hurt—so I can't be quite sure about it. Shall we come back into my office, Miss March, and resume our interrupted conversation? I don't think we shall be interrupted again."

"I'll have my lasso ready, sir, in case," said the helpful Albert.

"Put it away," ordered Tommy sternly.

He followed the girl into the inner office, and sat down at his desk whilst she took a chair facing him.

"I don't quite know where to begin," said the girl. "As you heard that man say, I was a passenger on the Nomadic.

The lady you advertised about, Miss O'Hara, was also on board."

"Exactly," said Tommy. "That we know already, but I suspect you must know something about her doings on board that boat or else that picturesque gentleman would not have been in such a hurry to intervene."

"I will tell you everything. The American Ambassador was on board. One day, as I was passing his cabin, I saw this woman inside, and she was doing something so extraordinary that I stopped to watch. She had a man's boot in her hand—"

"A boot?" cried Tommy excitedly. "I'm sorry, Miss March, go on."

"With a little pair of scissors, she was slitting up the lining. Then she seemed to push something inside. Just at that minute the doctor and another man came down the passage, and immediately she dropped back on the couch and groaned. I waited, and I gathered from what was being said that she had pretended to feel faint. I say *pretended*—because when I first caught sight of her, she was obviously feeling nothing of the kind."

Tommy nodded.

"Well?"

"I rather hate to tell you the next part. I was—curious. And also I'd been reading silly books, and I wondered if she'd put a bomb or a poisoned needle or something like that in Mr. Wilmott's boot. I know it's absurd—but I did think so. Anyway, next time I passed the empty cabin, I slipped in, and examined the boot. I drew out from the lining a slip of paper. Just as I had it in my hand, I heard the steward coming, and I hurried out so as not to be caught. The folded paper was still in my hand. When I got into my own cabin, I examined it. Mr. Blunt, it was nothing but some verses from the Bible."

"Verses from the Bible?" said Tommy, very much intrigued.

"At least I thought so at the time. I couldn't understand it, but I thought perhaps it was the work of a religious maniac. Anyway, I didn't feel it was worth while replacing it. I kept it without thinking much about it until yesterday when I used it to make it to a boat for my little nephew to sail in his bath. As the paper got wet, I saw a queer kind of design coming out all over it. I hastily took it out of the bath, and smoothed it out flat again. The water had brought out the hidden message. It was a kind of tracing—and looked like the mouth of a harbor. Immediately after that I read your advertisement."

Tommy sprang from his chair.

"But this is most important. I see it all now. That tracing is probably the plan of some important harbor defences. It had been stolen by this woman. She feared someone was on her track, and not daring to conceal it amongst her own belongings, she contrived this hiding-place. Later, she obtained possession of the bag in which the boot was packed— only to discover that the paper had vanished. Tell me, Miss March, you have brought this paper with you?"

The girl shook her head.

"It's at my place of business. I run a beauty parlor in Bond Street. I am really an agent for the 'Cyclamen' preparations in New York. That is why I had been over there. I thought the paper might be important, so I locked it up in the safe before coming out. Ought not Scotland Yard to know about it?"

"Yes, indeed."

"Then shall we go there now, get it out, and take it straight to Scotland Yard?"

"I am very busy this afternoon," said Tommy adopting his professional manner and consulting his watch. "The Bishop of London wants me to take up a case with him. A very curious problem, concerning some vestments and two curates."

"Then in that case," said Miss March, rising, "I will go alone."

Tommy raised a hand in protest.

"As I was about to say," he said, "the Bishop must wait. I will leave a few words with Albert. I am convinced, Miss March, that until that paper has been safely deposited with Scotland Yard you are in active danger."

"Do you think so?" said the girl doubtfully.

"I don't think, I'm sure. Excuse me." He scribbled some words on the pad in front of him, then tore off the leaf and folded it.

Taking his hat and stick, he intimated to the girl that he was ready to accompany her. In the outer office, he handed the folded paper to Albert with an air of importance.

"I am called out on an urgent case. Explain that to his lordship if he comes. Here are my notes on the case for Miss Robinson."

"Very good, sir," said Albert playing up. "And what about the Duchess's pearls?"

Tommy waved his hand irritably.

"That must wait also."

He and Miss March hurried out. Half way down the stairs they encountered Tuppence coming up. Tommy passed her with a brusque: "Late again, Miss Robinson. I am called out on an important case."

Tuppence stood still on the stairs and stared after them. Then, with raised eyebrows, she went on up to the office.

As they reached the street, a taxi came sailing up to them. Tommy, on the point of hailing it, changed his mind.

"Are you a good walker, Miss March?" he asked seriously.

"Yes, why? Hadn't we better take that taxi? It will be quicker."

"Perhaps you did not notice. That taxi driver has just refused a fare a little lower down the street. He was waiting for us. Your enemies are on the look out. If you feel equal to it, it would be better for us to walk to Bond Street. In the crowded streets, they will not be able to attempt much against us."

"Very well," said the girl, rather doubtfully.

They walked westwards. The streets, as Tommy had said, were crowded, and progress was slow. Tommy kept a sharp look out. Occasionally he drew the girl to one side with a quick gesture, though she herself had seen nothing suspicious.

Suddenly glancing at her, he was seized with compunction.

"I say, you look awfully done up. The shock of that man. Come into this place and have a good cup of strong coffee. I suppose you wouldn't hear of a nip of brandy."

The girl shook her head, with a faint smile.

"Coffee be it then," said Tommy. "I think we can safely risk its being poisioned."

They lingered some time over their coffee, and finally set off at a brisker pace.

"We've thrown them off, I think," said Tommy, looking over his shoulder.

Cyclamen Ltd. was a small establishment in Bond Street, with pale pink taffeta curtains, and one or two jars of face cream and a cake of soap decorating the window.

Cicely March entered, and Tommy followed. The place inside was tiny. On the left was a glass counter with toilet preparations. Behind this counter was a middle-aged woman with grey hair and an exquisite complexion who acknowledged Cicely March's entrance with a faint inclination of the head before continuing to talk to the customer she was serving.

This customer was a small dark woman. Her back was to them and they could not see her face. She was speaking in slow difficult English. On the right was a sofa and a couple of chairs with some magazines on a table. Here sat two men—apparently bored husbands waiting for their wives.

Cicely March passed straight on through a door at the end which she held ajar for Tommy to follow her. As he did so, the woman customer exclaimed. "Ah! but I think that is *an amico* of mine," and rushed after them, inserting her foot in the door just in time to prevent its closing. At the same time, the two men rose to their feet. One followed her through the door, the other advanced to the shop attendant and clapped his hand over her mouth to drown the scream rising to her lips.

In the meantime, things were happening rather quickly

beyond the swing door. As Tommy passed through, a cloth
was flung over his head, and a sickly odor assailed his
nostrils. Almost as soon however, it was jerked off again,
and a woman's scream rang out.

Tommy blinked a little and coughed as he took in the
scene in front of him. On his right was the mysterious
stranger of a few hours ago, and busily fitting handcuffs
upon him was one of the bored men from the shop parlor.
Just in front of him was Cicely March wrestling vainly to
free herself, whilst the woman customer from the shop held
her firmly pinioned. As the latter turned her head, and the
veil she wore unfastened itself and fell off, the well known
features of Tuppence were revealed.

"Well done, Tuppence," said Tommy, moving forward.
"Let me give you a hand. I shouldn't struggle if I were you,
Miss O'Hara—or do you prefer to be called Miss March?"

"This is Inspector Grace, Tommy," said Tuppence. "As
soon as I read the note you left I rang up Scotland Yard,
and Inspector Grace and another man met me outside here."

"Very glad to get hold of this gentleman," said the Inspector, indicating his prisoner. "He's wanted badly. But
we've never had cause to suspect this place—thought it
was a genuine beauty shop."

"You see," explained Tommy gently. "We do have to
be so very careful! Why should anyone want the Ambassador's bag for an hour or so? I put the question the other
way round. Supposing it was the other bag that was the
important one. Someone wanted that bag to be in the Ambassador's possession for an hour or so. Much more illu-
minating! Diplomatic luggage is not subjected to the
indignities of a Customs examination. Clearly smuggling.
But smuggling of what? Nothing too bulky. At once I thought
of drugs. Then that picturesque comedy was enacted in my
office. They'd seen my advertisement and wanted to put
me off the scent—or failing that, out of the way altogether.
But I happened to notice an expression of blank dismay in
the charming lady's eyes when Albert did his lasso act. That
didn't fit in very well with her supposed part. The stranger's
attack was meant to assure my confidence in her. I played

the part of the credulous sleuth with all my might—swallowed her rather impossible story and permitted her to lure me here, carefully leaving behind full instructions for dealing with the situation. Under various pretexts I delayed our arrival, so as to give you all plenty of time."

Cicely March was looking at him with a stony expression.

"You are mad. What do you expect to find here?"

"Remembering that Richards saw a tin of bath salts, what do you say about beginning with the bath salts, eh Inspector?"

"A very sound idea, sir."

He picked up one of the dainty pink tins, and emptied it on the table. The girl laughed.

"Genuine crystals, eh?" said Tommy. "Nothing more deadly than carbonate of soda?"

"Try the safe," suggested Tuppence.

There was a small wall safe in the corner. The key was in the lock. Tommy swung it open and gave a shout of satisfaction. The back of the safe opened out into a big recess in the wall, and that recess was stacked with the same elegant tins of bath salts. Rows and rows of them. He took one out and prised up the lid. The top showed the same pink crystals, but underneath was a fine white powder.

The Inspector uttered an ejaculation.

"You've got it, sir. Ten to one, that tin's full of pure cocaine. We knew there was a distributing area somewhere round here, handy to the West End, but we haven't been able to get a clue to it. This is a fine coup of yours, sir."

"Rather a triumph for Blunt's Brilliant Detectives," said Tommy to Tuppence, as they emerged into the street together. "It's a great thing to be a married man. Your persistent schooling has at last taught me to recognize peroxide when I see it. Golden hair has got to be the genuine article to take me in. We will concoct a businesslike letter to the Ambassador, informing him that the matter has been dealt with satisfactorily. And now, my dear fellow, what about tea, and lots of hot buttered muffins?"

23

The Man
Who Was No. 16

Tommy and Tuppence were closeted with the Chief in his private room. His commendation had been warm and sincere.

"You have succeeded admirably. Thanks to you we have laid our hands on no less than five very interesting personages, and from them we have received much valuable information. Meanwhile I learn from a creditable source that headquarters in Moscow have taken alarm at the failure of their agents to report. I think, that in spite of all our precautions, they have begun to suspect that all is not well at what I may call the distributing centre—the office of Mr. Theodore Blunt—the International Detective Bureau."

"Well," said Tommy. "I suppose they were bound to tumble to it sometime or other, sir."

"As you say, it was only to be expected. But I am a little worried—about Mrs. Tommy."

"I can look after her all right, sir," said Tommy, at exactly the same minute as Tuppence said, "I can take care of myself."

"H'm," said Mr. Carter. "Excessive self-confidence was always a characteristic of you two. Whether your immunity is entirely due to your own superhuman cleverness, or whether a small percentage of luck creeps in, I'm not prepared to say. But luck changes, you know. However, I won't argue the point. From my extensive knowledge of Mrs. Tommy, I suppose it's quite useless to ask her to keep out of the limelight for the next week or two?"

Tuppence shook her head very energetically.

"Then all I can do is to give you all the information that I can. We have reason to believe that a special agent has been despatched from Moscow to this country. We don't know what name he is travelling under, we don't know when he will arrive. But we do know something about him. He is a man who gave us great trouble in the war, a ubiquitous kind of fellow who turned up all over the place where we least wanted him. He is a Russian by birth, and an accomplished linguist—so much so that he can pass as half a dozen other nationalities, including our own. He is also a past master in the art of disguise. And he has brains. It was he who devised the No. 16 code.

"When and how he will turn up, I do not know. But I am fairly certain that he *will* turn up. We do know this— he was not personally acquainted with the real Mr. Theodore Blunt. I think that he will turn up at your office, on the pretext of a case which he will wish you to take up, and will try you with the passwords. The first, as you know, is the mention of the number sixteen—which is replied to by a sentence containing the same number. The second, which we have only just learnt, is an inquiry as to whether you have ever crossed the Channel. The answer to that is: "I was in Berlin on the 13th of last month." As far as we know, that is all. I would suggest that you reply correctly, and so endeavor to gain his confidence. Sustain the fiction if you possibly can. But even if he appears to be completely deceived, remain on your guard. Our friend is particularly astute, and can play a double game as well, or better, than you can. But in either case, I hope to get him through you. From this day forward I am adopting special precautions. A dictaphone was installed last night in your office, so that one of my men in the room below will be able to hear everything that passes in your office. In this way, I shall be immediately informed if anything arises, and can take the necessary steps to safeguard you and your wife whilst securing the man I am after."

After a few more instructions, and a general discussion of tactics, the two young people departed, and made their way as rapidly as possible to the offices of Blunt's Brilliant Detectives.

"It's late," said Tommy, looking at his watch. "Just on twelve o'clock. We've been a long time with the Chief. I hope we haven't missed a particularly spicy case."

"On the whole," said Tuppence, "we've not done badly. I was tabulating results the other day. We've solved four baffling murder mysteries, rounded up a gang of counterfeiters, ditto gang of smugglers—"

"Actually two gangs," interpolated Tommy. "So we have! I'm glad of that. 'Gangs' sound so professional."

Tuppence continued, ticking off the items on her fingers.

"One jewel robbery, two escapes from violent death, one case of missing lady reducing her figure, one young girl befriended, an alibi successfully exploded, and alas! one case where we made utter fools of ourselves. On the whole, jolly good! We're *very* clever, I think."

"You would think so," said Tommy. "You always do. Now I have a secret feeling that once or twice we've been rather lucky."

"Nonsense," said Tuppence. "All done by the little grey cells."

"Well, I was damned lucky once," said Tommy. "The day that Albert did his lasso act! But you speak, Tuppence, as though it was all over?"

"So it is," Tuppence. She lowered her voice impressively. "This is our last case. When they have laid the super spy by the heels, the great detectives intend to retire and take to bee keeping or vegetable-marrow growing. It's always done."

"Tired of it, eh?"

"Ye-es, I think I am. Besides, we're so successful now— the luck might change."

"Who's talking about luck now?" asked Tommy triumphantly.

At that moment they turned in at the doorway of the block of buildings in which the International Detective Bureau had its offices, and Tuppence did not reply.

Albert was on duty in the outer office, employing his leisure in balancing, or endeavoring to balance, the office ruler upon his nose.

With a stern frown of reproof, the great Mr. Blunt passed into his own private office. Divesting himself of his overcoat and hat, he opened the cupboard, on the shelves of which reposed his classic library of the great detectives of fiction.

"The choice narrows," murmured Tommy. "On whom shall I model myself to-day?"

Tuppence's voice, with an unusual note in it, made him turn sharply.

"Tommy," she said. "What day of the month is it?"

"Let me see—the eleventh—why?"

"Look at the calendar."

Hanging on the wall was one of those calendars from which you tear a leaf every day. It bore the legend of Sunday the 16th. To-day was Monday.

"By Jove, that's odd. Albert must have torn off too many. Careless little devil."

"I don't believe he did," said Tuppence. "But we'll ask him."

Albert, summoned and questioned, seemed very astonished. He swore he had only torn off one leaf—that of the day before. His statement was presently supported, for whereas the leaf torn off by Albert was found in the grate, the succeeding ones were lying neatly in the waste paper basket.

"A neat and methodical criminal," said Tommy. "Who's been here this morning, Albert? A client of any kind?"

"Just one, sir."

"What was he like?"

"It was a she. A Hospital Nurse. Very upset and anxious to see you. Said she'd wait until you came. I put her in 'Clerks' because it was warmer."

"And from there she could walk in here, of course, without your seeing her. How long has she been gone?"

"About half an hour, sir. Said she'd call again this afternoon. A nice motherly looking body."

"A nice motherly—oh! get out, Albert."

Albert withdrew, injured.

"Queer start, that," said Tommy. "It seems a little purposeless. Puts us on our guard. I suppose there isn't a bomb concealed in the fireplace or anything of that kind?"

He reassured himself on that point, then he seated himself at the desk and addressed Tuppence.

"Mon ami," he said. "We are here faced with a matter of the utmost gravity. You recall, do you not, the man who was No. 4. Him whom I crushed like an egg shell in the Dolomites—with the aid of high explosives, *bien entendu*. But he was not really dead—ah! no, they are never really dead, these super criminals. This is the man—but even more so, if I may so put it. He is the 4 squared—in other words, he is now the No. 16. You comprehend, my friend?"

"Perfectly," said Tuppence. "You are the great Hercule Poirot."

"Exactly. No moustaches, but lots of grey cells."

"I've a feeling," said Tuppence, "that this particular adventure will be called the 'Triumph of Hastings.'"

"Never," said Tommy. "It isn't done. Once the idiot friend, always the idiot friend. There's an etiquette in these matters. By the way, mon ami, can you not part your hair in the middle instead of one side? The present effect is unsymmetrical and deplorable."

The buzzer rang sharply on Tommy's desk. He returned the signal and Albert appeared bearing a card.

"Prince Vladiroffsky," read Tommy, in a low voice. He looked at Tuppence. "I wonder—Show him in, Albert."

The man who entered was of middle height, graceful in bearing, with a fair beard, and apparently about thirty-five years of age.

"Mr. Blunt?" he inquired. His English was perfect. "You have been most highly recommended to me. Will you take up a case for me?"

"If you will give me the details—?"

"Certainly. It concerns the daughter of a friend of mine—
a girl of sixteen. We are anxious for no scandal—you understand."

"My dear sir," said Tommy. "This business has been
running successfully for sixteen years owing to our strict
attention to that particular principle."

He fancied he saw a sudden gleam in the other's eye. If
so, it passed as quickly as it came.

"You have branches, I believe, on the other side of the
Channel?"

"Oh! yes. As a matter of fact," he brought out the word
with great deliberation, "I myself was in Berlin on the 13th
of last month."

"In that case," said the stranger, "it is hardly necessary
to keep up the little fiction. The daughter of my friend can
be conveniently dismissed. You know who I am—at any
rate I see you have had warning of my coming."

He nodded towards the calendar on the wall.

"Quite so," said Tommy.

"My friends—I have come over here to investigate matters. What has been happening?"

"Treachery," said Tuppence, no longer able to remain
quiescent.

The Russian shifted his attention to her, and raised his
eyebrows.

"Ah ha, that is so, is it? I thought as much. Was it
Sergius?"

"We think so," said Tuppence unblushingly.

"It would not surprise me. But you yourselves, you are
under no suspicion?"

"I do not think so. We handle a good deal of *bona fide*
business, you see," explained Tommy.

The Russian nodded.

"That is wise. All the same, I think it would be better
if I did not come here again. For the moment, I am staying
at the Blitz. I will take Marise—this is Marise, I suppose?"

Tuppence nodded.

"What is she known as here?"

"Oh! Miss Robinson."

"Very well, Miss Robinson, you will return with me to the Blitz and lunch with me there. We will all meet at headquarters at three o'clock. Is that clear?" He looked at Tommy.

"Perfectly clear," replied Tommy, wondering where on earth headquarters might be.

But he guessed that it was just those very headquarters that Mr. Carter was so anxious to discover.

Tuppence rose and slipped on her long black coat with its leopardskin collar. Then, demurely, she declared herself ready to accompany the Prince.

They went out together, and Tommy was left behind, a prey to conflicting emotions.

Supposing something had gone wrong with the dictaphone? Supposing the mysterious Hospital Nurse had somehow or other learnt of its installation, and had rendered it useless?

He seized the telephone and called a certain number. There was a moment's delay, and then a well known voice spoke.

"Quite O.K. Come round to the Blitz at once."

Five minutes later Tommy and Mr. Carter met in the Palm Court of the Blitz. The latter was crisp and reassuring.

"You've done excellently. The Prince and the little lady are at lunch in the Restaurant. I've got two of my men in there as waiters. Whether he suspects, or whether he doesn't—and I'm fairly sure he doesn't—we've got him on toast. There are two men posted upstairs to watch his suite, and more outside ready to follow wherever they go. Don't be worried about your wife. She'll be kept in sight the whole time. I'm not going to run any risks."

Occasionally one of the Secret Service men came to report progress. The first time it was a waiter who took their orders for cocktails, the second time it was a fashionable vacant faced young man.

"They're coming out," said Mr. Carter. "We'll retire behind this pillar in case they sit down here, but I fancy he'll take her up to his suite. Ah! yes, I thought so."

From their post of vantage, Tommy saw the Russian and Tuppence cross the hall and enter the lift.

The minutes passed and Tommy began to fidget.

"Do you think, sir. I mean, alone in that suite—"

"One of my men's inside—behind the sofa. Don't worry, man."

A waiter crossed the hall and came up to Mr. Carter.

"Got the signal they were coming up, sir—but they haven't come. Is it all right?"

"What?" Mr. Carter spun round. "I saw them go into the lift myself. Just"—he glanced up at the clock—"four and a half minutes ago. And they haven't shown up. . . ."

He hurried across to the lift which had just that minute come down again, and spoke to the uniformed attendant.

"You took up a gentleman with a fair beard and a young lady a few minutes ago to the second floor."

"Not the second floor, sir. Third floor the gentleman asked for."

"Oh!" The Chief jumped in, motioning Tommy to accompany him. "Take us up to the third floor, please."

"I don't understand this," he murmured in a low voice. "But keep calm. Every exit from the Hotel is watched, and I've got a man on the third floor as well—on every floor, in fact. I was taking no chances."

The lift door opened on the third floor and they sprang out, hurrying down the corridor. Half way along it, a man dressed as a waiter came to meet them.

"It's all right, Chief. They're in No. 318."

Carter breathed a sigh of relief.

"That's all right. No other exit?"

"It's a suite, but there are only these two doors into the corridor, and to get out from any of these rooms, they'd have to pass us to get to the staircase or the lifts."

"That's all right, then. Just telephone down and find out who is supposed to be occupying this suite."

The waiter returned in a minute or two.

"Mrs. Cortlandt Van Snyder of Detroit."

Mr. Carter became very thoughtful.

"I wonder now. Is this Mrs. Van Snyder an accomplice, or is she—"

He left the sentence unfinished.

"Hear any noise from inside?" he asked abruptly.

"Not a thing. But the doors fit well. One couldn't hope to hear much."

Mr. Carter made up his mind suddenly.

"I don't like this business. We're going in. Got the master key?"

"Of course, sir."

"Call up Evans and Clydesly."

Reinforced by the other two men, they advanced towards the door of the suite. It opened noiselessly when the first man inserted his key.

They found themselves in a small hall. To the right was the open door of a bathroom, and in front of them was the sitting room. On the left was a closed door and from behind it a faint sound—rather like an asthmatic pug—could be heard. Mr. Carter pushed the door open and entered.

The room was a bedroom, with a big double bed ornately covered with a bedspread of rose and gold. On it, bound hand and foot, with her mouth secured by a gag and her eyes almost starting out of her head with pain and rage, was a middle aged fashionably dressed woman.

On a brief order from Mr. Carter, the other men had covered the whole suite. Only Tommy and his Chief had entered the bedroom. As he leant over the bed and strove to unfasten the knots, Carter's eyes went roving round the room in perplexity. Save for an immense quantity of truly American luggage, the room was empty. There was no sign of the Russian or Tuppence.

In another minute the waiter came hurrying in, and reported that the other rooms were also empty. Tommy went to the window, only to draw back and shake his head. There was no balcony—nothing but a sheer drop to the street below.

"Certain it was this room they entered?" asked Carter peremptorily.

"Sure. Besides—" The man indicated the woman on the bed.

With the aid of a pen knife, Carter parted the scarf that was half choking her, and it was at once clear that whatever her sufferings, they had not deprived Mrs. Cortlandt Van Snyder of the use of her tongue.

When she had exhausted her first indignation, Mr. Carter spoke mildly.

"Would you mind telling me exactly what happened— from the beginning?"

"I guess I'll sue the Hotel for this. It's a perfect outrage. I was just looking for my bottle of 'Killagrippe' when a man sprang on me from behind and broke a little glass bottle right under my nose, and before I could get my breath I was all in. When I came to I was lying here, all trussed up, and goodness knows what's happened to my jewels. He's gotten the lot, I guess."

"Your jewels are quite safe, I fancy," said Mr. Carter drily. He wheeled round and picked up something from the floor. "You were standing just where I am when he sprang upon you?"

"That's so," assented Mrs. Van Snyder.

It was a fragment of thin glass that Mr. Carter had picked up. He sniffed it and handed it to Tommy.

"Ethyl Chloride," he murmured. "Instant anæsthetic. But it only keeps one under for a moment or two. Surely he must still have been in the room when you came to, Mrs. Van Snyder?"

"Isn't that just what I'm telling you? Oh! it drove me half crazy to see him getting away and me not able to move or do anything at all."

"Getting away?" said Mr. Carter sharply. "Which way?"

"Through that door." She pointed to one in the opposite wall. "He had a girl with him, but she seemed kind of limp as though she'd had a dose of the same dope."

Carter looked a question at his henchman.

"Leads into the next suite, sir. But double doors—supposed to be bolted each side."

Mr. Carter examined the door carefully. Then he straightened himself up and turned towards the bed.

"Mrs. Van Snyder," he said quietly. "Do you still persist in your assertion that the man went out this way?"

"Why, certainly he did. Why shouldn't he?"

"Because the door happens to be bolted on this side," said Mr. Carter drily. He rattled the handle as he spoke.

A look of the utmost astonishment spread over Mrs. Van Snyder's face.

"Unless someone bolted the door behind him," said Mr. Carter, "He cannot have gone out that way."

He turned to Evans who had just entered the room.

"Sure they're not anywhere in this suite? Any other communicating doors?"

"No, sir, and I'm quite sure."

Carter turned his gaze this way and that about the room. He opened the big hanging wardrobe, looked under the bed, up the chimney and behind all the curtains. Finally, struck by a sudden idea, and disregarding Mrs. Van Snyder's shrill protests, he opened the large wardrobe trunk and rummaged swiftly in the interior.

Suddenly Tommy, who had been examining the communicating door, gave an exclamation.

"Come here, sir, look at this. They did go this way."

The bolt had been very cleverly filed through, so close to the socket that the join was hardly perceptible.

"The door won't open because it's locked on the other side," explained Tommy.

In another minute they were out in the corridor again and the waiter was opening the door of the adjoining suite with his pass key. This suite was untenanted. When they came to the communicating door, they saw that the same plan had been adopted. The bolt had been filed through, and the door was locked, the key having been removed. But nowhere in the suite was there any sign of Tuppence or the fair bearded Russian, and there was no other communicating door, only the one on the corridor.

"But I'd have seen them come out," protested the waiter. "I couldn't have helped seeing them. I can take my oath they never did."

"Damn it all," cried Tommy. "They can't have vanished into thin air!"

Carter was calm again now, his keen brain working.

"Telephone down and find who had this suite last, and when."

Evans, who had come with them, leaving Clydesly on guard in the other suite, obeyed. Presently he raised his head from the telephone.

"An invalid French lad, M. Paul de Varez. He had a Hospital Nurse with him. They left this morning."

An exclamation burst from the other Secret Service man, the waiter. He had gone deathly pale.

"The invalid boy—the Hospital Nurse," he stammered. "I—they passed me in the passage. I never dreamed—I had seen them so often before."

"Are you sure they were the same?" cried Mr. Carter. "Are you sure, man? You looked at them well?"

The man shook his head.

"I hardly glanced at them. I was waiting, you understand, on the alert for the others, the man with the fair beard and the girl."

"Of course," said Mr. Carter, with a groan. "They counted on that."

With a sudden exclamation, Tommy stooped down and pulled something out from under the sofa. It was a small rolled up bundle of black. Tommy unrolled it and several articles fell out. The outside wrapper was the long black coat Tuppence had worn that day. Inside was her walking dress, her hat and a long fair beard.

"It's clear enough now," he said bitterly. "They've got her—got Tuppence. That Russian devil has given us the slip. The Hospital Nurse and the boy were accomplices. They stayed here for a day or two to get the Hotel people accustomed to their presence. The man must have realized at lunch that he was trapped and proceeded to carry out his plan. Probably he counted on the room next door being empty since it was when he fixed the bolts. Anyway he managed to silence both the woman next door and Tuppence, brought her in here, dressed her in boy's clothes, altered his own appearance, and walked out as bold as brass. The clothes must have been hidden ready. But I don't quite see how he managed Tuppence's acquiescence."

"I can see," said Mr. Carter. He picked up a little shining piece of steel from the carpet. "That's a fragment of a hypodermic needle. She was doped."

"My God!" groaned Tommy. "And he's got clear away."

"We won't know that," said Carter quickly. "Remember every exit is watched."

"For a man and a girl. Not for a Hospital Nurse and an invalid boy. They'll have left the Hotel by now."

Such, on inquiry, proved to be the case. The nurse and her patient had driven away in a taxi some five minutes earlier.

"Look here, Beresford," said Mr. Carter. "For God's sake, pull yourself together. You know that I won't leave a stone unturned to find that girl. I'm going back to my office at once and in less than five minutes every resource of the department will be at work. We'll get them yet."

"Will you, sir? He's a clever devil, that Russian. Look at the cunning of this coup of his. But I know you'll do your best. Only—pray God it's not too late. They've got it in for us badly."

He left the Blitz Hotel and walked blindly along the street, hardly knowing where he was going. He felt completely paralyzed. Where to search? What to do?

He went into the Green Park, and dropped down upon a seat. He hardly noticed when someone else sat down at the opposite end, and was quite startled to hear a well known voice.

"If you please, sir, if I might make so bold—"

Tommy looked up.

"Hullo, Albert," he said dully.

"I know all about it, sir—but don't take on so."

"Don't take on—" He gave a short laugh. "Easily said, isn't it?"

"Ah! but think, sir. Blunt's Brilliant Detectives! Never beaten. And if you'll excuse my saying so, I happened to overhear what you and the Missus was ragging about this morning. Mr. Poirot, and his little grey cells. Well, sir, why not use your little grey cells, and see what you can do?"

"It's easier to use your little grey cells in fiction than it is in fact, my boy."

"Well," said Albert stoutly, "I don't believe anybody could put the Missus out, for good and all. You know what she is, sir, just like one of those rubber bones you buy for little dorgs—guaranteed indestructible."

"Albert," said Tommy, "you cheer me."

"Then what about using your little grey cells, sir?"

"You're a persistent lad, Albert. Playing the fool has served us pretty well up to now. We'll try it again. Let us arrange our facts neatly, and with method. At ten minutes past two exactly, our quarry enters the lift. Five minutes later we speak to the lift man, and having heard what he says, we also go up to the third floor. At, say, nineteen minutes past two we enter the suite of Mrs. Van Snyder. And now, what significant fact strikes us?"

There was a pause, no significant fact striking either of them.

"There wasn't such a thing as a trunk in the room, was there?" asked Albert, his eyes lighting suddenly.

"Mon ami," said Tommy. "You do not understand the psychology of an American woman who has just returned from Paris. There were, I should say, about nineteen trunks in the room."

"What I meantersay is, a trunk's a handy thing if you've got a dead body about you want to get rid of—not that she *is* dead, for a minute."

"We searched the only two that were big enough to contain a body. What is the next fact in chronological order?"

"You've missed one out—when the Missus and the bloke dressed up as a Hospital Nurse passed the waiter in the passage."

"It must have been just before we came up in the lift," said Tommy. "They must have had a narrow escape of meeting us face to face. Pretty quick work, that. I—"

He stopped.

"What is it, sir?"

"Be silent, mon ami. I have the kind of little idea—colossal, stupendous—that always comes sooner or later to Hercule Poirot. But if so—if that's it—Oh! Lord, I hope I'm in time."

He raced out of the Park, Albert hard on his heels, inquiring breathlessly as he ran. "What's up, sir? I don't understand."

"That's all right," said Tommy. "You're not supposed to. Hastings never did. If your grey cells weren't of a very inferior order to mine, what fun do you think I should get out of this game? I'm talking damned rot—but I can't help it. You're a good lad, Albert. You know what Tuppence is worth—she's worth a dozen of you and me."

Thus talking breathlessly as he ran, Tommy reëntered the portals of the Blitz. He caught sight of Evans, and drew him aside with a few hurried words. The two men entered the lift, Albert with them.

"Third floor," said Tommy.

At the door of No. 318 they paused. Evans had a pass key, and used it forthwith. Without a word of warning, they walked straight into Mrs. Van Snyder's bedroom. The lady was still lying on the bed, but was now arrayed in a becoming negligee. She stared at them in surprise.

"Pardon my failure to knock," said Tommy, pleasantly. "But I want my wife. Do you mind getting off that bed?"

"I guess you've gone plumb crazy," cried Mrs. Van Snyder.

Tommy surveyed her thoughtfully, his head on one side.

"Very artistic," he pronounced. "But it won't do. We looked *under* the bed—but not *in* it. I remember using that hiding-place myself when young. Horizontally across the bed, underneath the bolster. And that nice wardrobe trunk all ready to take away the body in later. But we were a bit too quick for you just now. You'd had time to dope Tuppence, put her under the bolster, and be gagged and bound by your accomplices next door, and I'll admit we swallowed your story all right for the moment. But when one came to think it out—with order and method—impossible to drug a girl, dress her in boy's clothes, gag and bind another woman, and change one's own appearance—all in five minutes. Simply a physical impossibility. The Hospital Nurse and the boy were to be a decoy. We were to follow that trail, and Mrs. Van Snyder was to be a pitied victim. Just help the lady off the bed, will you, Evans? You have your automatic? Good."

Protesting shrilly, Mrs. Van Snyder was hauled from her place of repose. Tommy tore off the coverings and the bolster.

There, lying horizontally across the top of the bed was Tuppence, her eyes closed, and her face waxen. For a moment, Tommy felt a sudden dread, then he saw the slight rise and fall of her breast. She was drugged, not dead.

He turned to Albert and Evans.

"And now, Messieurs," he said dramatically. "The final *coup!*"

With a swift unexpected gesture, he seized Mrs. Van Snyder by her elaborately dressed hair. It came off in his hand.

"As I thought," said Tommy. *"No. 16!"*

It was about half an hour later when Tuppence opened her eyes and found a doctor and Tommy bending over her.

Over the events of the next quarter of an hour a decent veil had better be drawn, but after that period the doctor departed with the assurance that all was now well.

"Mon ami, Hastings," said Tommy fondly. "How I rejoice that you are still alive."

"Have we got No. 16?"

"Once more have I crushed him like an egg shell—In other words, Carter's got him. The little grey cells! By the way, I'm raising Albert's wages."

"Tell me all about it."

Tommy gave her a spirited narrative, with certain omissions.

"Weren't you half frantic about me?" asked Tuppence faintly.

"Not particularly. One must keep calm, you know."

"Liar!" said Tuppence. "You look quite haggard still."

"Well, perhaps I was just a little worried, darling. I say—
we're going to give it up now, aren't we?"

"Certainly we are."

Tommy gave a sigh of relief.

"I hoped you'd be sensible. After a shock like this—"

"It's not the shock. You know I never mind shocks."

"A rubber bone—indestructible," murmured Tommy.

"I've got something better to do," continued Tuppence.
"Something ever so much more exciting. Something I've
never done before."

Tommy looked at her with lively apprehension.

"I forbid it, Tuppence."

"You can't," said Tuppence. "It's a law of nature."

"What are you talking about, Tuppence?"

"I'm talking," said Tuppence, "of Our Baby. Wives don't
whisper nowadays. They shout. OUR BABY! Tommy, isn't
everything marvellous?"

AGATHA CHRISTIE

Mystery's #1 Bestseller!

"One of the most imaginative and fertile plot creators of all time!"
—Ellery Queen

Agatha Christie is the world's most brilliant and most famous mystery writer, as well as one of the greatest storytellers of all time. And now, Berkley presents a mystery lover's paradise—35 classics from this unsurpassed Queen of Mystery.

"Agatha Christie...what more could a mystery addict desire?"
—The New York Times

Available Now

181/a

___06778-5 **CARDS ON THE TABLE**
___06797-1 **THE PATRIOTIC MURDERS**
___06791-2 **MURDER IN MESOPOTAMIA**
___06793-9 **MURDER IN THREE ACTS**
___06803-X **THERE IS A TIDE...**
___06777-7 **THE BOOMERANG CLUE**
___06804-8 **THEY CAME TO BAGHDAD**
___06788-2 **MR. PARKER PYNE, DETECTIVE**
___06795-5 **THE MYSTERIOUS MR. QUIN**
___06781-5 **DOUBLE SIN AND OTHER STORIES**
___06808-0 **THE UNDER DOG AND OTHER STORIES**

___06787-4 **THE MOVING FINGER**
___06801-3 **SAD CYPRESS**
___06799-8 **POIROT LOSES A CLIENT**
___06776-9 **THE BIG FOUR**
___06780-7 **DEATH IN THE AIR**
___06784-X **THE HOLLOW**
___06796-3 **N OR M?**
___06802-1 **THE SECRET OF CHIMNEYS**
___06800-5 **THE REGATTA MYSTERY AND OTHER STORIES**
___06798-X **PARTNERS IN CRIME**
___06806-4 **THREE BLIND MICE AND OTHER STORIES**
___06785-8 **THE LABORS OF HERCULES**

All titles are $2.95
Prices may be slightly higher in Canada.

NGAIO MARSH

____	07507-8	NIGHT AT THE VULCAN	$2.95
____	06822-5	OVERTURE TO DEATH	$2.50
____	07505-1	PHOTO FINISH	$2.95
____	07504-3	WHEN IN ROME	$2.95
____	06014-3	COLOUR SCHEME	$2.50
____	07440-3	DEAD WATER	$2.95
____	06700-8	DEATH AT THE BAR	$2.50
____	06007-0	FALSE SCENT	$2.50
____	05967-6	THE NURSING HOME MURDER	$2.50
____	06179-4	SPINSTERS IN JEOPARDY	$2.50
____	06015-1	TIED UP IN TINSEL	$2.50
____	06012-7	VINTAGE MURDER	$2.50
____	06016-X	A WREATH FOR RIVERA	$2.50
____	06497-1	SCALES OF JUSTICE	$2.50

Prices may be slightly higher in Canada.
